DEB'S ALIENATION

DEB'S ALIENATION

Judy Lennington

DEB'S ALIENATION

iUniverse books may be ordered through booksellers or by contacting:

iUniverse
1663 Liberty Drive
Bloomington, IN 47403
www.iuniverse.com
1-800-Authors (1-800-288-4677)

ISBN: 978-1-5320-7642-8 (sc)
ISBN: 978-1-5320-7643-5 (e)

Print information available on the last page.

iUniverse rev. date: 06/05/2019

Thank you, David Lennington for all you do to make this possible. You are my inspiration and my life. I couldn't do it without you.

Thank you, Debby Mora and Lucille Huston for watching my back.
You are good at what you do, and I am proud to call you my friends.

CHAPTER ONE

Deb sat on the top step of the wooden porch, looking down at the second step from the top. A symbol had been carved into the wood. It was the same symbol she saw in her visions before the four strangers appeared to her. Who carved this symbol into this step? Was it possible that someone else saw the same symbols and numbers as Deb saw? Were there others out there like her?

Deb traced the symbol with her finger, repeatedly, as she recalled her home in Quincy, Pennsylvania. She had friends there. Friends she would likely never see again. She couldn't even call them to see how they were doing, for that would undoubtably put them in danger. She thought of her mother, Julie, and stepfather. She was certain that they were being watched by the FBI. She had promised to write to the McCall's using the name Candy McCall. She would pretend to be their niece, just in case their mail was being watched.

A bird shrieked overhead, and Deb looked up. It was a cloudy day, and the air felt humid. Rain was coming. She slid from the steps and went inside the two-room cabin. It had been built back into the woods near the lake by Mr. Patterson, years ago. It was leased by hunters and fishermen who came to the area during hunting and fishing season.

The cabin had been left unattended for two years while they cared for their son Richie. The symbols and route numbers Debbi saw in her head led her right to the Patterson's. It was here that she discovered their dying son, Richie. He was a few years older than Debbi and completely incapacitated due to a malignant brain tumor that was inoperable. Deb embraced him and, as in every other case, he shook violently for only a few moments. Of course, this gave the Patterson's quite a start. Then the shaking stopped, and Richie was cured.

This happened often as Deb traveled about seeking refuge from those who wanted to confine her and study her new capabilities. However, Richie was different. Somehow, he knew she was coming. He had seen the same symbols and knew she was being led to him. Why him?

At first, Deb thought there might be something between her and Richie. He was very handsome, and they had much in common. But as he continued to get his life back, it became apparent that his feelings for his old fiancée had rekindled and they were now planning their wedding day.

Richie continued to visit every day, delivering the mail or food. He had vowed to keep Deb's secret and the secret of the four space travelers who continued to speak to them both. Richie did not have the abilities Deb had however he did have a connection to the four travelers. Deb assumed because he had never actually encountered the travelers and she had, a few times, the new capabilities had not been passed on to him. His connection to the four strangers was a mystery to both of them.

The first few drops of rain began to fall upon her face as she went inside the cabin. She sat with the front door open, staring out into the thick forest across the lake, in the heart of Quebec, Canada. She could not remember her accident. She only knew what others had told her and what the newspaper article had written about that day. She was called the lady with angels riding in her back seat. They said she had been drinking, but her friends said she only had the one beer that night. Some said it was the strange lights in the sky. Debbi knew that had something to do with it, because the four strangers admitted they were responsible for her accident.

She closed her eyes and rubbed the back of her neck. Sometimes, her neck ached. She tried to recall her accident. She remembered working that day. She worked in a factory that built window and door frames for prefabricated homes. She recalled standing in line to punch out her time card for the day. She remembered she was meeting her friends Friday night at The Chaparral Tavern in Mont Alto. She drank one drink and left because she was going into work Saturday.

Angela wanted to leave early too, so they went outside and discovered everyone was looking at the strange lights in the sky. It appeared to be from some sort of space ship hovering overhead. It emitted bright green lights that shone down on the ground. Everyone was saying it was something new the military was using, and some said it was a UFO.

Deb recalled driving slowly, watching the strange lights in the sky as she moved onto Slabtown Road, where Angela lived. She remembered driving past Angela's house and deciding to turn right onto State Route 997 and looping back around. She stopped at the stop sign and looked both ways. It was clear. She remembered seeing many cars parked in the parking lot of Twin Kiss. The parking lot was full of people standing outside looking upward at the lights overhead. She looked toward the sky again. A truck had pulled up behind her, and the impatient driver blew his horn. She recalled taking her foot off the brake to pull out onto State Route 997 and seeing the bright lights of a car coming right for her. Everything from that moment on was gone, until she woke to find herself in the hospital.

She thought about the elderly man two rooms down from hers in the hospital. He was lonely and had nowhere to go. She often wondered if she could find Leonard again, and bring him with her. It would be risky going back to the states. The FBI, CIA, and probably the entire medical field were searching for her. If only Dr. Martelli had not witnessed her saving Eva's, daughter, Rachel.

The four strangers had visited her and explained that they were responsible for her new abilities. They apologized for inconveniencing her and explained that because of her new abilities she would have to leave her home and go somewhere where no one could find her. She was never to see her friends or family again.

Debbi leaned back in her chair and crossed her arms as the rain began to fall heavily. The four strangers were certainly odd. They were each identical, from what she saw of them. They were each the same height, weight, and built. Their voices were the same identical pitch and when they spoke, they all spoke together as one. It sounded more like a humming sound that only she could understand. They said they would guide her to safety, and they did. They sent signals and route numbers mentally until she ended up here, in Canada at the Patterson's.

Rich Patterson was dying from his brain tumor, yet he said, he knew she was coming. The voices in his head told him she would come, and he even knew what she would look like. Yet, Rich had never seen the four strangers or the strange lights. How was that possible?

It was quiet here in the forest that surrounded the lake. Deb watched as the trees swayed one way, and then back again from the wind. It appeared to be blowing in a storm. The clouds were dark and ominous above. The wind blew inside the cabin and the tattered curtains blew about. Deb stood up and closed the door. She sighed as she looked around.

The cabin had been a mess when she first came here. She spent many hours scrubbing the old gas stove to get it clean. Mr. Patterson brought a set of old wooden bunk beds he had stored overhead in the garage. He went to town and purchased two mattresses for them. Mrs. Patterson furnished the bedding, towels, and other linens she needed. They had decided to tell everyone a woman was leasing the cabin to write a book. All who inquired about leasing the cabin for hunting season was told it was not available.

No one knew who Deb was. She had never been to town. The Patterson's did all her shopping for her. Richie made a trip out to visit every other morning. She had no mailing address at the post office, and no one knew her name. She felt completely safe here, however, she was terribly lonely.

She recalled the night she met her friends at Chaps for drinks. They also met many times at another favorite place in Quincy, called Crackers. They drank and danced and gossiped, enjoying their time together. Deb smiled as she recalled her best friends and wondered where they were now and what they were doing. Did they ever think of her? Did they miss her as much as she missed them?

Debbi leaned over the sideboard where the porcelain dishpan sat upside down. A flash of lightning shot across the sky. She went to the bunk bed and laid down staring up at the underside of the bed overhead. She thought of her friend Brianna. From the first time she met Brianna, she recalled her to be on a diet. She was barely five feet tall and a little on the heavy side. Bri would watch her weight all week and then woof down junk food all weekend. She could not find a diet she could stick to. She ate way too much junk food and she was not looking well. Deb remembered embracing Bri before she left one day. As with every other incident, Bri began to shake and moan. When the shaking stopped, and Debbi released her, she said she felt fine. The last time she saw Brianna, she had lost nearly thirty pounds and was starting to jog. She looked healthier than Debbi had ever seen before. Deb wondered how Brianna was now. She missed her friends terribly.

She ran her fingers through the stubble on her head as she thought about her life in Pennsylvania. She had lived a wild lifestyle compared to her neighbors. The McCall's were an elderly couple who lived next door. They were caring for Debbi's pets now and Mr. McCall gave her his red pickup truck to drive when it became apparent that she had to flee to prevent them from locking her in a facility where they could study her.

Then there was Eva from across the street. She was a single parent who lived with her elderly father. They were Jehovah's Witnesses, and mostly kept to themselves. Deb met Eva when they had a yard sale one day. She was surprised to find that she liked Eva and was just beginning to understand her beliefs when everything happened.

It was because of Eva's little girl, Rachel, and Dr. Martelli, that Debbi had to flee her home. Dr. Martelli had called upon Deb, hoping to get her to agree to admit herself into a facility where they could monitor her brain activities. They claimed that her CT scan showed significant brain activity, which was highly unusual, especially, this soon after such a devastating trauma to the head. Debbi had refused to speak with Dr. Martelli and he was backing out of her driveway onto State Route 997, when Rachel's kitten darted onto the road and she ran after it. Dr. Martelli backed right over Rachel. She had died instantly from the injuries she sustained from his car.

Deb heard the screams as Eva realized what had happened. She hurried outside and quickly scooped Rachel into her arms. She had never brought anyone back from death before, but in the past, she had managed to heal every ailment she encountered by merely embracing the victims. Rachel shook violently. Deb heard Dr. Martelli's protests at the child being moved. Then Rachel blinked her eyes and smiled up at Deb. Deb released her grip on the child and she stood up, running into her mother's open arms, with no traces of an injury to her body anywhere.

Dr. Martelli was determined to report what he had just witnessed to the medical field. It was after that day, that the CIA and the FBI began searching for Deb, and the four strangers appeared to her in the cornfield beside her house, warning her that she had to run away and never return. They apologized for altering her life. They meant well, as they felt the need to revive her after her accident. The accident, they felt, was caused by their hovering in the skies the night she pulled out in front of another car, therefore they were responsible.

A flash of lightning shot across the room, causing Deb to jump. She sighed and closed her eyes. She concentrated on the sound of the rain falling upon the metal roof of the two-room hunting cabin. She began to feel groggy and tried to slow down her breathing. In the past, such actions would allow her to drift off to sleep. Her breathing was steady now, and she was close to sleep, when she heard a faint sound from outside. Deb quickly sat up and rubbed her eyes as she listened. She swung her legs over the side of the bed and went to the kitchen window to look outside. Richie's truck was parked behind Mr. McCall's pickup. He was sitting in it, obviously waiting for the rain to let up before he made a run for the porch.

Deb opened the front door and watched the pouring rain as it continued to pound upon the railing of the porch. Richie would have his arms full of supplies from town. She was preparing to dart outside to assist him in bringing the supplies in from the truck.

She became aware of the rain slacking as it fell onto the railing. She smiled toward the truck. She could not see into the window as the glare on the windshield prevented it. She took a deep breath and darted from the house, jumping from the porch, splashing water up her legs, as she ran toward the truck. Richie opened the truck door and began pulling plastic bags full of groceries from behind the seat. He held them out for Deb and she quickly grabbed them and turned to return to the cabin. She heard Richie splashing behind her as he followed. They entered the cabin laughing.

"Is it raining in town?" Deb asked, as Richie set the groceries on the table.

"It was just starting when I finished my shopping. It's a good thing it is spring. These fresh fruits and vegetables are getting harder to find. You might have to learn to like chips and dip before summer comes," Richie laughed.

"I've tried that stuff," Deb replied. "It leaves a bad taste in my mouth. Although, I recall a time when I lived on that kind of junk."

"I know what you mean," Richie said. "My first beer, after my recovery tasted like shit. But I kept at it, and now it's not so bad. I still prefer water though." They both laughed. "Donna says hello," Richie said.

"Oh, you saw Donna this morning?" Deb asked, placing the vegetables in the compact refrigerator.

"Yes, I stopped at the hardware store before I went to the grocery store," Richie said, sitting down near the table. "She's decided on peach and gray as the colors for the wedding. I didn't know there was so much to getting married," Richie said.

Deb sat down on the only chair in the room. "Wait until you get the bill," she said, laughing.

"It's a good thing her family has money," Richie said. "Although, I understand my parents are responsible for a portion of it, and they don't have the money to spare. I keep reminding her of that, and sometimes I think she isn't listening."

"Well, you two will work it out. Personally," Deb drew her legs up and rested her elbows upon her knees. "I don't see what is wrong with the two of you running off somewhere and having a private ceremony. You still aren't working anywhere. How are you going to live on her income alone?"

"That is another thing I can't seem to get through to her," Richie said. "I've been cleared by the doctor, but my old job is no longer available. Her father says I can work at the hardware store with Donna, but I think we need a break from one another every now and then."

"Donna likes the idea of you working for her father, I take it," Deb said.

"Oh, you know Donna. Remember how she nagged the hell out of me until I gave her your name. I kept trying to convince her I didn't know your name and that didn't work. She was going to come out here and meet you for herself," Richie said, shaking his head. "By the way, why did you choose Virginia Parks for your name?"

Deb smiled. "I remember visiting the historical battlefield park in Virginia with my parents, years ago. I always thought it was a beautiful place and the terrible things that happened there during the Civil War really stuck with me," she replied.

"Good choice for a name, I must say. However, she still questions me as to why she can't find anything written by Virginia Parks," Richie said. He shivered. "It's cold in here. Do you want me to bring another space heater down?"

"No, I'm not using the one I have," Deb laughed. "I'm really not cold."

"Well, I suppose I should get back to the house and check on Mom and Dad. Oh, by the way," Richie began. "Donna keeps asking me what kind of book you are writing. It seems you are the topic of discussion nearly all over town. Everyone is talking about the woman staying at the cabin, writing a book."

"What did you tell her?" Deb asked.

"I told her I don't know anything about you other than you are a writer, writing a book and you don't want to be bothered. She keeps asking me if we talk when I deliver your supplies," Richie said.

"Well, the less they know about me the better off everyone will be," Deb said.

"Okay, we will stick with what we've been saying all along. You don't like to be bothered and as long as you pay your rent, we don't bother you," Richie said.

Deb smiled. "That works for me. I don't feel comfortable lying and I hate putting your family on the spot, but believe me, they are much safer this way. Everyone is."

"I have to run, I'm sorry," Richie said. He turned and walked to the open door. "It looks like the prefect time to make my exit."

Deb went to look over his shoulder. The rain had let up. "I think you are right. Thank you for bringing my supplies. I'll drop by to visit with your parents when I feel the time is safe."

"I'll tell them. Oh, by the way, I brought a stool and a lawn chair. Now you have a chair for your guests to sit on," Richie said, laughing, without turning to look back at her. "They're on the porch. See you soon." Then he darted off the porch, splashing through the puddles as he made his way toward the truck.

Deb watched him as he backed up and turned around. Then the truck was bouncing down the rutted road toward civilization. Deb sighed. She was left alone again. She pulled the wet stool inside the cabin and placed it next to the table, leaving the plastic lawn chair on the porch in the rain. She went to the bunk and flopped down on it once again. She continued to stare up at the bottom of the upper bunk, hoping sleep would come. She was bored to death up here all alone. How much longer could she remain here, without anyone to talk to? Far off she heard a slight rumble of thunder. The storm would bring in a cold front. Soon the trees would be blossoming, and everything would be fresh and new.

CHAPTER TWO

The rain had stopped, and Deb decided to take a walk. The grass and weeds were nearly waist high, as she moved toward the lake. By the time she reached the area where she could see completely around the lake, she discovered that she was soaked to the skin from the waist down.

She stood looking across the lake. Somewhere in the distance a loon called out. She closed her eyes and smiled as she listened. It was a perfect addition to her walk. She took a deep breath of the damp air. The smells of rain lingered, highlighting the aroma of spring. Everything was new and freshly washed by the morning rain. She smiled to herself as she stood quietly listening with her eyes closed.

She spread her hands and reached out to touch the tops of the high weeds as she closed her eyes, filling her lungs for a second time. This was the perfect hiding place. At times the quiet solitude was boring. Time seemed to stand still as she lingered near the lake, taking in the fresh smells and sights.

With her eyes closed and her arms spread outward, she tilted her head to the left. She felt the wet grass touching her fingertips as it swayed to the left. She tilted her head to the right and the grass swayed to the right. She kept her eyes closed as she imagined herself floating upward. She felt a sense of weightlessness and imagined herself hanging in midair. She opened her eyes to find she was still standing on the bank of the lake with her hands outstretched.

How was it that she could lift something as heavy as an automobile, but could not levitate herself? She had tried many times in the past but was unable to lift herself from the floor. She sighed and turned to look behind her. After a few moments she began walking back to the cabin.

Deb changed into dry clothes and stepped out onto the porch again. Perhaps a brisk walk to the Patterson's would help break up the long day. She filled her lungs with fresh air again and began walking the rutted road that wound around the lake and forest leading to civilization. She was always careful to avoid coming close to the main road. Even though it was only a narrow dirt road, it was often traveled by neighbors who lived near the lake, most of whom rented out cabins to fishermen and hunters. Richie had told her the neighbors were curious about the woman staying in the cabin who was supposedly writing a book.

It was a long walk, but Deb did not mind. In fact, she welcomed it. It would help pass the time and break the boredom. She kept to the grassy mound on the center of the road, avoiding the water filled pot holes.

It was so quiet here she could hear the wind blowing through the tall trees. Most of the sounds were from various species of birds that frequented the area. A bubbling brook ran along the private road further up and she often stopped on a wooden plank bridge to listen to the running water. With the rain, the water would rush over the rocks, muddy and fast. In the summer she often sat on the bridge and allowed her feet to cool in the shallow brook. Today, however, the water would be high and rushing fast under the bridge.

How was it she was not able to levitate? She had lifted things as heavy as automobiles, and even other people, but not herself. Why not? She recalled lifting a car out of a snow bank during a snow storm once back home. Many times, she had closed her eyes and tried to lift herself, unsuccessfully. She was determined to find a way to levitate herself. She often practiced when she was alone, hiding out in her cabin near the lake.

She had come to the area where the wooden plank bridge stretched across the bubbling brook. There were no railings on the sides of this plank bridge and she recalled the first time she drove across it with the pickup truck Mr. McCall had given her to make her escape from those seeking to find her.

Reeds bobbed in the rushing water as the rain had caused them to bend and float in the brook with only their deeply seated roots keeping them from being washed away. The water was high, just inches from under the bridge. She stood gazing over the side at the rushing water. Deb looked back the way she had come. The white clouds clustered together, allowing rays from the hidden sun to stream down over the lake.

She moved on down the road. She was in an area where pines grew on both sides of the private drive. Beyond the pines the brook cut through the field, jutting left and right as it made its way to the lake cutting through the field of high grass and shrubs. It was not uncommon to find a moose or mule-eared deer standing in the tall grass. The boughs of the tall pines swayed in the breeze. The air smelled of pine needles.

Now she had reached the main road. A fence row here separated the private property and the road with a head rail to an old metal bed acting as a gate to keep strangers from passing. Deb lifted the chain over the wooden fence post and swung the gate open. After passing through the gate, she carefully replaced the chain. The last thing she wanted was to go home and find strangers lurking about.

She kept to the side of the road, dodging pot holes as she moved toward the Patterson's. This narrow dirt road was a side road that wound through the forest, past the homes and farms of the locals. This was wild country and nearly every home with any acreage had a cabin nestled somewhere they rented to hunters and fishermen to supplement their income. For some it was their only income, as one of the neighbors owned a string of cabins. They were nearly all filled with renters almost year-round.

It wasn't uncommon to walk all the way to the Patterson's without meeting one vehicle along the road. Deb seldom had need for the old pickup truck Mr. McCall gave her, as she had no need to go anywhere. Maxwell McCall still mailed her a new sticker to put on the plates just in case she needed to flee. She kept a backpack under her bed and ready to go at a moment's notice. She loved it here in Quebec. However, she knew better then to get too comfortable anywhere.

She was passing one of the neighbor's homes. She did not see anyone in the yard. This was the Hickman residence. They only owned four acres that had been cut out of the Patterson homestead. They were younger with two small boys, Larry and Liam. Debbi had watched them get on the school bus a few times, hidden back within the forest so no one could see her.

She moved quickly as she passed the home, for fear someone may be looking out the window. Everyone knew there was a single woman staying in the Patterson hunting cabin. They had all heard she was staying there for solitude while writing a book, and she did not want to be disturbed. Everyone was curious about her and the book she was writing.

She did not go to town. Richie made certain she had all the supplies she needed and often mailed letters for her. Of course, she only wrote to one person. She relied upon Maxwell and Lois McCall to keep her updated with all the news concerning her friends. She used the name of Candy McCall, who he claimed was his niece. When postal workers asked about Candy McCall, Maxwell would inform them she was a niece who visited now and then.

Debbi's mother Julie would often write to the McCall's and they would forward the letters to her, using the Patterson's address. Debbi felt safe and secure here in this cabin. The Patterson's had assured her that it was there for as long as she needed it, for they were grateful for her saving Richie's life.

Richie Patterson was a handsome young man, but deeply in love with his fiancée, Donna Staples. Their wedding was coming up soon and Donna had mentioned wanting to invite Deb. Everyone in town knew Debbi as, Virginia Parks, the author. Deb smiled to herself. If she were to write a book, what would it be about?

She giggled as she recalled standing in the corridor of the hospital looking into the room where the woman sat up in her bed in horror while a chair struck her abusive husband repeatedly, being wielded by some invisible person, until he was unable to move. It was Deb's way of rescuing the woman from her husbands' beatings and threats of more beatings if she told anyone. The last Debbi saw of the man, he was being wheeled out of the room on a gurney, on his way to the ER.

That wasn't the only time she used violence to protect someone. There were the two men at the bar who bought her and her friends a few drinks and then expected to be repaid with sexual favors. Deb broke a few arms that night as one of the men became violent toward her friends.

Deb did not like using her abilities in public. The less people knew about her the better. She wished she could help everyone. However, every time she used her abilities to help someone, she ended up running for her freedom.

The doctors at the hospital had noticed unusual brain activity. They wanted her to admit herself into a special clinic where they could monitor and test her. She knew what that meant. Then the FBI and government became aware of her abilities and made the connection to the UFO in the skies the night of her accident. Now her face was plastered on every television screen and in every newspaper in the country trying to locate her. An award had been offered to anyone who had information leading to her. They said she was a criminal, and even dangerous.

Deb swallowed the lump in her throat as she continued walking along the side of the dirt road. She could never go home again. She missed her friends and her mother. She knew the FBI was watching her mother and step-father. They had been screening their mail, and possibly listening in on every phone call. Deb had thought that was illegal, yet she was certain it was happening. They wanted her badly.

The Patterson's home came into view. A white picket fence enclosed the front yard. A single car garage sat off the left of the house. The house needed a coat of paint. The garage door hung crooked from a broken hinge. Deb studied the house as she neared. Why hadn't Richie done more for his parents? He wasn't working anywhere, and he was perfectly healed of his brain tumor.

Deb opened the gate and stepped inside. She heard a small dog barking from inside the house. It was the Patterson's little Yorkshire terrier, Ozzie. He was always excited to see Deb coming.

As she stepped up onto the front porch the front door swung open and Ozzie rushed out to greet her. Theresa Patterson stood smiling. "I knew it had to be you. He never gets that excited over a stranger," she said, laughing.

Deb reached down and scooped Ozzie up into her arms. He began licking her face, causing her to giggle. "You certainly are a happy boy this morning, Ozzie," she said, turning her face away.

"He didn't like that storm we had earlier," Mrs. Patterson said. "Is everything okay out there by the lake?"

Deb put Ozzie down and moved closer toward Mrs. Patterson. "Everything is fine. It just get's pretty darn quiet out there sometimes," she replied. "Do you mind if we step inside? I don't want anyone to see me out here."

"Of course, come on in. I was just baking some biscuits to go with our sausage gravy. Want some?" Mrs. Patterson asked.

"I didn't come here to eat. I have food at the cabin," Deb said, following Mrs. Patterson into the kitchen.

"Nonsense," Mrs. Patterson said. "Dick and I get tired of looking at each other all the time. A pretty face like yours is always welcome at our table."

Deb smiled. She had explained many times in the past that she only ate fruits and vegetables since her accident, because processed or cooked foods left a bad taste in her mouth. Now she found herself in an awkward position once again. She knew Mrs. Patterson was trying to be kind and hospitable. How could she insult this lady?

Deb smiled and said, "Well, I suppose I could use a good home cooked meal."

"Dick is out in the garage," Mrs. Patterson said. "I was just putting the biscuits in the oven. The gravy is simmering and all I need do is put the tea pot on the stove. Would you like a cup of tea with your lunch?" she asked, without turning around.

Deb smiled and said, "A cup of tea would be nice."

"Did you get much rain out at the lake this morning?" Mrs. Patterson asked, again, without turning around.

"We got plenty of rain. Everything smells fresh and new. I love that about spring. Soon the trees will be in full leaf and blossoms will be everywhere," Deb said.

Mrs. Patterson looked over her shoulder. "Oh, do sit down child. I totally forgot my manners," she said, pointing to a chair.

Deb pulled a chair out and sat down at the table. "I'm willing to help you with lunch Mrs. Patterson," she said.

"Nonsense, child. It's all done. All I have to do is set another plate on the table," she said, smiling back at Deb. "I always make more than we can eat. I never know if Richie is going to be here for lunch. I do hope he is out looking for a job. That boy needs to find something to do with himself."

"He seems to be happy," Deb said.

"Oh, he always did have a crush on that girl. I just hope he knows what he's getting himself into. It hasn't been that long ago he was dying, and she was off dating other men. Now it seems all is forgiven, and they are an item once again," she looked back at Deb and continued, "If you ask me, they are rushing into this wedding. In my day, you stuck with your man no matter what. Marriage used to be until death do you part. Now it's only if things are running smoothly. She's pushing this job at the hardware store mighty hard too. That is a whole other subject. Don't get me started on that one."

"You leave that boy be, Mother," Mr. Patterson said, from behind Deb.

Deb turned around to smile up at him. He pulled a chair out and sat down at the table across from her. "She is always on him about something or another. The boy is celebrating his life. You would think she would just be grateful he is still with us and let him be, so he can catch up on all he lost while he was sick," Mr. Patterson said.

Deb did not get a chance to respond. Mrs. Patterson spoke up right away. "He has the rest of his life to catch up on what he lost while he was sick. I don't see why he has to jump into marriage with both feet. It wouldn't hurt for him to show a little more gratitude to this young woman for coming along when she did."

"Oh, it wasn't all my doing, Mrs. Patterson," Debbi said, shaking her head. "I was drawn to this place by some unseen force I cannot explain. In fact, that is what I dropped by for. I have some questions about who rented the cabin before I came here," she explained.

"What kind of questions?" Mr. Patterson asked.

"Well, there is a strange symbol carved into the porch step. Do you know who carved it?" Deb asked.

"That's been there for a long time. I don't recall when I first noticed it," Mr. Patterson began. "I recall discovering it one day and wondering how long it had been there. So, you can see that I have no idea who could have carved it. We get all kinds of people up here renting that cabin. Sometimes it is just for a weekend and sometimes it's for months or even a whole season. In fact, we've had this feller calling us often of late, wanting to know when it will be available. He got mighty testy with me the last time we talked. He said he always stays at that particular cabin and he doesn't want to stay anywhere else."

"Do you recall his name?" Deb asked.

"Yes, I do, in fact. His name is Arthur Taylor," Mr. Patterson said.

"Do you recall who he is?" Deb asked.

"I believe so. He has rented it a couple of times. He gets pretty upset when it isn't available. I've told him repeatedly that there is usually a waiting list for renters. He doesn't like waiting, I take it," Mr. Patterson explained.

"Do you know where he comes from?" Deb asked, leaning forward.

"I probably have it written in the books somewhere. I used to keep better books than more recently. After Richie got bad, I sort of let all that go. Sometimes I remembered and wrote it down and sometimes I didn't. We really had our hands full right before you came along," Mr. Patterson smiled. "We didn't have time to keep up with things at that time. So, we rented it when it was empty and left it sit when it was not. That's why it was in such poor shape when you came along."

"I'd like to know more about this Arthur Taylor," Deb said. "I really would like to find out who carved that symbol on those steps."

"What is so special about that symbol, Dearie?" Mrs. Patterson asked, as she placed a cup of tea on the table in front of Debbi.

"It's the symbol I see in my head when something really important is happening. It is also the symbol that directed me here to your place," Debbi explained. "I find it strange that someone stayed in that cabin who knows about this same symbol."

"Oh, I see," Mrs. Patterson said, sitting down at the table. "Dick, would you mind saying a prayer before we eat?"

Mr. Patterson reached out and took hold of Deb's hand with his right hand and Mrs. Patterson's with his left hand. They bowed their heads and he prayed aloud before they ate their lunch.

After lunch, Mr. Patterson invited Debbi to sit on a chair near his desk while he went through his files. "Here it is," he said, flopping a heavy stack of papers on top of the desk. "His name is Arthur Taylor, like I said. He stayed here last in 2007. Let's see now," he said, as he went through the papers. "Yep, yep, he stayed in 2006, 2005, and twice in 2004. I can't find anything after 2007 though."

"How long did he stay each time?" Deb asked.

"Let's see now," Mr. Patterson said softly as he leafed through the stack of papers. "The first time he stayed two weeks. Oh, oh, I remember now. He just showed up one day knocking on my door and asked about the cabin in the woods. I remember the tenants we had at the time had to leave early because of an emergency back home. They had paid for a whole three weeks and they left a week early. He said he would pay them back for staying a week. I called the other tenants and they agreed. That is how he came to stay a week. He wanted to stay longer, but it was leased out to another tenant. He asked to be put on the list and when his turn came up again he stayed a month out there in the worst winter months we had seen in years. He stuck it out though. Then he asked about the next year and he was put on the list for every fall after that. According to this file, he stopped coming after 2007. Now he's wanting on the list again. He's a strange man this guy is."

"Does it say there where he's from?" Debbi asked, folding her hands in her lap.

"Ah, let me see," Mr. Patterson began. "He always paid cash in advance. I remember that. I gave him a receipt and he never filled out any paperwork. I didn't think much of it before. I get folks like that from time to time. They pay cash on the spot and sign the register. Sometimes they fill in the address and contact information and sometimes they don't. I see here he didn't. It looks like he never did." He shook his head. "I'm sorry, Dearie, I can't tell you where he hails from."

"That's okay. I certainly would like to meet this man," Debbi said, frowning.

"Well, if he calls again, do you want me to mention it to him?" Mr. Patterson asked.

"I'm not sure that is a good idea," Debbi warned. "You might suggest you need contact information in case there is an opening. Maybe I can get some information that way."

"I can do that. It would be my pleasure. Now that you mention the symbol and all, I'm kind of curious myself," Mr. Patterson said. He stood up and looked out the window. "It looks like it's clouding up out there again. Maybe I should give you a ride home."

"That won't be necessary," Deb said. "I don't mind getting wet. I won't need to bathe before bed tonight," she teased.

"Well, you be careful along that road if it starts to pour. Sometimes the folks around here don't watch where they are going as good as they should. That road is a bit on the narrow side," Mr. Patterson warned.

"I promise I'll be careful," Deb said, rising to her feet. She moved to the kitchen and called out to Theresa Patterson, "Thank you Mrs. Patterson. I enjoyed the lunch very much."

Mrs. Patterson rushed toward her. "You come back anytime, Dearie. You are always welcome here. Don't you forget that," she said.

"I won't forget. Thank you again," Deb said, smiling.

She walked quickly as she headed up the narrow road toward the private drive that led to her cabin. She looked to her right as she passed the little ranch style home of the Hickman's. There still wasn't anyone at home. The boys were likely still in school and the parents worked secular jobs. The house was quiet. A dog barked from somewhere in the back yard, but Debbi could not see it. She continued along, keeping to the left side of the road.

She heard a vehicle coming ahead. She moved over as far as she could making certain she did not slip off into the deep ditch that ran along both sides of the road. Both ditches were full of rushing rain water.

An old blue pickup truck was advancing toward her. She noticed two young men sitting in the front seat. They were watching her as they passed. Deb heard the brakes locking the wheels of the truck behind her and the tires sliding on the gravelly road. She turned to look behind her. The truck was moving toward her in reverse, with both men hanging out the windows, looking back at her.

"Hey there," the passenger was calling out to her. "Wait a minute."

Deb paused, not quite certain what she should do. She did not feel threatened by these two men. Even if they did try something, she could hold her own. There were always her secret abilities that would render them both powerless to do anything harmful to her.

"Hey, you," the driver called out, climbing from his pickup. "Are you the book writer that is staying at the Patterson cabin?" he asked.

Deb took a deep breath. "That depends on who is asking and why they want to know," Deb replied.

"My name is Larry, and this is my brother Henry. We live on down the road here. My parents have a few cabins on the other side of the lake. We heard the Patterson's had a woman renting their cabin who was writing a book. Everyone in town is wondering who this woman is. Would that be you?" Larry asked.

"That would be me," Debbi replied.

Larry pointed to his head and asked, "You got cancer or something?"

Deb reached up and placed her hand on the scarf she wore wrapped around her head. "I don't have it now, but I did," she lied.

"Sorry to hear that," Larry said. "I didn't mean it that way. I'm glad you don't have it anymore. I'm just sorry you had cancer, that's what I meant," he said, stammering. "So, what kind of book are you writing?"

"You ain't staying up here to write a cook book or something like that, are you?" Henry asked.

Deb smiled. "No, I'm not. I'm what they call a ghost writer. I write books for other people. They get most of the credit. That is why you never heard of me before."

"What's your name again?" Henry asked.

"Virginia Parks," Deb replied.

"Well, Virginia Parks," Larry began, "We are having a get together with some of our friends in town at Pappy's Bar and Grill. It's right on Main Street, you can't miss it. We certainly would be honored if you could drop by for a couple of drinks and meet some of the young locals up here. There's no reason for you to keep yourself locked away out there in that dinky little cabin day after day. How long you been out there, anyway?" he asked.

"I came in last fall," Debbi replied.

"Well, we certainly would love to introduce you to some of our friends in town. Like I said, at Pappy's, say, around 7:00 this evening?" Larry asked.

"Well, I thank you for the invitation, but I really do have a lot of research work to do before I can finish this book. I'm sorry, I don't think I can make it; however, I do thank you for the invitation," she lied.

"Okay," Larry said, throwing his hands in the air. "If you change your mind, just come on into town." He smiled and turned to walk back to the truck. "Come on Henry. Let the lady get back to work."

"Nice to meet you Miss Virginia Parks," Henry called out to Deb before following his brother to the truck.

"Nice to meet the two of you," Deb called out to them. She continued walking toward the private drive. She heard the truck pulling away and soon it was silent again.

She had reached the fence row, and as she opened the gate and stepped inside, she looked down the road both ways. It was quiet with the exception to the sounds of the many bird's shrills echoing through the forest.

She stood on the wooden plank bridge looking at the water rushing underneath. The water level had gone down some since her last visit. She kept to the high grassy mound in the middle of the rutted road as she moved toward the cabin. The dark clouds were moving quickly eastward. She felt certain the rain would blow past them. She reached the cabin and paused to look at the carving in the step. Then she went inside.

Her stomach ached from the heavy lunch she ate at the Patterson's. She needed to eat something green and leafy. Then maybe a short nap, for there certainly wasn't anything else to do.

She looked at the milky white mirror that hung on the wall. She reached up and pulled the scarf from her head. She recalled dying her hair auburn on her journey to this place in hopes of hiding her identity, for her picture was being plastered on every television screen in the states. After settling here, she found her blonde roots were becoming a problem, so she shaved her head. She rubbed the top of her head before replacing the scarf.

She contemplated writing a book. Could she do it without anyone finding out who she was? Maybe she should give it a try. She would need a computer. She looked around. There was no electric in this cabin. It would require a hand written document. She laughed to herself and went to the bunk bed, stretching out. So much for that. Perhaps she should start with a journal.

CHAPTER THREE

Deb woke after a short nap. The humidity was heavy even though the temperature was in the mid 50's. She sat on the side of her bunk trying to decide what she was going to do with her day. She rose and went to the only door in the cabin. As she opened it, she heard a grunting from somewhere in the tall grass between the cabin and the lake. Something was out there.

It was not unusual to come across a moose, elk, or deer during the day. She thought about walking to the lake but decided against it. Even though there was nothing out there that was a threat to her, she did not want to frighten or interrupt the feeding or grazing of the wild life. She would wait a while.

She left the door open as she stepped out onto the porch and sat on the plastic lawn chair Richie had left, leaning her back against the outside wall of the cabin. She raised her feet to rest them on the railing of the porch. As always, she glanced down at the symbol that had been carved into the step. Did Arthur Taylor carve that symbol into the step? Was there someone else like her out there?

She heard voices from afar echoing through the trees that lined the lake. It was probably fishermen on the lake. Maybe someone who had leased one of the other cabins. She longed to hear the voice of another human being. She wished she had stayed longer at the Patterson's.

After some time, she stood up and stretched. It was quiet now. Perhaps a walk to the lake would do her good. It always seemed to calm her. She closed the door to keep the raccoons and vermin out before descending the steps.

Deb waved her hands as she moved through the high grass, causing it to part as she made her way to the lake. The grass was still wet as the humidity lingered after the morning rain. Deb looked about for any signs of the sounds she had heard earlier. All was quiet and still.

She reached the grassy bank where she made it a habit of visiting every day. From this spot she was able to see all the way around this end of the lake. Off to the east the lake curved and stretched another two miles. She was not able to see that end of the lake from here.

A fish jumped out of the water and splashed upon re-entering only a few feet away from her. The lake was very deep and cold. The cold didn't bother Deb much since her recovery from her accident, but this water was cold enough to make her shiver this time of year. In the summer she often swam in the lake.

She had started her journey late in the summer. It was last fall when she arrived here. She had survived one full winter here on the lake. Now spring was here, and she longed to see her mother and friends. The solitude was nearly too much for her to bear.

Deb stretched her legs out, crossing her ankles as she sat quietly on the bank. A gaggle of Canadian Geese flew overhead, squawking loudly as they went. She watched as they flew over the lake and turned eastward toward the other end of the lake. It was quiet again.

The sounds of voices echoed around the lake. The fishermen were out there somewhere. She couldn't see them, and with the echoing, they could be anywhere. She sat upright, looking out over the top of the glistening water. The wet ground had soaked through her jeans, but she didn't mind. Where were the voices coming from? She did not want to be seen. Perhaps she should return to the cabin.

Deb stood up and looked out over the water one more time before turning to go back to the cabin. Again, she parted the wet grass using her hands in a waving motion. A slight breeze blew against her face and she closed her eyes, lifting her face upward.

Something startled her. It was a huffing sound. The grass was moving and whatever it was, it was coming right toward her. It couldn't be a moose or deer for their heads would be visible above the grass. She stopped and waited.

A black bear cub rushed right past her. She watched it as it passed, not even pausing to take notice of her. Before she could move, another cub appeared in the grass. This one stopped and cried out at the sight of her. "Oh no," she said aloud. She began to look around.

Off in the distance she heard it coming. The grass was parting, and it was coming fast. Deb began to back up. Still the cub cried out. She began moving in the opposite direction, hoping to avoid a confrontation with a mother black bear.

She heard it coming, and it was coming fast. It grunted and snorted as it followed her. She knew she could not outrun it. If ever there was a time for levitation, it was now. She continued to move quickly, closing her eyes and imagining herself drifting upward. She felt the wet grass cutting at her arms as she moved along. She was still on the ground. It was useless. She knew she could not outrun the bear.

Deb turned and waved her hands high in the air, trying to appear taller than the bear, as she waited for it to appear through the tall grass. There it was. It had stopped just a few feet away.

Deb waved her hands and shouted, "Bear! Bear!" hoping to scare it off. From behind her she heard the first cub cry out. It was close, and she was standing between the cub and its angry mother. "Oh, no," she moaned, softly.

The mother bear reared up and stomped both front feet while snorting and showing her teeth. It swayed from side to side, growling and stomping as she inched closer. Deb took two steps backward, trying to move away from the sounds of the cub calling out to its mother. Still the mother bear stomped and growled at her.

Deb knew she was in trouble. She waved her hands and the bear arose off the ground only inches. It did not seem to notice what was happening as it was so angry, trying to protect its cubs. Deb pushed her hands toward the bear and it began moving away from her. Now the bear sensed something was off and began rolling its head from side to side, growling and howling at the same time. The cub came into view and rushed toward its mother. Deb continued pushing the bear off into the distance slowly, so the cub could keep sight of its mother. Soon they were far enough away that Deb would no longer be a threat to them.

Deb looked around for the second cub. She heard the mother crying out and heard the cub calling back as it moved toward the mother bear's voice. Deb sighed. That was a close one. She began walking back toward the cabin now, keeping a close watch at her surroundings as she went. She hoped the bear would not come looking for her.

The cabin was in sight now. Deb quickened her pace as she hurried up the porch steps. She turned and looked out over the tall grass. Off in the distance she saw the grass parting and thought it might be the mother bear and her cubs. They were moving toward the pine grove on the eastern side of the lake. Deb sighed and went inside the cabin.

She stood in the center of the main room. She stretched out her arms and closed her eyes. When she opened her eyes, everything that was not nailed down was floating in mid-air. Deb took in a deep breath and exhaled slowly. All the dust and leaves that had blown in from the open door began to move. She moved to the side of the room, with her arms still outstretched, and blew toward the open door. Once all the dirt was on the porch, she lowered her arms slowly and everything returned to where it was before. She went outside and blew the debris off the porch. Then she went inside and closed the door behind her.

Deb closed her eyes and concentrated hard. Once again, she tried to imagine herself floating above the floor. She felt the sensation of being weightless and floating upward. She opened her eyes to find herself still standing with both feet firmly planted on the plank floor of the cabin. Her heart sank. If only she could lift herself upward. She would have been able to float out of sight of the mamma bear and cubs. She flopped down upon a chair and crossed her arms on the table, dropping her face into her folded arms.

She lost track of the time. Had she fallen to sleep? She heard the engine of a vehicle coming up the dirt path that led from the main road to the cabin. It couldn't be Richie, he had been there already today. She rose to her feet and went to the door, swinging it open to peer outside.

A green Jeep came bouncing toward the cabin. Deb could see the silhouette of a person behind the wheel of the jeep. Deb stepped out onto the porch and waited for the jeep to come to a stop behind the pickup truck Maxwell McCall had given her.

The door of the jeep opened, and a tall thin brunette stepped out. She waved and smiled as she walked toward the porch. Her brunette hair was a cluster of soft curls that shined even though it was a cloudy day. She wore blue jeans and a long-sleeved flannel shirt.

"Hello, you must be Miss Virginia Parks," the young lady called out from the bottom of the porch steps. "I'm Richie Patterson's fiancée, Donna Staples," she said, as she began to climb the steps. She extended her hand and Deb slowly reached out to shake hands with the young woman.

"Nice to meet you," Deb said, cautiously.

"I've been wanting to meet you for some time," Donna said, laughing. "I suppose if I were honest I would have to admit the whole town has been wanting to meet the woman staying out here writing a book." She smoothed out her flying hair. "You have been the topic of every breakfast conversation at the diner at one time or another."

"Oh, I don't know why," Deb said softly. "I'm certainly nobody special."

"Well, everyone is curious about this book you are writing. I keep asking Richie and he keeps insisting he doesn't know anything about it, but I know my Richie. I can tell when he is trying to avoid something, and he certainly changes the subject every time your name comes up," Donna said. "So, he either has something he is trying to hide or something he doesn't want to talk about."

"If you are implying there is something between Richie and me, let me put your mind to rest, Miss Staples," Deb began.

"Oh, call me Donna, please," Donna interrupted. "Don't worry, I know there is nothing going on between you. Although, you are certainly the mystery woman around here."

"I'm nobody special, as I said before," Deb said.

"Well, I have asked Richie to extend an invitation to our wedding. He keeps putting me off, so I thought I would drive out here and invite you myself," Donna said, handing Debbi an envelope. "I brought you an invitation. If you have any trouble finding the place, just ask the Patterson's."

Deb took the envelope and stood quietly staring down at it, unsure as to what she should say.

Donna took a deep breath and asked, "What kind of book are you writing?"

"I can't discuss that with anyone," Deb replied.

"Oh, I see. You don't want to lose the element of surprise," Donna said, laughing. "I get it." She took another breath and said, "I've been googling authors under Virginia Parks and I can't find anything. Do you write under another name?"

"No," Deb said, shaking her head. "I am what they call a ghost writer."

"Oh, I know what that is. You write books for other people," Donna said, smiling. "Cool. That must be hard, I mean, you never get credit for all the hard work you do," Donna said.

"Well, sometimes your name comes up," Deb replied. She must be very careful because she really didn't know how all of this worked. Donna may know more about ghost writing than Deb did.

"I work at my Dad's bait shop and hardware store. There is just Dad and me. Mom is a teacher at the school. She helps in the summer, but most of the time it is just Dad and me. I've been trying to get Richie to come help out at the store, but he doesn't seem interested in that line of work. It sure would help if he had a job before we got married," Donna said.

Debbi did not feel comfortable commenting on this subject. She did not know this woman very well. Personally, she felt this was a private matter between Donna and Richie and did not want to be drawn into the middle of anything.

"I noticed the scarf around your head," Donna said, pointing to the top of her head. "Do you have cancer or something?" she asked.

Deb sighed and smiled. "Not anymore," she lied.

"Oh, I'm so sorry," Donna said. "Oh, not that you don't have it anymore. I didn't mean it that way. I'm sorry you had to go through all of that. I'm very happy to hear you don't have it anymore."

Deb smiled. "Thank you," she said, with a nod of her head.

"What kind was it?" Donna asked. "Cancer, I mean. What kind of cancer did you have?"

Deb stammered, not sure how to respond. Donna noticed it and flushed. "I am sorry, that is a personal thing. I didn't mean to pry. You don't owe me an answer. I apologize again. I wasn't thinking," she was wringing her hands.

Deb fell silent, deciding not to say anymore than she had to.

Donna looked around. "Well," she sighed. "I suppose I should be getting back to town. I do hope you will come to the wedding. The date, time, and location are all right there in the invitation. We would love to have you share our special day, if you can." She swayed, waiting for Deb to reply, and when she did not, Donna waved and said, "Well, I have to get back. Have a nice day. It was nice meeting you." Then she turned and walked to the jeep. Deb watched as she turned around and bounced down the rutted path toward the main road. Then Deb turned and went back inside.

Deb placed the envelope on the table. She stood staring down at it. She opened it and read it to herself, replacing the invitation into the envelope and placing it on the table once more. She had received two invitations today. One for the meeting at a local bar tonight and one for Richie and Donna's wedding.

Dare she make an appearance? No, that would not be a good idea. She didn't know if they were still showing her picture on the television and in the papers. She needed to be cautious. It wasn't safe to be seen out there by anyone.

She sighed. The days were so long here all by herself with no one to talk to. How she missed gossiping and laughing with her friends. She sat down and covered her eyes with her hands.

CHAPTER FOUR

A fog began to drift into the area. Deb stepped out onto the porch again, sitting on the white plastic lawn chair with her back leaning against the wall and her feet propped up on the railing of the porch. She closed her eyes, hoping that a brief nap would help pass the time.

"What are you thinking?" she said aloud. "You're growing old here, hid from everyone and everything that you love." She stood up and stretched. The risk of being recognized was great but hiding out from the world was not the answer. She was young and full of life, as well as something else. She had several hours before the meeting at Pappy's Bar and Grill in town. She would need to clean up some.

Deb went to the metal medicine cabinet that hung on the wall over the wash board. The medicine cabinet had rusted away, but the mirror on the door was as good as new. In fact, it was probably the only thing holding the old medicine cabinet together. She pulled the scarf from her head and rubbed the stubble of new hair. Should she shave her head again?

In the past she had shaved her head and eyebrows in an effort to hide her identity. Because of that, someone who met her for the first time always assumed she was a victim of cancer and treatment that caused her to lose her hair. She debated shaving her head before leaving the cabin, but then thought against it. She had already announced to two people that she no longer had cancer, so it was normal to expect new hair growth.

She rubbed at her eyebrows. They could certainly use a tweezing, but she didn't have any tweezers. She went to the paper list she kept on the rough table and wrote TWEEZERS on the list of things she needed for the next week.

She turned to look at herself in the mirror again. Should she risk going into town tonight? Richie had been bringing everything she needed to the cabin to keep her from having to go into town. Perhaps it would be a mistake to do something so foolish at this point. It would soon be a year that she had been living out here with no inkling of being discovered. A trip to town could change all of that.

She sat down at the table and held her head in her hands. She had felt so happy at the thought of conversation with other human beings. Would an hour make that much difference? Perhaps, she shouldn't risk it after all. If she was discovered, she would have to flee this place. Where would she go?

Numbers were constantly flashing in her head. Sometimes, she knew what they meant, and sometimes she did not. Like the number 2 flashed when the baby bear cub rushed past her. She knew there was another one close by. Then the 2 turned to 3 which flashed rapidly, which usually indicated danger. That was when she became aware of the mother bear and the two cubs.

Then there were the symbols. Those she did not understand. The symbol carved into the porch step she knew. It was the symbol she saw when she was being directed by the four strangers from the space craft. It had been weeks since she had seen this symbol. Could it be that the four strangers went back to wherever they came from? Perhaps she would never see or hear from them again.

Other symbols often accompanied this symbol and she had no idea what they meant, but often found them connected to moving away or toward something. This morning she saw a variety of symbols as she stood near the water's edge looking across the lake. It had become common to see such symbols, yet she still did not know what any of them meant.

She went to look outside again. The door was standing open and she stood just inside the threshold, looking out at the fog which seemed to be sitting upon an invisible ledge, hanging just above the tall grass. She wondered where the bear and cubs were at this moment. She wondered if the fishermen were still drifting out on the cold water of the lake in the thickening fog. That would not be a wise move on their part. Should she venture out to the lake?

She turned and went back to the table. Any grown adult would know better than to linger out there in this fog. They could possibly float all night and most of tomorrow trying to find their way to shore. Then there was always the danger of hitting a floating log and sinking in the icy water. As cold as that water was, they would go straight to the bottom and possibly never be found.

Now she was beginning to worry. What if they were still out there? She went to the door again and stared out into the tall grass. She went to the wash board and grabbed her scarf, wrapping it around her head. She pulled on her rubber boots and began walking toward the lake.

The fog was thick and felt like millions of tiny beads of water on her face as she moved through the tall grass. The closer she got to the lake, the thicker the fog seemed to be. She held her hands out, touching the tops of the tall grass as she moved. Soon her fingertips were brushing against reeds and her boots sunk in the soft mud. She was near the water's edge. She stopped and listened. Only sounds of birds and an occasional fish jumping in the water could be heard. She moved to her right keeping close to the reeds. All was quiet. After some time, she turned and began making her way back to the cabin.

As she moved through the tall grass she heard an engine. It was a familiar sound. It was Richie. He had already made his run today. Something must be up. She quickened her pace and soon she was walking up the rutted path behind his vehicle.

Richie was just getting out of his truck. He did not see her coming. She watched as he darted up the steps and into the cabin, calling out, "Company coming."

"I'm out here," Deb called out.

Richie stepped out onto the porch and waved down at her. "Where were you?"

"I walked out to the lake," Deb replied.

"In this fog?" he asked.

"Yeah, that was why I went to the lake. I heard fishermen on the lake earlier today and thought they may be in trouble with the fog coming in so quickly," Deb began climbing the steps. She looked down at the symbol carved into the wooden step. "They weren't there. All is quiet on the water," she said, smiling at him.

"Well," Richie began, "if they are out in this neck of the woods, they certainly should have enough sense about them to get off the lake when it gets foggy."

Deb laughed. "I agree," she said. "I just thought it best to check. You never know."

"No, I suppose you don't," Richie said. "Was Donna out here?"

Deb smiled and nodded her head. "She was. She gave me an invitation to the wedding," she announced.

"I was afraid she might do something like that," Richie said. "She's been bugging the heck out of me to invite you to the wedding. I'm sorry. I've tried to be very stern about you not being disturbed."

"It's alright," Deb said. "In fact, it was the second invitation I got today."

"What? Who?" Richie asked, frowning.

"I met two locals along the road earlier. I was walking back from your parent's house. Their names were Henry and Larry," Deb explained. "I believe they said they were brothers."

"Larry and Henry Escott," Richie said, nodding his head. "They are brothers."

"Well, they invited me to come into town and join them and some other friends at a place called Pappy's," Deb said, leaning against the wall.

Richie sat down at the table. "Larry and Henry are alright. They keep out of trouble as far as I know. They are well known in these parts, and I haven't heard anything bad said about either of them. Larry went to college in Ontario, but he dropped out in his second year and came back home. Now that you mention it, I do recall seeing them at Pappy's on occasion. They play pool and drink a few beers. I've never known them or their friends to be a problem," he explained.

"So, do you think there would be any harm in my going to town tonight and meeting them?" she asked.

"I don't know," Richie said, rubbing his chin. "I haven't seen or heard anything about you on the telly lately. Your picture hasn't been in the papers in a long time. I'm not so sure about hanging on a wall somewhere in one of our local lodges or supply shops. That is always a possibility."

Deb sighed and flopped down on the chair opposite him. "It gets mighty quiet and boring out here day after day. I certainly could use some conversation and a few drinks might be nice too," she said.

"Yeah, but then folks will start talking about you all over town, and you never know who might be listening," Richie warned. "I'm not trying to stop you from going into town, but I think you might want to consider the consequences."

"I've been rolling that around in my head for the last couple of hours. Should I, or shouldn't I? That is the question," she said, covering her face with her hands. She allowed her hands to drop onto the table top. "Do you think anyone would recognize me now?" she asked.

"Probably not," Richie said. "Want me to drop by just to help if you need me?" he asked.

"I don't think I need a babysitter, and I certainly can take care of myself," Deb said, laughing.

"I know you can," Richie said, leaning forward. "That is what I'm worried about. Right now, you are just an author writing a book secluded out in the middle of nowhere. If you pull off some miraculous act and someone notices it, then we have a problem."

"I understand," Deb said, covering her face again. "I suppose I should stay away from people." She sighed and moaned as she lowered her head to rest upon her folded arms. "I'm so bored," she moaned. She raised her head again and asked, "What brings you back out here today?"

"I wanted to know what you and Donna talked about before I drop by the hardware store. I don't like being blindsided," he explained. "We need to keep our stories straight."

"She asked me if I had cancer," Deb said, pointing to the scarf wrapped around her head. "I told her I used to have it, but I don't anymore. I didn't go into detail about what kind of cancer or anything like that. Thank goodness she didn't pry because I don't have a clue what I would have told her. She gave me an invitation to the wedding and said she would like for me to come. I did not reply either way. She asked about the book

I'm writing, and I told her I was a ghost writer and I was writing for someone else. She bought that and said that explained why she couldn't find anything written under my name. That is about it."

"Okay," Richie said, rising to stand up. "I have to get to the hardware store. Her father wants to talk to me. I think he is going to ask me to go to work for him."

"You could do worse," Deb said. "There isn't anything wrong with that kind of work."

"I don't want to work in a hardware store all my life," Richie said.

"It would do until you found what you do want to do with the rest of your life. You need to be doing something soon. You're going to be married in a few weeks," Deb smiled.

"I know, but since I've had those visions, I think there is something out there I should be doing, and I haven't figured out what it is yet," Richie explained.

"Well," Deb began, "I certainly understand that. I don't think those strangers led me here to hide out for the rest of my life."

"Now, you understand what I'm saying. Or at least what I'm trying to get across to Donna. I can't tell her about the visions. That wouldn't go over very well," Richie said, walking toward the door. He stopped and turned to face Deb. "You know, if you want to go into town tonight, I don't suppose it would hurt. Just limit your time to an hour or two and don't give out too much information. They will be talking about you for a long time after meeting you. I know these people."

Deb smiled. "I haven't decided yet. I might, but again, I might not."

Richie nodded his head and left. Deb remained seated at the table, resting her head on her folded arms. She wanted to go to town so badly. She looked over at the battery powered clock. She had two hours to decide. Maybe a bath while she was thinking about it.

Deb bathed and changed into a clean pair of jeans and a flannel shirt. She rolled the sleeves up to her elbows. She carried her boots outside and pounded them together to get all the dried mud off them. Then she tied a clean scarf around her head and stuck two twenty-dollar bills into her jeans pocket. She climbed into the truck and turned the key. The truck started without hesitation. Deb smiled and turned around, facing the path that led to the plank bridge and on toward the main road. She hesitated, not sure she was doing the right thing. The desire for human interaction drove her to put the truck in gear and press down on the accelerator.

The truck bounced along the rutted path, splashing muddy water on both sides as it went. The fog hung just above the hood of the truck. Soon she heard the wooden plank bridge under her. She kept her eyes on the path ahead, for fear of slipping over the side into the rushing stream beneath. Again, she was bouncing and splashing until she reached the gate. She put the truck in park and slid from the truck, lifting the chain over the post and swinging the gate open. She climbed into the truck and stopped on the other side, sliding from the truck again, to secure the gate once more.

Now she was bouncing along the main road in the direction to town. She had only been in town twice in the time she had been staying at the cabin. She did not know her way around very well but did know that Main Street went right down the middle of town. She felt certain that she would find Pappy's Bar and Grill well enough.

Deb pulled into a small parking lot of a log building with a ground level plank porch. Pappy's Bar and Grill flashed in bright red and amber lights over the roof of the porch. As Deb exited the truck, she heard music coming from inside. She stood looking around the parking lot. There were about seven trucks and one lone car parked in the lot. She saw the number 7 and the number 1 and then the number 8 floating within her mind. As she stood staring at the entrance the numbers 14, 2, and 18 came into view. She took a deep breath and stepped toward the porch.

"Hey, look who decided to show up," someone called from behind her.

Deb turned to see Larry and Henry walking toward her. She smiled as the number two floated ahead of the other numbers within her mind. "I decided I could use a couple of hours away from writing," she said.

"Well, come on in and meet everyone," Larry said, stepping up onto the porch. He held the door open and waited for her to enter ahead of him and his younger brother.

"Hey everyone," Henry called out after entering behind Deb. "I want you all to give a hearty welcome to Miss Virginia Parks, here. She decided to take a break from writing that book and join us for a spell."

Larry entered behind his brother and walked ahead of them to a group of people sitting in two booths near the pool tables.

Deb looked around the room. She counted 14 people in the room. With Larry, Henry, and herself, there were a total of 18, including the bartender. The bar had four men seated who had all turned to look back at them.

"Welcome, Miss Parks," a young woman said. "Come sit over here with me." She slid out of the booth and into the one behind it. Deb smiled at the faces watching her as she slid into the booth across from the young woman.

"My name is Jenny Calvin. It is so nice to finally meet you. We have all heard so much about you," the young lady said.

Before Deb could respond, Larry called out, "Hey, Miss Parks, what are you drinking?"

The bartender was making his way toward them. She took a deep breath and smiled. "Do you have bottled water?" she asked.

Everyone began hooting and laughing. "You come to a bar for bottled water, Lady?" the bartender asked. "If it's water you want, you need to go to the market two blocks down. We only serve beer, whiskey, and wine in here."

"I'm sorry," Deb felt her face flushing. "I'll have a draft, if you have it."

"Draft it is," the bartender said, shaking his head as he walked away.

"Pay no mind to Stoney. He gets cranky, but he's a good guy," Jenny said.

Larry slid into the booth next to Deb. "I take it you aren't a drinker, Miss Parks," he said.

Deb shook her head. "No, I'm afraid I never liked the taste of spirits much," she lied. If only he had known her before her accident.

A man turned in the booth next to them and asked, "What kind of book are you writing out there on the lake?"

Deb swallowed the lump in her throat. She had gone over and over this in her head on the way over here. She smiled and said, "I'm afraid I am not at liberty to say. You see, I am what they call a ghost writer. I write books for other people who get the credit for the books. I am not supposed to give out any information about the books I write beforehand."

"That sucks!" the man said, turning in his seat again.

Deb sighed. She had managed to get through the first hurdle. She smiled at Jenny who was watching her closely.

Larry slid his arm over the top of the bench, behind her. He leaned close and said, "Have you eaten? The food here is the best around."

"I haven't eaten. I'm afraid I'm not much for eating out. I'm a vegetarian," she said, smiling.

"Oh no, now that may prove to be a problem," Larry said, allowing his head to fall back against the high back of the booth. He laughed out loud. "We will not tell Stoney. We'll find something on the menu you can eat."

Soon Deb was staring at a tall glass of beer and a platter of French fries. She knew she would not be able to eat or drink what sat before her. But she did enjoy the company.

Jenny pointed to her head and asked, "Are you taking Chemo for cancer?"

Deb smiled and shook her head. "Not anymore. I was, but I am now cancer free. The hair hasn't grown in yet, and it's kind of weird looking. I've been wearing the scarf until it gets long enough to do something with."

Jenny reached across the booth and squeezed Debbi's hand. "I'm glad you are cancer free. My aunt went through that and had such an awful time. She wasn't as lucky as you were, I'm afraid," she explained.

"I'm very sorry to hear that," Deb said, swallowing the lump in her throat.

The sound of pool balls banging against one another was a sound that she hadn't heard in a long time. The juke box played loudly, and cigarette smoke drifted in the air. Before long, two hours had passed, and it was time for her to exit.

"I'm sorry, I have to get back," she said, smiling up at Larry.

She noticed Jenny was watching him too, and got the sense that Jenny had feelings for Larry.

"So soon?" Larry asked.

"I'm sorry, I need to get an early start in the morning and I don't like being away from the cabin too long," Deb explained.

"Then there's that bridge out there," Jenny said. "No way would you catch me driving over that bridge after dark."

"Maybe I should follow you home," Larry suggested.

Deb noticed the blood draining from Jenny's face as he spoke. She shook her head and replied, "That won't be necessary. I don't have any problems crossing the bridge. I've had a good time, but I need to keep my thoughts trained on researching this book I'm writing. I can't allow too many distractions. I did have a good time and I appreciate the invitation. If you don't mind, I think I should leave now."

Larry slid out of the booth and waited for Deb to follow. "I'll walk you to your truck," he said.

Deb sighed and smiled over at Jenny. "I am so glad I got to meet you Jenny. Thank you for your kindness," she said. She looked up at Larry and said, "I can find my own way to the truck, thank you." She reached into her pocket and pulled out the two twenties as she made her way to the bar.

"You didn't eat or drink a thing," Stoney said.

"I'm not hungry. I ate dinner before I came. But I had such a good time," Debbi said, smiling across the bar at Stoney.

Stoney took a twenty and held it high in the air. "We got us an American," he said waving the twenty-dollar bill. He smiled and said to the guy sitting at the bar, "This here is a writer. She's leased the Patterson's cabin out on the lake. You know, the one you've been asking about?"

The man sitting at the bar turned to look at Deb. "How long you gonna be out there, Lady?" he asked.

"I suppose I'll be there until I get this book done," Deb replied.

"How long does it take you to write one of them books?" he asked.

"A while, I suppose. It all depends upon the book. Some books take a couple of years," Deb said, smiling.

"Years?" he asked, spinning around to stand up.

"You need to get that book wrote and move outta there. I lease that cabin every year. That's my lucky cabin and I need to get in there as soon as possible," he said, glaring down at Deb.

Deb stepped back. She was aware of Larry moving toward her. "I'm sorry, Sir," she began. "I'm afraid I'm not quite ready to leave yet."

"Oh, you're gonna get ready real quick like," the man said.

"Hey, Buddy, we will have none of that in here," Stoney said.

Deb realized she had made a mistake by coming into town. She smiled and quickly turned to make her way toward the door. The man took two steps toward her and Henry and another man he had been playing pool with stepped in front of the man, barring his way. Deb quickly went for the door, with Larry right behind her.

She moved toward the truck. "I'll keep an eye on him, to make sure he doesn't follow you, but if I were you, I would lock up tight before you go to bed tonight," Larry said, as she climbed into the truck.

"Thank you," Deb said. She turned the key and quickly pulled from the parking lot.

CHAPTER FIVE

Deb paced the floor of the small cabin, often stepping outside onto the narrow porch to listen to the sounds of the night. It was so quiet here. There were no traffic sounds or neighbors close by. There were no city lights to obscure the view of the stars in the enormous sky overhead. Even the milky way was plain to see from the porch. She stared up at the night sky, searching for a luminous green light flashing across the sky. There was nothing but sparkling stars filling the darkness of the night. A cloud obscured the moon briefly. The fog was not as dense as she expected it to be.

The quiet safety of this cabin is what brought her here. At least that was what she thought in the beginning. Now she was wondering if it might be something else. She looked down at the carving in the step. Someone put that carving there. It was identical to the symbols she often saw in her mind. She saw many symbols and it was true that she didn't understand half of them. However, this symbol was one she saw every time she felt urgent danger was near. She was very certain that it was a very important symbol. And someone else knew of this symbol. Therefore, she was confident that she was not alone. Someone else out there knew about what she was going through and possibly was sharing in her experiences. Who?

The quiet seemed to be engulfing her. She paced more rapidly, scratching at the itching inside her head. It was a common itch she got when something was bothering her. It was an itch that she couldn't scratch, and it was most annoying.

She felt the stubble of new hair growth every time she reached up to scratch. She also felt the scars from the injuries she sustained in her accident. Funny how things work out. While she was unconscious, her mother would not let them cut her long blonde hair. She was afraid Deb would be upset over losing her beautiful golden locks when she woke from her coma. Now here she was, shaving her head regularly to hide her identity.

That man at the bar, the one that became agitated with her because she occupied his lucky hunting cabin; was it possible that this man was Author Taylor? Could he have been the man Mr. Patterson said kept calling about renting the cabin? She scratched at her head with both hands. Her brain was itching intensely. She shook her head to stop the itching, but it was to no avail.

She had suspected that Mr. Taylor was responsible for the carving in the wood step. She had hoped to talk to him about the carving, but the man she met at Pappy's Bar and Grill did not appear to be very conversational. "I wonder where he is staying?" she asked aloud. She paced some more.

The sound of a loon calling near the lake caught her attention. She looked up. The sun would be up soon, and she had not slept all night. She went inside and dropped down on the bottom bunk. Staring at the bottom of the bunk above her, she sighed. Maybe she needed to change beds.

She climbed up onto the top bunk and curled up into a fetal position. She tossed and turned until sleep finally overtook her. Still, even in her slumber, the itching continued. After a brief nap, she sat up, allowing her legs to hang over the side of the bunk. "What a night!" she moaned, covering her eyes. The sun was up, and it was a new day. A new day filled with nothingness.

Deb did not walk to the lake this morning. She continued pacing, anxiously waiting for Richie to arrive with news from town. She sat on the front porch staring out over the field of tall swamp grass, listening for the familiar engine sounds of Richie's truck.

She was beginning to drift off to sleep when finally, she heard the truck bouncing across the planks of the wooden bridge. She sat up straight, staring over the wooden porch railing. Richie's truck came into view. He was not alone. She stood up, waiting for him to park the truck. A glare across the windshield prevented her from seeing who was in the passenger seat. The door opened, and Mr. Patterson climbed from the truck. He and Richie walked toward the porch together.

"I say there, you look like you didn't sleep well," Mr. Patterson called up to her from the bottom step of the porch. As he climbed the steps he pulled himself with the help of the wooden railing. He pointed to the carving on the step. "This be the carving you were talking about?" he asked.

Deb nodded her head. "It is," she replied.

Mr. Patterson nodded his head as he continued climbing. Richie followed taking one step at a time behind his father.

"I went over all my old records and receipts after you left yesterday," Mr. Patterson said, easing himself down into the chair Deb had occupied only moments ago.

Richie handed her a white box. "Mom sent you some donuts. They are store bought. I keep reminding her that you only eat raw fruits and vegetables, but you know how that goes," he said, laughing. "I'll put these on the table inside."

"Did you learn anything about Author Taylor?" Deb asked.

"Nothing except he rented the cabin same time every year," Mr. Patterson replied.

"Do you recall what the man looked like?" Deb asked.

Mr. Patterson frowned. "I can't recall. I might know him if I see him again, but to give you a description of the guy, I'm not sure I can. I'll have to think on that a spell," he said.

"I met a man last night who seemed to be upset that I was staying out here in the cabin. He referred to it as his lucky cabin," she explained.

"Now," Mr. Patterson began, shaking his index finger at her. "I do seem to recall a guy calling this his lucky hunting cabin a time or two. It might or might not be the same guy."

"Where did you see this guy?" Richie asked.

"I went into town last night. I met Larry and Henry at Pappy's Bar and Grill, like I said. He was at the bar. The bartender, Stoney, I believe his name was, said he and the guy had been talking about the cabin and

Stoney told him I was the writer staying out here. He became very upset at my being in his lucky cabin," Deb explained.

"You ought not hang out in town like that if you don't want folks to see you, Missy," Mr. Patterson declared, nodding his head.

"I'd like to learn more about this Mr. Author Taylor," Deb said, looking down at Mr. Patterson and then over at Richie. "I'm not quite sure how to go about it, but I think I'd like to talk to him. I suppose I'd like to know if he is the guy who carved that symbol in the steps, to begin with."

"That symbol is connected to what happened to us, isn't it?" Richie asked.

Deb nodded her head. Mr. Patterson interlocked his fingers and took a deep breath. "Be careful what you wish for, Missy," he said. "You may be getting yourself into something you want no part of. You may find yourself exposed and running again. You know, you've been lucky out here since you arrived. You're safe and no ones knows anything about you. This could all go sour really quick. You might want to keep that in mind."

"That sounds like good advice if you ask me," Richie said.

"I know, you are both right," Deb began. "It's just that I'm going nuts out here. Last night the itching in my head about drove me nuts. That happens whenever something is about to happen. Something isn't right."

"Maybe the itching is a warning. You know, maybe you shouldn't go asking questions about Mr. Taylor," Richie said.

"But what if he carved that symbol? And if he did, how did he know about it? Why that symbol? Where did he see it? Whoever did that, must know something about what has happened to me," Deb replied.

"Well, if I was you, I wouldn't be going back into town anytime soon," Mr. Patterson said. "That Taylor man got mighty belligerent on the phone. If he is that man you met last night, he may be dangerous."

Deb looked over at Richie, who smiled back at her. "I don't think I have anything to worry about," she said.

"Maybe not, but what if he did carve that symbol and what if he has abilities of his own? Who is to say that they aren't stronger or more powerful than yours?" Richie asked.

"He has a point," Mr. Patterson added.

Deb sighed as she thought about what Richie had just suggested. The man at the bar was most definitely angry. She could see him becoming aggressive to the point of hurting someone. She nodded her head and said, "You may be right. Perhaps I should stay out here away from the public."

"I'll ask around town about the man at the bar last night. Maybe someone knows who he is or where he comes from. Even if I get a name to go by, it would be helpful," Richie said.

"If Mr. Taylor calls again, I will see if I can get any information, too," Mr. Patterson said, standing to his feet. He stood looking out across the tall grass. "You ever see any bears out there?" he asked.

"I saw a cow and two cubs yesterday," Deb replied.

"From here or somewhere out there?" Mr. Patterson asked, turning to look back at Debbi.

"From out there. She wasn't but a few feet away from me. I was standing between her and a cub," she said smiling. "See, I told you I could handle myself just fine."

"How did you manage to get away?" Mr. Patterson asked.

"Oh," Deb smiled over at Richie before finishing. "I have my way." She smiled.

"Well," Mr. Patterson said, scratching his head. "You are either very lucky or very talented. I recall when Richie was a baby we had a couple of hunters staying in the cabin and one of them got mauled by a cow with cubs right out there in that tall grass. It's not likely to be the same bear, but I recall it was a bad mauling. They flew him outta here, and as I recall, he didn't make it. You might want to keep that sort of thing in mind before you go traipsing off in that high grass all by yourself."

"I'll keep that in mind," Debbi said.

"Well," Richie said, patting his father on the back. "What do you say we go see what Mom is up to? As I recall, she was making chicken and dumplings for dinner today."

"Maybe, Virginia would like to join us for dinner? We certainly welcome a new face at the table from time to time," Mr. Patterson said.

"I was just there yesterday," Deb laughed. "I certainly would hate to wear out my welcome."

"Oh, that isn't going to happen, Missy," Mr. Patterson laughed, as he hoisted himself to his feet. "We love having you."

"Well, I will admit, it gets awfully quiet out here day after day," Deb said. "However, I certainly don't want to put any extra work upon Mrs. Patterson. You have been so kind to me."

"It isn't any extra work," Mr. Patterson said, smiling back at Deb. "I'll tell the missus to set an extra plate."

"Can I bring anything?' she asked.

"You best stay outta town, Dearie," Mr. Patterson said. "If you need anything, you let Richie here fetch it for you. I'm not so sure about that man you met at Pappy's. I think we best wait until we are sure who he is and if he is dangerous."

"You don't have to worry about me, Mr. Patterson, although I am very honored that you do," Deb explained. "If I can handle a bear, I think I can handle the likes of that man I met at the bar."

"It's not wise to tempt fate," Mr. Patterson said.

"Who said anything about fate?" Richie asked. He laughed and added, "We would be honored to have you join us for dinner."

Deb nodded her head. "In that case, I would be honored to join you," she said.

"See you around 6:00 then," Mr. Patterson said. "Oh, I almost forgot." He reached inside his vest and pulled out a book. "The missus sent this. She thought you might like something to read to pass the time out here all by yourself."

Deb took the book. She held it between her palms and without blinking an eye, she was able to read the entire book in a matter of seconds. She smiled back at the two men watching her and asked, "What's it about?" as she did not want to give away what she had just done.

"Danged if I know," Mr. Patterson said, throwing his hands into the air. "I didn't read it."

Richie was smiling. Something told Deb he suspected she had done something, but he wasn't certain what it was exactly. She smiled back at him. "I'll see you around 6:00," she said.

"Six it is," Richie said, as he waited for his father to descend the wooden steps. "Watch Dad, the steps are still a bit wet and may be slippery," he said.

Mr. Patterson frowned as he looked back at Deb. She winked and smiled at him as he turned and proceeded down the steps again. Richie looked over at her and shook his head before following his father down the steps and to the truck.

Deb stood on the porch and watched as they pulled away. She remained on the porch even after they were no longer visible. She could hear the truck bouncing across the wooden plank bridge. It was then she turned and went inside.

She looked down at the book lying upon the rough tabletop. She smiled. She was able to read the entire contents of the book without turning a page. Her visitors were unable to discern what she had done. She smiled. It was best to keep some things a secret. After all, it may be best that they know as little as possible.

What about this Mr. Taylor? What was she going to do if he showed up out here? She certainly would like to talk to him, but he didn't appear to be the friendly sort. She would have to think about it. For now, she would take a dip in the freezing water of the lake and prepare to go to dinner at the Patterson's.

CHAPTER SIX

Deb walked to the Patterson's. She decided it was best to leave her truck parked at the cabin should anyone be lurking about. The thought of coming home to an empty cabin after dark was disturbing to her. She did not fear for her own safety, even though the element of surprise was unsettling. However, she was not fond of hurting anyone, even in self-defense. She feared being exposed and having to leave this place. Especially now, as she was intent on learning more about the person who carved the symbol into the wooden step.

The sun was going down over the tall pine trees that lined the horizon to the west. The sky was a brilliant display of bright colors tonight. It was one of these nights when she liked to sit on her porch and stare up at the horizon until the sunlight was totally gone from view. Tonight, she sat at the dinner table with Mr. and Mrs. Patterson and their son Richie.

"Dick was telling me you had a run in with a she bear out there in that tall grass," Mrs. Patterson said.

"I did," Deb said, smiling. "It wasn't anything to go on about. She backed away, and her cub followed her," Deb lied.

"Oh, my, Dearie. You really must be more careful. I'm supposing you got lucky this time," Mrs. Patterson said.

"Now Theresa, don't start preaching to the girl. She knows the dangers of being out there in that tall grass. I already talked to her about it. You know I did. Don't you recall my telling you about talking to her concerning the dangers of being out there in that tall grass? Remember, I said I told her about the guy that was mauled when Richie was a baby?" Mr. Patterson asked, holding his fork in his right hand.

Deb looked across the table at Mrs. Patterson. Her milky blue eyes appeared to be glazed over as she looked up at her husband. Was she confused? Was there something wrong with her? Deb took a deep breath and smiled before saying, "Maybe I should give Mrs. Patterson a big hug for going to all this trouble on my account," she said, looking across the table at Richie.

"Oh, she's alright, Dearie," Mr. Patterson said. "She just gets confused from time to time."

"Well, it couldn't hurt," Deb suggested, waiting for Richie to say something. Instead, he continued staring across the table at his mother.

"How's the wedding plans coming?" Mr. Patterson asked.

"Oh, not before I've eaten," Richie said. "It will upset my stomach."

"What's wrong, Dear?" Mrs. Patterson asked.

"Donna is driving me crazy with all the planning. I never knew there was so much to getting married," Richie said, covering his eyes with his hands.

"What did I tell you, Son?" Mr. Patterson said. "You stand up to that girl and tell her if she wants to get married to climb into the truck and the two of you will ride off into the sunset together. You don't need all that fancy stuff. It ain't going to make your wedding any more special or last any longer, and you'll have more money in your pocket when it's all over."

"I've tried talking to her, Pop," Richie said. "She comes back with how special a girl's wedding is and the memories she will have of the most special day in her life."

"Weddings are a special day, dear," Mrs. Patterson said. "Mine was. I remember it like it was yesterday. I wore my mother's wedding dress and we were married under a big oak tree in the back yard of my grandparent's farm. Neighbors came from everywhere. All the ladies brought covered dishes and we had a big party. Do you remember Dick?" she asked.

Mr. Patterson frowned over at his wife. "I remember, Theresa," he replied. "I was there, remember?" Just then, the phone rang. "I'll get that," Mr. Patterson said, pushing his chair back and rising.

It grew quiet at the table as he spoke into the phone that hung on the kitchen wall. "Yes, this is Richard Hugh Patterson." He quickly looked back at Debbi and pointed to the phone. "Oh, yes, Mr. Taylor. Yes, I do recall who you are, yes sir," he said, nodding his head.

Debbi rose from her chair and quickly went to stand near Mr. Patterson as he spoke into the phone. "Yes, Sir," he said. "The writer is still staying at the cabin." There was a pause. "I don't know how much longer she is going to be out there. I suppose I could talk to her tomorrow sometime. Where are you now?"

Debbi nodded her head as she waited for a response.

"Oh, you are in Connecticut, I see. Oh yes, you teach at a high school down there. No, I don't recall you telling me that before," Mr. Patterson said. "So, you say you are in Connecticut right now?" He nodded his head. "I see. Well, give me a number and a time to call you back. I'll go out there tomorrow and speak with the young lady and see what I can find out. I'll call you back after I've spoken with her. That's right. Oh, by the way, you wouldn't happen to know who carved a symbol into one of the wooden steps out there would you?" he asked.

It got very quiet as everyone stared at Mr. Patterson while he leaned against the wall looking across the kitchen at them all. "Oh, no, Mr. Taylor, it isn't like that at all. There isn't any problem with the carving. It's just that it is such a unique symbol and I was wondering if it had any significant meaning, that's all," he explained.

"So, you didn't carve that symbol into the step? I see, well, would you happen to know who did or about when it was put there?" Mr. Patterson asked. "No, we had no idea it was even there. The writer brought it to our attention. I was wondering how long ago it was done."

Deb sighed. So, apparently Mr. Taylor did not carve the symbol.

"Oh, I understand Mr. Taylor," Mr. Patterson said. "I'll give you a call right after I talk to Miss Parks. Yes, Miss Parks, that is her name. Miss Virginia Parks." There was a pause and Mr. Patterson stepped closer to the wall phone. "Okay, until tomorrow then," and then he hung up the phone.

"Well, that was obviously Mr. Taylor. He said he was calling from Connecticut. At least, that is what he said. I'm supposed to call him back tomorrow after I talk to you about how long you're staying at the cabin. I suppose you heard that," Mr. Patterson said, as he returned to the table. "If what he said was true, he is not the same man you met at the bar. He also said he didn't know anything about a carving on the steps. He didn't sound surprised when I brought it up, so I'm not exactly sure what that means."

"So," Richie began. "We have two men insistent upon renting the cabin. We still aren't sure if they are the same man, but it sounds like they aren't. One may be dangerous. Of course, it is possible the guy had too many drinks under his belt and that is why he got aggressive at the bar."

"It's possible," Deb said, rubbing her forehead.

"Are you alright dear?" Theresa Patterson asked.

"I'm fine," Deb said, smiling.

"What do you want me to tell Mr. Taylor?" Mr. Patterson asked.

"Tell him she pre-paid in advance for the next year. That should buy us plenty of time and keep him off your back for at least another year." Richie said.

"I don't want to be the cause of so much trouble," Debbi said, walking back to the table.

"You are no trouble Dearie," Mrs. Patterson said. "We owe you so much. It is the least we can do for you."

"You let us worry about these guys. You have enough to worry about for the time being," Richie said.

Deb shook her head as she carried her plate to the sink. "Like what? I sit out there day after day, doing absolutely nothing. You could be renting that cabin and making money from it. Maybe all of this is someone's way of telling me it is time to move on," she said.

Mrs. Patterson hurried to the sink. "Oh, I'll get these, Dear," she said. "You sit down and relax."

"That's what I'm trying to tell you all. I am relaxed. More than relaxed, I am bored to death out there all by myself," Deb said.

"But you must stay out of sight. That cabin is the perfect place," Richie argued.

"What good is having all of these abilities if I can't use them to help people?" Deb asked.

"And if you go around helping people, you will be noticed by the very people you are hiding from," Richie replied. "You can't do that. You must not do that."

"I just feel so useless out there," Deb said.

"Then do something useful," Mrs. Patterson said.

"Like what?" Debbi asked, smiling down at the elderly lady.

"I don't know. Join a club or something. You know, something local and low key. Maybe something like our quilting classes or maybe buy some paper and a typewriter and write a book. That is what we are telling everyone you are doing out there. Do that," she said, straightening her back and smiling.

"A book huh?" Deb asked, chuckling. "I did think of that, but I don't think I am the sort of person to do something like that. I wouldn't know where to begin."

"When you write a book, Dearie, you always start at the beginning," Mrs. Patterson said.

Debbi chuckled. She embraced Mrs. Patterson and held her for a few moments. Mrs. Patterson began trembling. Her feet lifted off the floor and her eyes rolled back into her head. When Deb lowered her to the floor, she released her embrace slowly, carefully, so the elderly woman wouldn't collapse. Mrs. Patterson staggered backwards, leaning on the sink. She was panting, and sweating. Deb's suspicions were correct. There was something wrong with her.

When she looked up at Debbi, her eyes were clear. She smiled and looked down at her hands, holding them out in front of her. "My hands aren't trembling," she said, smiling up at Deb. "What did you do to me?"

"I just hugged you, the same way I hugged Richie when we first met," Deb replied.

"I feel so good," she said, looking over at her husband. "I almost feel weightless, like I'm floating or something. However, I feel very sleepy."

"Well, I'm glad you are feeling better," Deb said, smiling.

"Maybe you should hug Dick, there," Mrs. Patterson said, pointing to her husband.

"There ain't anything wrong with me!" Mr. Patterson barked.

"You don't know that," Mrs. Patterson said. "I didn't think there was anything wrong with me either. What harm could it do?"

Deb smiled and opened her arms. Mr. Patterson shook his head and frowned before crossing the room toward Deb. He towered over Debbi. She wrapped her arms around his waist and tightened her embrace. He quivered slightly. It wasn't the same reaction she got from Mrs. Patterson, but there was something there. When the quivering stopped, she released her grip and stepped back.

"How do you feel?" Mrs. Patterson asked.

"I feel exhausted," he said. "I feel fine!"

"Oh, pay him no mind, dear. He wouldn't admit it even if he felt wonderful. It's just the way he is," Mrs. Patterson said.

Debbi laughed. "Well, I suppose I better get going. It's getting dark and I need to get home. I mean back to the cabin."

"That is your home for as long as you want it," Mr. Patterson said. "And don't worry about Mr. Taylor. I will tell him like Richie said. You paid in advance for the next years rent. That should buy you some time to figure out what you're going to do."

Thank you," Deb said, smiling. "And thank you for the lovely meal," she added.

"I'll give you a lift home," Richie said. "It isn't safe walking these back roads after dark. You might run into that old bear again."

"Oh, she was no problem," Debbi said, waiting for him to open the door for her.

They walked to his truck and Debbi climbed inside. The moon was high in the sky tonight. The dark clouds had moved out of view and the sky was filled with bright stars. It was a beautiful night.

Richie drove down the road and pulled off at the dirt road that led to the cabin. Deb got out and opened the gate. She climbed back into the truck leaving the gate open for his return. They bounced across the wooden plank bridge.

"Has this area ever flooded before?" Deb asked, to break the long silence between them.

"A couple of times. There used to be a big bridge that crossed the creek back there. Pop replaced it so many times he gave up and just put a plank crossing over it. Some of the people who have rented the cabin in the past have complained about that old bridge. They don't like the thought of no side rails. I suppose it seems scary if you aren't used to crossing something like that," Richie explained.

"Well, maybe it will keep the curious at bay," Deb laughed.

"Maybe, but if they are locals, they are used to that sort of thing. You would be surprised at how many bridges there are around here like this one," Richie said, parking the truck. "I'll come inside with you, just to be safe."

Debbi laughed. "If I can handle a mad she bear, I think I can handle an irate stranger."

"But what if he surprises you and catches you off guard? What if he's packing a gun or some other weapon? I'll go inside and make sure you are safe before I leave. You have no say in the matter," he declared.

They entered the cabin together. Deb lit the oil lamps and stood smiling as Richie determined the cabin was secure. She waited for him to leave and then she dressed for bed. Her stomach rumbled from the heavy meal she ate at the Patterson's. She sat on the porch in her pajamas, looking up at the stars until she assumed it to be late. Then she went to bed.

CHAPTER SEVEN

The hooting of an owl woke Deb from sleep. She covered her eyes with her arm as she lay upon her back. It had taken her so long to get to sleep and now she found herself awake. She rolled over onto her side and looked out the only window in the back room. A full moon hung in the cloudy sky, making it appear to be fall. Was it going to rain again? She closed her eyes and rolled over onto her back, staring up at the wooden plank ceiling.

She tried going back to sleep. If only she could push all thoughts out of her mind and relax. She heard a creaking sound. It was probably a tree limb swaying in the breeze, or possibly something or someone walking on the wooden porch.

Instantly she sat upright. She listened for any sound in the still of the night. She heard the wings of the owl fluttering as it flew away. Had something startled it?

Deb swung her legs over the side of the top bunk. She remained motionless for a few moments, concentrating on the sounds around her. Again, a creaking. It wasn't coming from the porch at all. It was coming from the front room.

Had she remembered to lock the door before retiring for the night? It wasn't all that uncommon for raccoons and other creatures to enter the cabin in search for food. Could it be the old she bear?

Deb gently lowered herself to the floor and tiptoed to the door. The latch on the door had been broken and it was slightly ajar. Deb leaned close to peer through the opening. A shadow moved across the wall facing the gas stove. It was a tall lean shadow. Someone was in the cabin and it was a two-legged intruder.

Deb placed her index finger upon the door and moved it slightly. It made a soft squeaking noise and the shadow stopped moving. "Okay," Deb thought to herself. "It's do or die." She swung the door open and called out, "Whose there?"

It appeared as if all sound had vanished at that moment. It was dead still within the cabin. "I know you're there. Come out where I can see you!" she called out.

Suddenly the dark figure standing near the table turned and darted toward the door. Deb concentrated on the front door, causing it to shut firmly. The figure fought with the door trying to force it open, but it was useless. Deb remained focused on the door as she stepped closer into the front room of the cabin.

"Who are you?" she asked. "What do you want?"

The dark figure turned to lean its back against the door. The intruder was dressed in black with a hooded sweat shirt pulled over his head, hiding his face from view.

"Who are you?" Deb repeated. "What do you want?"

The figure reached up to remove the hood. In the darkness, Deb realized it was the obnoxious man from the bar.

Deb reached for the lantern and box of matches on the table. As she lifted the globe on the lantern the figure quickly turned and opened the door. Once again, Deb focused her attention on the door, causing it to slam shut. In the process, the man's fingers became caught in the door, causing him to cry out in agony. He managed to free his hand, bending over to hold his broken fingers in his other hand. He moaned, cursing softly, as he rocked back and forth in pain.

"That door can be tricky," Deb said, smiling as she lit the lantern. She replaced the globe and nodded toward a chair with no back. "Have a seat, and let me take a look at that hand," she said.

"You stay away from me, you witch!" the man shouted.

"That is no way to talk to your host, now is it?" Deb asked, sitting on a stool opposite where the man stood. "I think it would be very rude of you not to explain yourself. You owe me that much," she said, calmly, while he continued to curse at her.

"I've never had a problem with that door before," the man moaned.

"So, you admit being here before," Deb said.

"You know I have. I told you that in the bar," the man said.

"Yes, you did at that. You knew the cabin was occupied and you came in without knocking anyway. That tells me you did not have good intentions behind your visit," Deb said.

The man looked up at her for the first time. "I told you to move on. I told you I need to lease this cabin," the man said, rubbing his broken fingers.

"There are other cabins in the area," Deb said. "Many of them have access to that lake out there. It isn't like this is the only cabin around."

"It has to be this cabin!" he barked. "I told you this is my lucky cabin."

Deb swallowed the lump in her throat and forced herself to smile across the room at the man. "Why don't you have a seat and we will discuss it like grown adults," she said.

"I ain't sitting at the table with you. You need to pack up your shit and move to another cabin," the man huffed, still rubbing his fingers.

"Well, now we have a problem," Deb began. "You see, I have paid in advance for this cabin. I am quite certain that the Patterson's have long spent the money I gave them. So, you can see why I cannot just up and move on so you can settle in here. I am afraid you will have to settle for another cabin this time. Maybe by next season this one will be available."

"I have to stay here. I can't settle for another cabin. You've got to go, Lady!" the man shouted. "Besides, I've been looking around, and I don't see any signs of a computer or typewriter. How is it you are writing a book with no computer or typewriter?" He leaned forward and jutted out his bottom jaw as he said, "Sounds to me like you been lying to a lot of folks about why you are here."

"Well," Deb said, straightening herself to sit erect. "Aren't you the know-it-all about the literary world!" She noticed he was wiggling his fingers freely. Perhaps they hadn't been broken after all.

The man shifted from side to side. She had struck a nerve. "What other ways are there to write a book?" he asked.

"I don't see why I owe you any explanation," Deb said. "You forget that you are an intruder. I could very well shoot you where you stand, and no one would question my motives at all. Everyone at the bar saw and heard you threatening me to leave here. For all I know, you came here fully intending to do me harm."

"I don't see any gun," the man declared, looking around. "What you going to shoot me with?"

Deb pointed her index finger at the man, as if it were a gun. "Be warned, Mister. You are in more danger than you think."

"Maybe it should be me warning you, Missy smart ass," the man said, leaning forward again.

As he moved forward, he glared at her. She felt her chair lifting from the floor. Suddenly she realized she was floating in the air.

Deb's jaw dropped as she looked around her. She looked over at the man as his lips curled up into a smile.

"You're not so full of yourself anymore, are you now?" the man slurred.

"Who are you?" Deb asked.

"I'm the man telling you to get your shit and get the hell out of my cabin before I hurt you!" the man said.

Deb narrowed her gaze and glared back at the man. Suddenly he lifted from the floor. She continued concentrating on moving him upward until his head touched the ceiling.

"What the hell?" the man shouted. "How is this possible?"

Suddenly, Deb's stool hit the floor hard. She nearly tumbled from it, breaking her concentration, so that the man fell to the floor.

"Agh!" he shouted, folding his tingling fingers under his arm.

He held his hand outward and closed his eyes. His fingers straightened out and the bruises cleared up right before her eyes.

"You've seen them," Deb said. "It was you who carved the symbol in the step."

"Apparently, I am not the only one who knows about our four friends," the man said, sitting astride the backless chair opposite Debbi. "I thought I was the only one."

"When did you encounter them?" Deb asked.

"It was right here in this cabin," the man said. "I saw a green glow in the sky out yonder in the tall grass. It moved out over the lake and appeared to go down on the other side of the pines. It was dark and I didn't want to run into a bear out there, so I stood on the porch, watching the lights. It was late, or early, I suppose. After a while, these four look alike strangers appeared right out there. They started chanting something, I couldn't understand. Then suddenly, it was like someone turned the volume up and it was in French. I understood French right enough," he explained.

"What did they say?" she asked.

"They said, I was to tell anyone who asked about the lights that it was a meteor that went down in the lake. I wasn't sure anyone would buy that if they happen to see what I saw, but they insisted. They kind of lifted me in the air, sort of like you just did. Then everything went black. I woke up out there in the wet tall grass, but I wasn't cold or even chilled. I felt better than I've felt in years. After that, I began noticing some changes and I realized I could do things I never did before," he explained. "What about you?"

"I was in an accident. I was in a coma for a long time. I am told I was pronounced dead by the coroner at the scene of the accident. My friend said these four strangers appeared and chanted over me. I woke up in the hospital pretty much like you did, only different. They appeared to me in a corn field one day and told me I had to run because people were coming after me. They led me here to this cabin," Deb sighed. "I keep seeing this symbol in my head. It's the same symbol carved out there on the steps."

"I carved that symbol. I see it too," the man said. He reached his hand across the table. "I'm Joseph Kearney. You can call me Joe," he said.

"I'm Debbi Farlow. My friends call me Deb," Deb said, shaking the man's hand.

"Well, now what?' Joe asked, looking around. "I take it you aren't writing a book after all."

"No, no book," Deb said. "I just needed a story for the locals."

"So, the Patterson's think you're writing a book?" Joe asked.

"No, they know about me. They are the only ones. I was led to them and found their son, Richie, was dying. I healed him and they moved me in this cabin and told everyone I was a writer to get the locals off my back. Funny thing, Richie saw the four men in a vision while he was dying. They told him I was coming, and I would heal him. They told him to protect and help me," Deb explained.

"So, there are a few people who know about you," Joe said, rubbing his chin.

"Does anyone know about you?" Deb asked.

The man shook his head. "Nope! Not a soul. No one cares either. I'm a retired school teacher from New Hampshire. No family, no friends," Joe said.

"How is that even possible?" Deb asked.

Joe squirmed in his seat. "I sort of got involved with a student years ago. They moved me from school to school until word got out. It wasn't anything dirty like folks thought. Me and this student really cared for one another. She was a senior and we planned to marry when she graduated. Her folks had other ideas, though. Anyway, I had to retire early, and I moved up near the border. I started drinking a lot and rented this cabin to be alone in my misery when I met the four strangers."

"I see," Deb said, looking away. "I'm sorry things haven't gone well for you. The four strangers must have seen something worthy in you to bestow such a gift, or should I call it a curse?"

"It's a curse. If you haven't figured that out by now, you will soon enough," Joe said. "I think they mean well, but here on earth, it just isn't normal and if it isn't normal it isn't acceptable."

"I understand completely," Deb said. "What do we do now?"

Joe rubbed his chin again. "Well, you said the four strangers led you here. They led me here as well. I keep getting signals that this is where I am to be. I don't suppose we could come to an arrangement where we both can stay here," Joe suggested.

Deb chuckled. "I don't know the locals in these parts, but if they are anything like the locals where I came from, we are going to raise a few eyebrows," she said. She laughed. "I don't care what people say. If you want to bunk out here in the corner that is fine with me, but the bedroom is mine and it is off limits. I don't want you getting any funny ideas because I'll tell you straight up, it won't go over well, and you will find yourself out there." She nodded her head toward the door.

"I have a car. I'll sleep in the car if that's alright with you," Joe said.

"That is better yet," Deb said. "At least for tonight. We can move one of the bunks out here tomorrow after the sun comes up. There must be a reason the four aliens want us both to be here. Let's find out what they want."

"Aliens?" Joe asked.

"What?" Deb asked. "You don't think they are aliens?"

Joe laughed and nodded his head. "I suppose I have always thought they're aliens, but that is the first time I've heard them described that way."

"Well, whatever or whoever they are, we best not piss them off," Deb said. "If we have special gifts because of them, just imagine what they are capable of." She stood up and stretched. "I need to get some sleep. Are you going to be alright?" she asked.

"Yeah, my car is parked on the other side of the stream. I'll pull it up close to the cabin and call it a night," Joe said.

"Fine, good night then," Deb said, turning to return to the back room. She laid on the top bunk staring up at the ceiling again. The bottom bunk was empty. Had the intruder been a woman she would have suggested she sleep in here. Tomorrow they could separate the bunks and move one out to the front room. Oh well, it was too late and too confusing to think about now and she was too tired. Perhaps tomorrow.

The next morning Deb awoke to the smell of scrambled eggs. She wrapped a flannel shirt around her and went into the front room to find Joe standing at the stove.

"So, you are a late sleeper," he smiled over his shoulder.

"Not usually," Deb replied. "Something, or someone, kept me up late last night."

Joe laughed. "Daylight's burning. I need to get out on the lake and catch a couple of fish for dinner."

"You eat meat?" Deb asked, sitting down on the backless chair.

"No, never," Joe replied. "I hate the stuff. I do eat fish, though. Good for you, you should try it sometime."

"I did," Deb said. "I can't stand the stuff. In fact, since my exposure to our four friends, I find I can't eat anything except fruits and vegetables. I prefer them raw. I can get that other stuff down, but it makes me miserable. Richie should be along this morning with some provisions."

"So, Richie comes by often?" Joe asked.

"Every other day," Deb replied.

"Well, if he's coming out here today, I should probably hide my car somewhere," Joe said, placing a plate on the table. "I made enough for two, but if you don't eat eggs, I suppose I'm going to have to eat enough for both of us."

"I'll have a carrot," Deb said. "That's plenty."

Joe shook his head. "I don't know how you keep going on just a carrot for breakfast."

"I'm not much of an eater first thing in the morning," Deb said. "I'm sorry. Where did you get the eggs?"

"I had them in the car. I bought some groceries yesterday before I came out here," Joe explained.

"What about the night at the bar?" Deb asked. "You don't seem to have trouble drinking alcohol."

Joe laughed. "As a matter of fact, I do have a problem with alcohol as you plainly witnessed. I don't process it well at all," he said, taking a bite of eggs. "I only had one beer."

"One beer did that to you?" Deb asked.

"Yep!" Joe replied. "Just one."

Deb shook her head. "I'm going outside. I like to spend my mornings on the porch listening and watching to the sights and sounds of nature. You go on and eat your breakfast." She reached into the refrigerator and held a carrot up for him to see before moving past him toward the door.

A light fog hung over the area this morning. She took a deep breath and closed her eyes. "Well," she thought to herself. "So much for being lonely."

She stared across the field of high grass in the direction of the lake. She closed her eyes and took a deep breath. A Loon called out in the morning fog. Deb smiled. She sat down in the plastic lawn chair to the left of the door.

Only yesterday she was thinking how lonely she was. "Be careful what you wish for," she thought to herself.

Joe stepped out onto the porch. He allowed the door to remain open and the aroma of scrambled eggs still lingered in the air.

"What do you do all day out here if you aren't writing a book?" he asked.

"You are witnessing it," Deb said, placing her feet upon the wooden railing of the porch. "What did you do all day out here?"

"I fished in the beginning. After my encounter I still fished, only I sold the fish to the bar in town. It gave me some spending money and something to do while I hung around waiting for our four friends to appear again," he explained.

"And did they?" Deb asked.

Joe went to lean his elbows upon the railing, looking out across the tall grass. "No. They didn't. But somehow I had this feeling that they were going to show up at any moment."

"So, you hang around here day after day waiting for them to show up because you have a feeling?" Deb asked.

"Well," Joe began with a smile. "When you put it that way it does sound a little strange."

"Do you think?" Deb asked.

"Why are you hanging around?" he asked. "You said last night you had a feeling they were leading you to this place. Isn't that sort of the same thing?"

Debbi shrugged her shoulders. "I suppose," she said. "My case is a little different than yours. They are searching for me."

Joe looked back at her. "Who? Who is searching for you?"

"Doctors, scientists, FBI, you name it. They've posted my face on every news channel in America. They claim I am wanted by the law, but the truth is I am wanted because they want me in a facility to test my abilities," she explained.

"How did they find out about you?" Joe asked.

"I told you I was in a coma, right?" Deb asked.

Joe nodded his head.

"Well, they kept running tests on me in the hospital and apparently my brain activity was higher than normal. Also, I healed way faster than anyone before with my kind of injuries." She dropped her feet onto the porch and laced her fingers behind her head. "These doctors kept coming to the house asking me to admit myself into their research facilities for testing. One day one of the doctors backed out of my driveway and over a little girl that lived across the street. She was dead."

"And you revived her in front of this doctor?" Joe asked.

"Yep. That's pretty much what happened," Deb said.

"Well," Joe began. "I can see how that could be a problem."

"What was I supposed to do? I can't go home again. I can't even call home because the FBI is watching my parents' place. I had a group of friends that were like family and I can't even contact them. I'm sure everyone is wondering if I am alright," Deb said.

"Isn't there anyone you can trust?" Joe asked.

"There is this older couple that were my neighbors. They said I could write to them using an alias, but I'm not sure that is really safe," Deb declared. "I don't want to cause any problems for them. They've been very good to me."

"I might be able to help you, but not until I find out why I am supposed to be here," Joe said. "Let me ponder on it a while."

"That is very kind of you," Deb said.

"Well," Joe said, taking a deep breath. "I need to take a walk to the lake. I'll move my car around back first."

Deb watched him as he descended the porch steps and moved toward the car. Should she trust this guy? She didn't know much about him with exception to what he told her. Could this be a trap? Could he be part of the establishment that was searching for her? Had they discovered her hiding place and sent him to get information? What about his ability to lift her off the floor and heal his broken fingers?

She concluded that she would be very careful about any information she shared with him. She would keep a close watch on his activities. For now, she needed to brush her teeth, comb her hair, and get dressed for the day.

CHAPTER EIGHT

Deb stood looking out across the tall grass that grew between the cabin and the lake. She scanned the area for signs of Joe but didn't see anything out of the normal. She thought about the mother bear and her two cubs. She had forgotten to warn Joe about her encounter with them.

After a time, she went down the steps and began walking through the tall grass toward the lake. The sun was warm and shown down upon her head. She reached up, scratching her head through the scarf she had tied around her head. She felt the stubble of new hair growth under the scarf. Soon it would not be necessary to wear the scarf any longer. Would they still be searching for her when her hair grew out?

She had reached the shore line now. She saw a canoe off in the distance, gliding across the crystal-clear water near the bend in the lake. She stood silently watching it until it was no longer in sight. She looked around, hoping to see Joe somewhere, but there was no sign of him.

She looked toward the grove of tall pines off to her left. She knew there were several cabins nestled back in the pines that belonged to other land owners in the area. She decided to walk toward the many varieties of tall trees to her right. She would have to keep on the watch for the mother bear for she was last seen moving in this direction.

There were places where the ground was soft and swampy. The mud sucked at her boots as she kept the shoreline in view. From time to time, she would look back toward the cabin, judging how far she had traveled. Still there was no sign of Joe.

What would she do if she encountered a hunter? She should have worn her orange vest to make herself more visible. Now she began to have doubts about her plans. She may be able to fend off an attacker, but she was certain she would not fend off a bullet. She turned and began moving back toward the cabin. She had not planned ahead, and this was a very bad idea.

She continued moving through the tall grass. Here she would be out in the open and stand tall enough to be seen by any hunter who may be passing this way. The ground was soft as the warmer weather thawed the frozen marsh, allowing water to ooze to the surface.

A gaggle of Canadian Geese flew overhead, squawking as they went. She stood motionless watching them fly over a cluster of trees and landing upon the lake. If only she could levitate. It would be almost like flying. Wouldn't that be wonderful? She smiled to herself and resumed her walk back to the cabin.

As she neared the cabin, she heard Richie's truck bouncing across the plank bridge. She quickened her pace, hoping to reach the cabin before he left. She tried running, but it was useless in the tall grass and marshy ground. Again, she was reminded of how convenient it would be to be able to levitate over the top of the grass and move quickly to the cabin.

She heard the engine stop. She was panting as she struggled through the grass. What if he noticed Joe's car behind the cabin?

After a few moments of silence, she heard the engine start again. She was so close. If only he took the time to look across the grass, he might see her head bobbing toward him.

"Hey, over here!" she called out, moving as quickly as she could. "I'm right here."

Richie's truck backed up and he swung the back end toward the back of the cabin. It stopped. He had seen the car. He got out of the truck and walked back to where the car was parked. He was walking around the car when Deb reached the opening near the porch. She bent down, placing her hands upon her thighs as she tried to catch her breath.

"Oh, there you are," Richie said, walking toward her. "Whose car is this?" he asked, pointing toward the green Subaru.

"His name is Joe Kearney," Deb said, still panting.

"Where is he?" Richie asked, looking around.

"Out there somewhere, I suppose," Deb replied, pointing toward the lake. "I honestly don't know where he went."

"What's he doing here?" Richie asked.

"Come on inside and I'll try to explain," Deb said, waving her hand as she walked past him toward the steps. She pointed to the symbol and said, "He's the guy who carved that symbol in the steps."

"What's he doing here?" Richie asked, again.

Deb went inside and sat down upon the stool Richie had brought her. "We now have two seats at the table, remember?" Deb said, smiling as she pointed to the backless chair. "Have a seat."

"Do you know anything about this guy?" Richie asked.

Deb shook her head. "Only what he told me."

Richie sat down on the backless chair and looked around. He noticed the bunk against the wall and raised his eyebrows as he asked, "He's staying here now?" He was becoming flushed.

"Don't get your drawers in a twist, Richie," Debbi said. "I certainly can take care of myself."

"I have no doubt," Richie began. "I thought you didn't want anyone to know anything about you. I thought that was the whole purpose in you staying out here all alone. Now, you meet some stranger and he's sleeping here? What's up with that?"

Deb was surprised at his reaction. "What is this?" she asked, frowning. "Why are you upset, really?" she asked.

"What do you mean?" Richie asked. "I've been lying to everyone about who you are and why you are out here. I've been bringing supplies out here every other day because you said you didn't want anyone in town to know anything about you. Now, I come out here and find some strange guy just happened by and, oh, yeah, by the way, he's staying here with you."

"You certainly are behaving strangely," Deb said, leaning forward.

"Well, yeah," Richie said, throwing his hands in the air. "Who is this guy? Do you even know?"

"Sort of," Deb said.

"Sort of?" Richie asked. "What kind of answer is that?"

"You seem awfully upset for some reason," Deb replied. "I haven't had a chance to explain anything to you, and you have already begun ranting and raving like I've committed some crime or something. You do know, I can take care of myself, don't you?"

"Against a bullet? Or what if he stabs you in your sleep? Is he dangerous? Did you even check him out?" Richie was waving his hands in the air. He rose from the chair and began pacing the room.

"Well, are you going to let me explain, or not?" Deb asked.

"Go ahead!" Richie said, returning to the chair. "Let's hear it."

"I found this guy in the cabin during the night, nosing around," Deb began. Richie began to protest, and she interrupted. "I know how that sounds, but it wasn't that bad. He was checking me out. You know, to see if I was really writing a book."

"Oh, like that isn't cause for concern," Richie said, slapping the table.

"Are you going to listen, or bitch?" Deb asked.

"Go on, I gotta hear more of this shit," Richie said, shaking his head.

"When I discovered him lurking around out here in the middle of the night, I was concerned as well. We sort of had a confrontation," she scratched her head and smiled. "He said he always stayed in this cabin and he wanted me to leave. We argued and suddenly I found myself floating in the air," she smiled.

"What, so you finally levitated? You've been working on that, right?" Richie asked.

"No, I wasn't levitating, Richie. He was doing it. So, I did it right back to him. There we were, both hovering in midair. That is when we discovered that he is just like me. He had an encounter with the four strangers just like I did. We both have the same abilities," Deb smiled. "Get it?"

Richie stared at her blankly for a moment. He rose from his chair and paced the room again. "That doesn't mean that he isn't dangerous. Did that ever occur to you?" he asked.

"Well, yeah, it occurred to me," Deb said. "I'm not certain he's being totally honest with me, but how else am I going to find out?"

"Isn't there some way you can check out his story? Where did he have his encounter? When was it? You know, do some investigating before you go off and let the guy move in with you," Richie barked.

"Oh, I see," Deb said, rising from her stool. "He does have the same abilities as I have, Richie."

"That doesn't make him a saint and it doesn't mean he isn't dangerous," Richie said, pacing the room.

"He said he had his encounter here. He said it was while he was renting this cabin. He also said the voices told him he was to come here. They called him here for a reason, just like they did me," Deb said. She was pacing also now.

"We don't even know that much about these voices or aliens as you called them," Richie said.

"Well they can't be evil, Richie!" Deb barked. "They brought me here to save your life, didn't they?"

Richie's face was flaming red now. He was speechless as he continued pacing without making eye contact with Deb. "So, you're just going to let the guy stay here?" he asked, after a while.

"I am for now. I must sort this through in my mind. I figure it is better to have him where I can keep an eye on him," Deb said, more calmly.

"I don't know," Richie said. "I still don't like it."

"Why?" Deb asked. "What is really bothering you, Richie?"

"I have to go," Richie said. "I just came by to drop those groceries off." He pointed to the bags of produce sitting in the wash basin.

"What's your hurry?" Deb asked.

"I have to get back to town. I told Donna I would train to be the cashier at the hardware store," he said, standing in the open doorway staring out at the grass field.

"Are you okay with that?" she asked.

"What difference does it make? I need some type of employment and until something else comes along, this will help," Richie said, tugging on his jacket. "I can't loaf around for the rest of my life."

"You don't sound very happy about it," Deb said.

He looked back at her. "You be careful out here. I don't trust this guy and you shouldn't either. Lock that door at night when you are sleeping," he said, nodding toward the back room.

Deb smiled. "He is like me," she said. "Do you really think a locked door will keep him out?"

"That's what bothers me," Richie said. "I'll drop by tomorrow before I go into town just to check on you. I wouldn't mind meeting this guy for myself."

"Okay, if you must. We agreed not to tell anyone about his abilities. So just keep that in mind when you talk to him," Debbi said.

"So why did you tell me?" Richie asked.

"Because you are my friend and I trust you," Deb replied.

Richie nodded his head and said, "I'll drop by early tomorrow." Then he left.

Deb watched him pull away until his truck was no longer visible. She sat in the plastic lawn chair and listened to his truck bounce across the wooden plank bridge. She stood up and gazed across the grassy field toward the lake, wondering where Joe had vanished off to. Then she went back inside and opened a bottle of berry juice, drinking it straight out of the bottle.

CHAPTER NINE

Deb filled the basin with warm water she had heated on the small stove. She removed her scarf and bent over the basin wetting her head before adding a drop of shampoo. Soap dripped onto the floor and all about her shoulders. She scrubbed at her scalp with her nails. Her hair had grown to about an inch in length. She was rinsing her hair when Joe stepped through the open door.

"You really should close the place up before you start doing that stuff," Joe said, dropping down onto the backless chair.

"Why?" Deb asked. "I'm fully dressed."

"You shouldn't leave the door open like that regardless," Joe said. "Anyone could walk in here."

"Oh, yeah, and apparently some people can get in here even if the door is locked," she wrapped her head in a towel. "Like you did last night."

Joe shrugged his shoulders. "I saw your friend brought your groceries."

"Yes, he was here," Deb replied, carrying the basin of soapy water outside and tossing it over the railing of the porch. She returned and wiped the basin dry, placing it back on the wash board, upside down. "Where were you?" she asked.

"I was out there," Joe said, tipping his head toward the door.

"Doing what?" Deb asked.

"You certainly ask a lot of questions. You're beginning to sound like my wife or something," Joe replied, frowning up at her from where he sat.

"I'm not all that sure I should be trusting you," Deb replied.

"I told you I was going to the lake," Joe said, shrugging his shoulders.

"I went to the lake. I didn't see you anywhere down there," Deb said, sitting on the stool on the opposite end of the table. She folded her hands on the table in front of her, waiting for him to respond.

"Were you checking up on me?" Joe asked.

"Should I have been?" Deb asked.

"I thought we cleared all the hostility in the air last night," Joe said, smiling.

Deb smiled back and said, "I'm still not sure I trust you. Just because you have the same abilities I have; doesn't mean you use them for good. I've seen a bad side to you."

Joe chuckled. "Well, I only have your word that you use your abilities for good. You could have been lying to me last night too."

Deb stood up and began to pace the room. "I think I'm going out for a while," she said.

"Going to get your hair done, are you?" Joe asked.

Deb smiled and shook her finger at him. "Now that is exactly what I was talking about. There is a mean streak in you. Why our four friends would bestow special abilities on someone like you baffles me."

"You have a point there," Joe said, nodding his head. "I won't deny that I'm not Mr. Nice Guy. I never was and probably never will be. However, everything I told you about myself last night is the God's truth. And, for your information, if I didn't keep getting these annoying visions of that symbol in my head, I would be perfectly happy to go about my own way."

"Well," Deb began. "That makes two of us." She reached for her orange vest that hung on a nail near the door and stepped outside onto the porch.

Deb jumped from the third step to the ground. She began walking through the high grass toward the lake once again, pulling the vest on as she went. She could feel Joe's eyes upon her back as she moved toward the lake for the second time this morning.

She held her hands outward, tilting her head from left to right, causing the grass to sway as she went. She knew he was watching. She wanted to demonstrate her power. Was he able to do this? Did he have all the same powers as her or was his different?

She heard a sound and instantly thought about the bear and her cubs. She stopped and listened. It was a pair of Canadian Geese nesting in the tall grass, warning her to keep her distance. She kept moving away from them, making a conscious effort not to disturb them as she went. It was spring and new birth was everywhere.

It was her first spring here at the cabin. The winter had been harsh, but tolerable. It seemed to stretch on forever, and the isolation was nearly all she could bear. Somehow, she managed, but she was dreading another year here all alone.

She thought about Joe. Perhaps she had made a terrible mistake in allowing him to stay. Simply because he said he had visions and callings that he was to be at the cabin didn't necessarily mean she should allow him to stay. She should have thought it through more thoroughly before agreeing to it. Now she was in a pickle. She couldn't just say, "Oh, I'm very sorry, but I've changed my mind."

Then again there was always the possibility that he wouldn't be happy staying there. Maybe if nothing happened, he too would become bored and decide to leave. She smiled at the idea of making his time at the cabin miserable. Her friends back home would like that idea.

She had reached the lake again. She stood at the waters edge gazing across the crystal-clear water. Geese bobbed up and down off in a distance. Squawking as more geese landed nearby. She turned to her right and began following the bank of the lake, watching for any signs of the bears, or anything else that she might frighten unexpectedly.

Muddy water sucked at her boots. She moved further into the grass where the ground was firmer. In the distance the calling of a moose shrieked in the mist. She was nearing the tall trees that grew along the wooded area near the lake. Once she stepped beyond those trees she was no longer on the Patterson's property. She had never been this far before.

She smelled smoke and suspected it was coming from another hunting cabin near the lake that had been leased. Perhaps it was the two men she had seen canoeing on the water yesterday. She turned to look behind her. It was still. Should she turn around? She was wearing an orange vest to stand out in the terrain. Was she in danger of being shot?

She heard voices. She came upon a clearing and two men were pulling on orange vests and gearing up to go hunting. They were laughing about someone named Cecil who apparently stunk up the out house the night before. She smiled and shifted her weight, snapping a twig. The men grew silent.

"Maybe it's that bear," one of them said, raising his gun.

Deb sighed and raised her hands. "No, it's no bear, gentlemen. It's only me, your neighbor, out for a morning walk," she said, stepping out where they could see her.

"It's a woman!" the short stalky man said.

"Yep, I'm a woman, alright," Deb said, smiling. "I hope I didn't startle you. I was only taking a walk and I must have wondered off the limits of my cabin."

"Are you staying in a cabin near here?" the short man asked.

Deb nodded her head. "Yes, I am. My name is Virginia Parks. I'm leasing the Patterson's cabin over that way," she explained pointing toward her cabin.

"Well, lady, you want to be more careful about walking up on people like that. There is a bear with some cubs in the area. If you don't get yourself shot you might get eaten by them," the tall thin man said.

"Yes, I know about the bears. I saw them a couple of days ago," Deb said.

"You saw them you say?" the short man asked.

Deb nodded her head. "Yes, I did."

"Well, you are lucky you lived to tell about it," the short man replied.

"Forgive me for my poor manners," the tall man said. "I'm Terry Parsons from Long Island, New York. This here is Carl Neighbors, a long-time friend and co-worker of mine. We have another friend, Cecil Roman inside the cabin. We all work together, and we come up here hunting and fishing every spring. Are you with a hunting party?"

Deb smiled and shook her head. "No, I'm not hunting or fishing. I'm a writer. I'm up here working on a book," she explained.

"Oh, we heard about you," the shorter man, called Carl Neighbors said, looking over at his friend.

"Yeah, we did hear about you," Terry Parsons said, smiling. "Everyone at the bar in town was talking about you. They said you were a ghost writer or something like that."

Deb smiled and nodded her head. "Yes, that's right."

"Well," Terry Parsons said, extending his hand and walking toward her. "As I said, I'm Terry Parsons and this here lump on a log is my longtime friend, Carl Neighbors."

Deb shook his hand and the hand of Carl Neighbors. "Hey, what's going on out here?" someone asked from the cabin.

"Come on out here and meet that writer everyone was talking about in town," Terry Parsons said. "This here is Cecil Roman." Deb extended her hand to shake with Cecil. "This is Virginia Parks, Cecil."

"Nice to make your acquaintance, Ms. Parks," Cecil said. "Clever name, Virginia Parks. Were your parents from Virginia?" he asked.

Deb smiled. He was the first person to make the connection with the name. She nodded her head. "I was born in Virginia," she lied.

"Virginia has some mighty fine parks. Beautiful state Virginia is. What are you doing up here?" Cecil asked.

"I'm writing a rather difficult book, and I needed a place where I could get away from the front door and telephone," she lied again.

"Well, you came to the right place, didn't she, Cecil?" Terry asked.

"I suppose she did," Cecil said, smiling.

"Well, I didn't mean to interrupt. I just felt a need for some exercise this morning. I'll let you gentlemen get back to your day," Deb said, backing away.

"Good to have met you Ms. Parks," Cecil said. "You be careful out here. There's a sow and some cubs wondering about. I wouldn't want to stumble upon them in that tall grass out yonder. Also, watch yourself that you don't stumble near that bull moose. He's young and on the prowl and that makes him a might crazy this time of year."

Deb nodded, "I understand. Thank you. Good day gentlemen," she said, turning to walk away.

"She knows about the bear, Cecil," she heard Carl explaining as she moved away. "She said she saw them a couple of days ago."

Once Deb was out of sight of the cabin, she once again turned right. She had a strange suspicion that this was the area Joe had gone this morning. She remembered him saying the alien craft landed beyond the tree line. Had he gone in that direction? She was curious to find out for herself. She recalled the bull moose calling out from somewhere out this way. He would stand tall enough for her to see at a distance in this terrain, but once she reached the trees and wooded area, he would be difficult to spot.

Deb leaned against a large oak tree and scanned the area. Her hearing was quite acute, and she picked up a variety of animal sounds all around her. She did not hear anything to indicate the moose or bear were near. She moved deeper into the woods, often stopping to close her eyes and listen. What if the hunters were coming this way? She knew she would hear them before they saw her, still, there was always the danger of being shot. She could possibly save someone who had been shot, but could she save herself? She moved on.

Now she had reached a clearing. The grass had been severely burnt, but strangely had not begun to regrow. She stood in the center of the large burnt circle looking around. Nothing on the perimeter had been damaged to indicate something had moved into the area. Whatever did this had to have dropped directly onto the ground from above.

She bent down and touched the black ground. Everything had been burnt away leaving even the soil dark and dry. She allowed the dark powdery soil to sift through her hand. It was obvious that this was the place the alien craft had landed the night Joe had told her he met the four strangers.

Time seemed to stand still as she allowed her thoughts to linger on their conversation the previous night. How much time had passed she did not know? She was no longer paying attention to the sounds surrounding her. A loud crack shot through the forest and seemed to echo on and on.

Something hit her in the right side of her chest and knocked her off her feet. She reeled around as she hit the ground hard. She gasped but was unable to get air into her lungs. Her arms were waving into the air and she tried to sit up but could not. She was dizzy and struggling for air.

Out of nowhere, Joe appeared. He knelt and smiled at her. "Told you to be careful, didn't I?" he asked, grinning an awkward smile.

Had he done this to her? Was it his intention to kill her? What had happened?

"Calm down, you've been shot," he said, placing his hand upon her chest.

Deb felt everything growing fuzzy with a heavy fog. Unable to breath she felt herself drifting away. She was dying. She felt herself getting lighter and floating upward. "Oh, now you levitate," she thought to herself. She felt herself begin to tremble before losing consciousness.

Suddenly her eyes opened, and she looked up at Joe. He smiled down at her. "How do you feel?" he asked.

Deb sat up and took a deep breath, holding the air in her lungs a moment before exhaling. "I feel fine," she said, standing up. "Tired, but fine." She looked down at her orange vest. Blood had stained the area around a small hole in the vest. "Did someone shoot me?" she asked.

"Sure enough," Joe said. "Good thing I was nearby."

"What were you doing out here?" she asked. "Were you following me?"

"Good thing I was," Joe said, frowning. "You'd be a goner if I hadn't."

"Why were you following me?" she asked.

At that moment the three men she had met at the cabin came rushing toward her. "Are you alright, Ms. Parks?" Terry called out, as they neared.

"I'm fine," Deb said, smiling.

"I could have sworn I hit you," Terry said, trembling as he spoke. He fell to his knees. "Oh God, I was certain I killed you."

"I'm fine," Deb said, touching his shoulder.

"You got some blood…," Carl said, pointing to his own shoulder.

Deb looked down at her stained vest and said, "Oh, that. That's nothing." She pulled her collar aside to reveal her shoulder where the bullet had pierced earlier. "See? Nothing."

"Where did that blood come from?" Carl asked.

Terry was still on his knees with his head hanging. He was sobbing uncontrollably. Deb went to him and placed her hand upon his shoulder. "Terry, you did not shoot me. If you were shooting at me, you obviously missed. Maybe you should work on your aim," she teased. He could only reach out and take her hand. "It's alright," she said.

"Who are you?" Cecil asked, looking over at Joe.

"I'm Joe," Joe replied, smiling. "I'm a friend of Ms. Parks. I followed her out here."

Terry began to retch, as he vomited onto the ground. "I think you boys should take Terry back to the cabin," Deb said.

"I'm going home. I'm going home," he repeated. "I'm done out here."

"Terry don't let this spoil your trip," Deb said, placing her hand upon his shoulder. She watched as he began to tremble. The others thought it was his reaction to what had happened, but Deb watched his eyes roll back and his mouth drop open. When she removed her hand, he dropped face down into his own vomit.

"Oh," Cecil said. "That's got to smell."

Deb smiled. "I think you boys should take Terry back to the cabin and let him get some sleep. He'll feel better after a little rest."

The men got on each side of Terry and helped him to his feet. They began walking back toward their cabin. Deb smiled over at Joe and said, "Thanks for saving my life."

"My pleasure. I knew I was sent here for a reason," Joe replied.

Deb looked around at the burnt ground and asked, "Is this the place where the craft went down?"

"It is," Joe replied.

"Is this where you went this morning?" she asked. He nodded his head. "Why did you come out here?"

"I knew I was getting the messages to be here for a reason. With you being here too, I just thought maybe I would find the answer out here," Joe explained.

"Did you?" Deb asked.

He shook his head. "No. Maybe I was called here to save your life," he said, smiling.

"But if you hadn't been here, I wouldn't have known about this place and I wouldn't have come all the way over here, and wouldn't have been shot," Deb said.

"Maybe you would have been shot somewhere else," Joe said, shrugging his shoulders.

"Come on, let's go back to the cabin."

They walked together, side by side, without saying a word. Deb kept listening for sounds of the bear or bull moose. Oddly she felt better than she had in years. Is this what others felt after she helped them recover? She closed her eyes as she moved along, imagining herself floating upward above the tall grass, looking down from somewhere high above. She opened her eyes to find herself standing amidst the tall grass.

"What is it?" Joe asked.

"Nothing," she said, smiling as she hurried to catch up with him.

CHAPTER TEN

They were climbing the steps to the cabin. Deb glanced down at the symbol. "I know there has to be a reason why we were both called to this place," Deb said, pausing to look out across the tall grass toward the lake. "Do you suppose there are others like us out there?"

"I've often wondered that," Joe said, turning to look back at her. "It is highly probable."

Deb glanced over her shoulder at him. "I wonder where they are," she said.

"Who? The aliens or the people like us?" Joe asked.

"Both, I suppose," she replied, looking out toward the lake again.

"I don't know. I've stopped mauling over it a long time ago. Sometimes, it comes to mind, but I try hard to push it way back in my mind. I know the visions won't let up, and if I do what they want me to do, I get some relief. If I don't, I can't sleep. They won't let me. Is it like that for you too?" Joe asked.

"Yes," Deb replied. "I get this horrific itching inside my head. There's a crackling sound sometimes, too. Do you get anything like that?"

Joe shook his head. "No, I can't say I've experienced anything like that."

"Maybe it has something to do with the injuries from my accident. I had five skull fractures when I was ejected from the car," Deb explained.

"That had to hurt," Joe said, straddling the backless chair.

Deb stepped inside the cabin and sat down upon the stool. "Actually, I never felt a thing," she said, smiling. "I was in a coma for a time. I was put on a life support system until I regained consciousness. There was some pretty weird stuff that went on in that hospital while I was recovering."

"Weird how?" Joe asked.

"None of the electrical machines would work when I was awake. As soon as I took something to put me out everything began working again. Even the television wouldn't work. They kept taking me down for CT scans and X-rays and the machines would malfunction. They took me back to my room and everything was up and running again. No one at the hospital made the connection except for my mother. She noticed it right away. Finally, she persuaded the doctor to give me something to help me sleep while they ran tests and that is how they discovered an unusual amount of brain activity and rapid healing. That was what brought Dr. Martelli to the house the day I revived Eva's daughter, Rachel," Deb explained.

"Now I can relate to the mechanical thing," Joe said, nodding his head. "I noticed early on that radios and TV's don't work in my presence. I'm not sure how that works, or doesn't work, but it's the same with me." He laughed. "Of course, what goes on when I'm sleeping, I can't say."

"You said you don't sleep much," Deb said.

Joe shook his head. "No, that's why I drink. Helps me to relax and when I've gone about as long as humanly possible without sleeping, it helps me go down. You don't seem to have trouble sleeping," Joe said.

"No, I don't," Deb replied.

"Do you take medication for your injury?" he asked.

Deb shook her head. "No."

"Is the injury why you don't have any hair?" he asked.

Deb shook her head again. "No. I shaved my head. They had pictures of me all over the country, so I shaved my head and eyebrows. So far, it's worked," she smiled.

"I'm trying to picture you with hair," Joe said. "I think you were probably a red head."

Deb shook her head and laughed. "No, I was a natural blonde."

"So, are you smarter now?" Joe teased.

"I'm not even going to respond to that," Deb said, frowning. "That isn't very nice."

Joe pursed his lips. "Sorry about the remark, but it wasn't very smart of you to go out there knowing there are hunters everywhere in those woods."

"You went out there," Deb said.

"Right," Joe said, nodding his head. "You got me there."

"So," Deb began. "What happened to the senior you were going to marry?"

"I don't know. I left without a word," Joe explained. "Her parents threatened to have me thrown in jail. I thought maybe it was best that I moved on, maybe wait a couple of years before I try to contact her again."

"Aren't you afraid that she will be in a relationship with someone else by the time you get around to going back?" Deb asked.

"I thought about it," Joe said. "All of that was before my encounter. Now I hope she has found someone else."

"You never tried to contact her to explain why you ran off?" Deb asked.

Joe shook his head. "Nope. Just up and left in the night. Drove until I couldn't hold my eyes open any longer and settled there. Applied for a teaching position, and when someone learned about my past, I climbed in the car again. Finally, I decided to do some fishing in Canada, and came here. You pretty much know the rest," he explained.

Deb smiled. "You said you were going fishing this morning. You walked off without a pole or tackle box. You came back empty handed too," she said, watching him. "You lied to me. If this is going to work, you can't do that."

"I didn't want you to follow me," Joe began. "I knew you were curious. I didn't want you out there. I was hoping for an encounter, and I thought my best chance was to go out there alone."

"Well," Deb said, throwing her hands in the air. "So much for that theory." She studied him a moment. "What now? Where do we go from here?" she asked.

"You do what you normally do. As for me, I'll be around. I won't say anything about you, and I would appreciate it if you showed me the same courtesy," Joe said. He paused a moment before asking, "You said there's nothing between you and the Patterson guy. So, did you leave anyone behind?"

Deb smiled. "No love life, that's me. I've had relationships in the past, but nobody special." She stood up and threw her hands in the air. "Doesn't look like there's anyone in my future either."

"Why don't you come into town with me and have a drink?" Joe asked. "Might do you some good to get out and socialize with some of the local guys."

Deb shook her head. "That would definitely raise some eyebrows, you and me having a couple of drinks. I don't think so. You go on. I'll stay here and work on my book," she smiled back at him.

"Have it your way, Miss Virginia Parks," Joe said. "Me? I'm going into town. I'm not one for hiding out. Hell, I wouldn't be here at all if it wasn't for that darn symbol and the nagging number thing."

Deb smiled and nodded her head. She turned the dishpan over upon the washboard and stared down into it with her back to Joe. She heard him step through the door and descend the steps. She listened as he started his car and drove down the rutted road. She heard his car bouncing across the plank bridge and move toward the road. She sighed and sat down upon the stool again. She crossed her arms upon the table top and buried her head in them. She was lonely. She wanted to go out and party like old times with her friends. It was the middle of the day and she was already bored out of her mind.

Deb retreated into the back room. She pulled off the orange vest and inspected the hole where the bullet had penetrated through the fabric. She felt fortunate that Joe had followed her. She felt sorry for Terry. He was so overcome with grief over what he had done. Of course, his actions were horrific, and the outcome could have been so much more tragic had Joe not been there. The words Richie had spoken earlier came rushing back to her. She might not be able to save herself from a bullet or a stabbing. Deb dropped down onto the bunk and stared up at the ceiling.

She closed her eyes and tried to breathe slow and steady. If only she could go back to sleep. It was the only way to pass the time. She drew her arm up over her face. She rolled over to face the wall and pulled her pillow over her head. After a few moments she was sitting up again.

"Agh!" she moaned.

Deb stood up and walked back out to the front room. Perhaps another walk. This time she would stay close to the rutted road. She pulled her mud boots on and began walking toward the plank bridge.

She stood watching the muddy water rush under the bridge. After a while she walked toward the gate that led to the main road. She kept to the grassy middle to avoid the puddles. She took notice of the muddy tire tracks made by Joe leaving earlier. She had reached the gate and passed through it not sure where she was going or why.

Soon she found herself standing in front of the Hickman home. One of the boys was playing with a border collie in the front yard. He looked up to see her standing on the road. He waved, and the dog rushed toward her. Deb froze. Was the dog friendly? Would it feel a need to protect the boy? Maybe this was a mistake.

"Hello," the boy called out as he approached. "Daisy, come back!"

The dog stopped but continued to bark. "This is Crazy Daisy. She won't bite, but she might jump on you and lick you to death," the boy said, laughing. "Are you the lady writing a book?"

Deb took a deep breath and smiled. "I am the writer. My name is…,"

"Virginia Parks, I know," the boy said. "Everyone knows."

Deb smiled and nodded her head. "I see," she said. "And your name?"

"I'm Larry Hickman," the lad said, extending his hand. "It's nice to meet you Miss Parks."

Deb shook the young man's hand. "It's my pleasure," she replied. She reached down and began to stroke Crazy Daisy's head. "Crazy Daisy is an odd name, especially for a border collie. They are one of the most intelligent canines."

"She's smart. We named her Crazy Daisy because she acted so crazy when she was a puppy," Larry said. "Would you like to come in and meet my parents?"

"Oh, I don't want to intrude," Deb protested.

"Oh, you won't be intruding. Mom said we should take a gift back to the cabin and introduce ourselves," the boy said. "The only reason we haven't is because everyone said you want your privacy and we don't want to bother you."

Deb smiled. "Well, that is certainly kind of your family," she replied.

"Larry, who are you talking to?" a woman called from the front porch.

"It's Miss Virginia Parks, Mom," Larry called back. He looked back at Deb and said, "Please, come meet my Mom."

Deb took a deep breath. She wanted to object, however, the woman was approaching them. "Miss Parks," she called ahead. "It's so nice to finally meet you."

Deb smiled. "I was just out for some air. Sometimes I need to clear my head after a lot of researching," Deb lied.

"I totally understand," the woman said, extending her hand. "I'm an accountant. My name is Charlotte. Charlotte Hickman."

Deb shook her hand. She smiled and started to speak, but Charlotte interrupted, "Virginia Parks. We know."

"Yes, that's right," Deb said. She felt her face flushing.

"You must be chilled. This air is still a bit nippy even though spring is in the air," Charlotte said. "Won't you come inside?"

"I don't want to intrude," Deb protested. "I was just out for some air."

"Oh, nonsense, Miss Parks. It's a bit nippy as I said. Come inside and have a cup of tea to warm yourself," Charlotte insisted.

"Come on, Miss Parks," Larry urged. "You need to meet my brother, Liam. He wants to be a writer."

Deb felt her spine go rigid. She knew nothing about writing. Liam was going to want information from her that she could not give. What should she do? This was a mistake.

"I really can't come in right now," she said, smiling. "I would love to meet the family and I do appreciate the offer of tea, but I can't be gone long. I have so much work to do and I've been stuck on something, I need to work out," she lied, backing up. "Please forgive me for rushing off, but I just had a thought and I need to get it down before I lose it. Thank you and again, I do apologize." She turned and began walking back toward the gated drive that led to the cabin.

"Darn!" she said to herself. It would have been nice to have a conversation with another adult female. What harm would there have been in a short visit? After all, it was just the length of time to drink a cup of tea. How odd she must have appeared rushing off that way.

She found herself standing upon the plank bridge staring down at the rushing water. It was murky and flowing rapidly underneath her. She sighed. What was done was done. There was no going back now. She sighed and moved toward the cabin.

As Deb reached the porch, the sound of a vehicle bouncing across the plank bridge caused her to turn around. A familiar pickup truck was approaching with three adults sitting inside. It pulled up to a stop and she instantly recognized Larry and Henry Escott. She did not recognize the third person.

Deb stood near the steps and waited for them to approach. "Good afternoon, gentlemen," she said, smiling.

"Good morning," Henry said, smiling. "It isn't noon yet. Do you have a clock out here?"

Deb smiled. She stood up and extended her hand to the younger Escott brother. "No, I have a clock in the cabin, but I'm not in the cabin at the moment."

"Well, we will have to do something about that, won't we Larry?" Henry asked, turning to look back at his older brother.

Larry walked up to stand directly in front of Deb. "You need a wristwatch. We were at the trading post when two guys came in and said you had been accidently shot. Henry and I thought we should come out here and check on you."

Deb smiled. "I'm fine. It was just a graze and there was no damage done," she replied.

"That's what he said, too. He said he was there, and it knocked you off your feet. He said there was blood on your vest, but you showed him your shoulder and there was no sign of injury. He said he was baffled by the whole thing. He was pretty upset when he described the event," Larry explained.

"I'm fine. I just got back from a walk, in fact," she said, smiling. "I met a couple of my neighbors. Mrs. Hickman and her son Larry."

Larry smiled. "That's our sister, Charlotte. Her son Larry was named after me," he said.

"Oh my," Deb began. "It's a family thing."

"Sure is," Henry said.

Deb looked at the third man, leaning against the grill of the truck. "Is this gentleman another family member?" she asked.

"Oh!" Henry said, turning to look back at the smiling stranger. "No, he isn't related. Just a friend of ours."

Larry turned to look back at the stranger. "This is Marshall Nemmans. He happened to be with us when the men came into the trading post," he explained.

"It's a pleasure to meet you, Mr. Nemmans," Deb said, rising and extending her hand.

Marshall moved toward her, taking her hand. As their hands touched, Deb instantly felt a static electric shock between them. Marshall pulled his hand back quickly and shook it. "Wow!" he exclaimed.

Deb rubbed her hand. Her head was spinning as messages flocked toward her faster than she could process them.

"What was that all about?" Henry asked.

"I don't know," Marshall said, rubbing his hand. "Did you feel that?" he asked Deb.

Deb smiled and nodded her head. She had to remain composed. She wasn't certain what had just happened, but somehow, she had a connection to this man. She smiled and said, "It must be the flannel shirts."

"It was something," Marshall said.

"Are you sure you are okay?" Larry asked. "Maybe we should take you in to see the Doc. You are kind of isolated out here and maybe you should have him look at you, just to be safe."

Deb shook her head. "No, I feel fine. I just got the wind knocked out of me for a moment. I swear to you that I am fine."

"That stranger that gave you a hard time at the bar has been hanging around in town," Henry said. "Thought maybe we should warn you about him."

"I know," Deb said, smiling. "He's been out here. He isn't a problem. In fact, I put a bunk in the front room for him. He is harmless and it appears to be so important to him that he be in this particular cabin."

"He's staying here?" Larry asked.

"Yeah," Deb replied. "Like I said, he is harmless."

"Maybe if he's sober, but that night at the bar, he didn't appear harmless. I'm not sure that is wise on your part," Larry said.

"Well, he stayed last night, and we didn't have any problems," Deb said. "In fact, he came in pretty handy after Terry Parson's shot at me. I'm thinking it might be a good idea to have someone else out here."

"You are rather isolated out here," Marshall said.

Deb smiled, as she looked into his soft blue eyes. "Yes, I am."

"Well," Larry said, clearing his throat. "Some of us are getting together at Pappy's again tonight. Why don't you join us for a couple of hours?"

Deb smiled. "I think I will. I could use the fresh air and a break," she replied.

"Good," Larry said. "See you around 7:00?"

Deb nodded her head. "7:00 it is," she replied.

"She doesn't have a watch, Larry," Henry said.

Larry removed his watch, holding it out toward Deb. "Take this. You can give it back tonight at Pappy's," he said, smiling.

Deb took the watch. "Thank you," she replied, smiling. "I can assure you my battery clock works just fine. I really hate taking your wristwatch."

"Nonsense, you don't want to hang out in the cabin all day watching the clock and you certainly don't want to carry a big clock around with you when you're out here," Larry said.

"See you there," Marshall said, smiling over at Deb. He paused as Larry and Henry moved toward climbing into the truck. Larry cleared his throat and Marshall quickly climbed into the front seat next to Henry.

Deb watched as the truck turned around and they moved down the rutted, muddy road toward the plank bridge. She heard the truck bouncing across the wooden planks. Soon the engine revved as it reached the main road. Deb smiled to herself. She had something to look forward to.

She looked down at the watch she held in her hands. It had stopped. She smiled and carried it inside, placing it upon the table. She sang to herself as she twirled around the front room. What had started out as a bad day, was quickly beginning to change. Who was Marshall Nemmans? What was his connection to her?

CHAPTER ELEVEN

The rest of the afternoon seemed to drag. As the sun was setting, Joe returned. He entered the cabin and flopped down upon his bunk.

"Do you have the time?" Deb asked.

He opened one eye and looked over at her. "Are you expecting someone?" he asked.

Deb shook her head. "No, I'm not expecting anyone. I've been invited to join some friends at Pappy's around 7:00, and the battery is dead in the clock," she said.

"Oh, so now you're suddenly the social butterfly," Joe jeered.

"What's up with you?" Deb asked, walking to stand looking out the door at the sunset in the distance. "I don't own a watch, and it wouldn't work if I did. I have a battery clock and the one time I need it the battery is dead."

"Well, I suggest you be on your way, if you want to meet them by 7:00," Joe smirked.

"Oh, really?" Deb said, looking back at him. "Is it that close?"

"This time of year, sunset is around 7:15," Joe said, pulling his ball cap over his eyes.

"Oh," Deb replied, looking down at her worn jeans and flannel shirt.

"Don't worry, you look fine. In fact, you'll fit right in. Everyone wears tattered jeans and flannel shirts these days. People don't dress like they used to," Joe said.

"Why are you back so soon?" Deb asked, pausing at the door.

"Don't worry about me. I need a power nap and then I'll hit the bar again. You'll probably see me around before the night is over," Joe said, rolling over to face the wall.

Deb frowned as she grabbed her shoulder pouch and moved through the door. She climbed into her truck and turned the key. The engine turned over immediately, and she soon was bouncing across the wooden plank bridge.

The sunset was beautiful this evening. She pulled into Pappy's parking lot and parked nearest the road. The lot was full of vehicles tonight. She could hear the music before she reached the bar. As she opened the wooden door, everyone turned to look at her.

"Over here, Virginia!" Henry called out.

Deb smiled as she moved toward the small crowd sitting at two tables that had been placed together to form one long one. There were many faces she did not recognize.

Marshall Nemmans stood up and pulled a chair out next to him. "Have a seat," he said, smiling down at her. Deb felt her neck growing hot as she smiled up at him before sitting down.

"What are you drinking?" Larry called out from the end of the table.

Deb sighed. This always presented a problem for her. "I'll have a draft," she said, not knowing what else to say. She was aware of Marshall bouncing his leg nervously next to her. She watched Larry as he turned and made his way toward the bar. She noticed that Jenny had been sitting next to Larry, and she too was watching him as he moved away from the group. He soon returned with a draft mug, placing it on the table in front of her.

"Stoney said he will be over in a minute for grill orders," Larry said, smiling down at her. "I'm glad you came."

Deb glanced over at Jennifer's face, which seemed to pale as she watched Larry talking to Deb. She smiled up at him and said, "Thanks' Larry, but I'm not hungry. I just needed to clear my head and get a change of scenery."

"Hey, Virginia," a thin bearded man called from the other end of the table. "We hear that fisherman who calls himself Joe Kearney is sharing the cabin with you."

Larry waved at the man and said, "Do you remember Willy? Willy Goldman? He was here the night you stopped in."

Deb shook her head. "I don't remember him," she replied. "Why did he refer to Joe as the fisherman who calls himself Joe Kearney?" she asked.

"Oh, don't pay Willy no mind," Larry said.

Marshall leaned close and said, "Willy is one of those conspiracy people. He swears aliens visit us from time to time. Nobody pays any attention to him. We just more or less tolerate him. Besides, he's already hammered."

Deb smiled as she looked down the table at Willy who was already draining the last of the beer in his bottle. He slammed the bottle upon the table and waved toward the bar. "I'm empty over here, Stoney," he called out.

"I see," Deb replied, smiling.

At that moment someone had selected a song on the juke box and music filled the air. Jennifer rose from her seat and approached them. "Dance with me, Larry," she coaxed, smiling up at Larry.

"Maybe later, Jen," Larry said.

Jennifer's face showed her disappointment.

"Oh, go ahead and dance with the lady," Marshall said. He rose from his seat and smiled down at Deb. "May I have this dance Miss Virginia Parks?" he asked."

Deb felt her face growing hot. It had been nearly two years since she had danced. How she missed the old days. She smiled up at Marshall and took his hand. "I would love to," she replied, as she moved toward the dance floor.

Jennifer and Larry were dancing to their right. At first it was quiet between them, and then Deb cleared her throat and asked, "Are you from around here?"

Marshall nodded his head. "Nearly all my life. I work for a company that does commercial welding. I find myself on the road a lot, but most of the time, I'm right here," he replied.

"So, you've known Larry and Henry all your life," Deb said, nodding her head.

"Yep, I live the next place down the road from them. My older sister, Carol was best friends with Larry's sister Charlotte, and Larry and I have been best friends since first grade. Maybe even before that," Marshall explained.

Deb smiled. "It seems everyone knows everyone here."

"Yep," Marshall replied. "They either know them or are related to them."

"So," Deb began. "You have an older sister, Carol."

"Yep," Marshall replied, with a nod of the head. "I also have a younger sister, Paulette, who is married and lives in Harrisburg, Pennsylvania. She works for an insurance firm down there. Her husband is a Highway Patrolman." He spun her around. "What about you, Miss Virginia Parks? Where are you from and what about your family?"

Deb smiled. "I don't have a family. My parents are both gone, and I was an only child," she replied. It was all a lie, but she didn't dare tell this man the truth.

"Where are you from, originally?" Marshall asked.

"I'm from North Carolina," Deb lied.

"Oh really?" Marshall asked. "That's odd. The plates on your truck are Pennsylvania plates."

"Oh," Deb smiled. "The truck belongs to my Uncle. I didn't have a vehicle, so he gave me his truck. My aunt and uncle are my only relatives." Deb hoped he bought her story. She tried to control her crackling voice.

"That's very rare," Marshall said, smiling.

"What is rare?" Deb asked.

"Having so little family. I can't imagine. Up here, everyone is related to someone, somehow. I guess it's the small-town thing," he laughed.

"I suppose that would explain it," she replied.

"That, and the fact that we are so isolated from the rest of the world," Marshall said. "The nearest town is thirty-two miles west."

"That far?" Deb asked. "Wow!"

"You didn't know that?" Marshall asked. "How on earth did you come to pick this area to write your book?"

Fortunately for Deb, the song ended then and Larry turned to them. "How about we switch partners?" he asked Marshall.

Marshall smiled and nodded his head before turning to dance with Jennifer. Larry smiled down at Deb and said, "I promise not to step on your toes."

"I'm afraid I can't promise you I won't step on yours," she replied, smiling back at him. "I'm very much out of practice, I am afraid."

"Well, we will have to do something about that," Larry said, spinning her around. "I'm very glad you came tonight."

"I'm glad I came too. It feels good to get out," Deb said. She noticed that Jennifer was watching them from over Marshall's shoulder as they danced. "By the way, I have your watch, but for some reason it stopped working. I hope it wasn't something I did."

"Oh, it was just a cheap digital watch. One of those things you pick up at any Walmart. I have a couple of them," Larry laughed.

"Are you and Jennifer a couple?" Deb asked. Larry began to chuckle, and Deb said, "Pardon my frankness. I didn't mean to stick my nose where it doesn't belong. I am just trying to figure out who belongs to who and where everyone fits in."

"I understand," Larry said, smiling down at her. He sighed and said, "Jennifer and I go out from time to time, but I wouldn't classify us as a couple. Not technically anyway."

"Does she know that?" Deb asked, looking over at Jennifer who was still watching them. "I mean, it's written all over her face."

"This is a very small community, in case you haven't noticed," Larry said, pulling her close to him. "There aren't many to choose from. She probably feels an attachment to me because there isn't anyone else available."

Deb sensed that he was dodging the subject. "What about Marshall?" she asked.

"Marshall is my best friend," Larry began. "There isn't any reason why Jennifer couldn't date Marshall officially."

"He seems like a nice enough person," Deb said.

Larry leaned back and looked down at her. "Nice enough for who? Are we still talking about Jennifer?"

Deb smiled up at him. "For anyone," she said, laughing.

The door opened and Richie and Donna walked in. Everyone shouted out a greeting as the two of them made their way to the table.

"What about Richie Patterson? Is he a nice enough guy?" Larry asked.

"There isn't anything wrong with Richie Patterson, with the exception to the fact that he is already spoken for," Deb replied, with a broad smile.

"That he is," Larry said, spinning her around again. "He is very much spoken for. Donna is a good catch. Just ask Marshall."

"Why should I ask Marshall about Donna?" Deb asked, frowning.

"Donna was dating Marshall while Richie was sick. Everyone thought he wouldn't pull through," Larry began to explain. "When Richie suddenly got better and started coming around again, Donna brushed Marshall aside."

"Oh," Deb said. "How did Marshall feel about that?"

"Well," Larry said, looking back at the table where his friends sat, drinking. "He swears he wasn't that serious about Donna, but I think she's beginning to have second thoughts about her feelings for Richie. Something happened one night after Richie got better and Donna moped around town for a few days, crying at the drop of a hat. Marshall swears he hasn't any idea what the problem was. He thinks it was between Donna and Richie, but everyone else thinks it had something to do with Marshall."

"Oh," Deb said, looking over at Marshall and Jennifer dancing.

The music stopped and they made their way to the table where they each greeted Donna and Richie.

"Look who came out after dark," Richie said, smiling over at Deb.

"Hello, Miss Parks," Donna said, smiling across the table at Deb. Deb noticed that her eyes briefly shifted upon Marshall and quickly back to Deb.

"Good evening, Donna. It's good to see you again," Deb said, with a slight nod of her head.

Stoney approached, wiping his hands upon his white apron. "Okay, who all wants something from the grill?" he asked.

Everyone ordered something. When it came Deb's turn she smiled and said, "I'll just stick with my beer, thank you. I ate earlier."

"Then bring her another beer!" Henry called out.

Stoney took all the grill orders before leaving. Deb listened to the conversation around the table. She noticed Marshall's leg bouncing nervously once again. Soon Stoney returned with a tray of bottles, mugs, and one wine glass. Now Deb had two full mugs of draft beer sitting in front of her.

"You better drink up, Miss Parks," Willy Goldman called out from the end of the table.

Deb smiled at him and lifted her mug in a toast to Willy before taking a drink. It burnt going down and the bitterness almost caused her to gag. She was able to hide her dislike for the taste, as she smiled at everyone watching.

Marshall smiled as he leaned close and said, "You can drink something else if you want. I'll see to it you get home alright."

Deb smiled and said, "That shouldn't be necessary. Water is my preferred drink. It's just difficult to come into a place like this and order water, if you know what I mean."

"I understand," Marshall said, laughing. "That wouldn't go unnoticed in here."

"I'm certain it wouldn't," Deb said, smiling back at him.

She felt Donna's eyes upon her. As she sat looking around the table, she noticed Donna watching her closely. Every time Larry said something to her, she noticed Jennifer watching her closely. She sighed, for she felt like she was making enemies by association.

"Well," she said, rising. "I'm afraid I should get back to the cabin."

"What's your hurry Miss Parks?" Willy called out. "I wanted to talk to you about some of the strange things that have gone on out at that lake."

"And we shall talk, Willy. Drop by sometime and we will talk," she smiled.

Marshall leaned close. "That might not be such a good idea, Virginia," he whispered.

Deb looked down at him and smiled. She was not certain how to respond. "Well, I better go," she said, sliding her chair under the table.

"I'll see you to your truck," Marshall said, following her toward the door.

When they reached the truck he asked, "Are you sure you'll find your way back alright? Maybe I should follow you home."

"I think I can find my way," Deb said, smiling.

"I'm not sure about that guy staying out there with you," Marshall began. "He's displayed some very erratic behavior. You are very isolated out there should something go wrong."

"Oh, Joe is harmless. His bark is far worse than his bite," Deb declared. "I'll be fine."

"If you don't mind, I would feel much better if I followed you home," Marshall insisted."

"Suit yourself, but I feel terrible taking you away from the party," Deb said.

Marshall waved his hand in the air. "Don't worry about that. I see that gang every day. Fact is, I won't be missed," he laughed.

"Really?" Deb asked. "I get the feeling that there is one person in there who will miss you."

Marshall chuckled. "What? What are you talking about?"

"Donna. I think she will miss you," Deb replied.

"Richie's Donna? Donna Staples?" he asked.

"That's the one," Deb replied.

"What…, where did you get the idea that Donna Staples would miss me?" he asked.

"Just a feeling I got when she walked into the bar. There was something about the way she looked over at you. And you, there was something about the way that you avoided eye contact with her. Then there was the nervous bouncing of your leg," Deb explained.

"I bounce my leg like that all the time," Marshall said. "That certainly doesn't mean there is anything between me and Donna Staples. She and Richie are getting married soon."

"I'm aware of that," Deb said. "I was merely making an observation.'

"Well, lady, this time you got it all wrong," Marshall said, leaning against the grill of the truck. It reminded Deb of her meeting him for the first time earlier that day.

"I don't want to cause any problems. I am here to finish this book and then I'll be leaving. I don't want to cause any grief or hurt anyone's feelings, and I certainly don't want to make any enemies while I'm here," Deb said.

Marshall threw both hands in the air. "I got you Miss Virginia Parks. Okay, okay. I'll just mosey right on back in there and you can go on back to the cabin. It was nice talking to you," Marshall said, pushing himself away from the truck and walking toward the bar.

Deb wanted to call out to him. She didn't want him to leave, but she knew it was for the best. She climbed into the truck and drove back toward the narrow road that led to the muddy side road. She bounced across the plank bridge, swallowing the lump in her throat. She felt a heaviness in her heart as she pulled to a stop in front of the cabin. Joe's car was gone. Good, for she didn't feel like conversation. She just wanted to curl up on her bunk bed and have a good old-fashioned cry.

The next morning Deb woke to the sound of Joe's snoring. She tiptoed out onto the front porch. As she passed him the smell of sweat and alcohol filled the air. He was in a desperate need of a good bath.

She leaned her elbows upon the porch railing and looked out over the tall grass toward the lake. A faint smell of smoke lingered in the air. Deb closed her eyes and concentrated on the numbers and symbols flashing in her minds eye. She saw the numbers, 3, 2, 3, 3, repeatedly. It could mean three people were nearby and one leaving then coming back. It could have something to do with the tree bears she had met earlier last week. It could mean anything, she thought as she ran her fingers over her head and closed her eyes.

Her head had begun to itch inside. Since her accident this had happened many times. She had concluded that it was her brain healing or adjusting to the rapid healing rate the doctors had wanted to investigate.

Deb descended the porch steps and walked between her truck and Joe's dirty car. There was trash all over the seats and floor boards of the car. A few road maps had been opened and tossed about the car. Two empty beer bottles were lying upon the floor behind the driver's seat. Deb shook her head as she moved away from the car. She envisioned that the inside of the car most likely smelled as bad as he did.

She followed the rutted drive down toward the bridge. The morning fog was light this morning. She reached the bridge and stood looking over the side at the rushing water underneath. She heard the revving of an engine and recognized the sound of Richie's truck coming toward her. She reached up to adjust the scarf on her head and realized that she wasn't wearing any head covering. It was too late to run toward the cabin now, as the truck was visible moving toward her. She had no recourse but to stand there and wait for him to reach her.

Richie pulled up to a stop and exited the truck. "What are you doing out here so early?" Deb asked.

He reached into the truck and held out a letter. "This came in the mail. You said your contact name would be Candy McCall," he said.

Deb took the letter and turned it over in her hands several times while staring down at it.

"Should I wait for you to read it in case you need my help?" Richie asked.

Deb pursed her lips and drew a deep breath. "Just give me a minute," she replied, as she turned and moved to the bridge again. She stood in the center of the bridge and took a second-deep breath before opening the envelope. It was a letter from Lois McCall.

> Dear Candy,
>
> We continue to be in excellent health for a couple our age. Most of our friends are amazed at how well we are and how we don't seem to have deteriorating health like most of them. We think of you often.
>
> We have heard from our friends. They seem to be doing well and so far, they have been quite capable of avoiding any difficulties with the neighbors. They have had several visits from them and continue to feel that they are far better off keeping their association to a minimum.
>
> We haven't heard from you in a while and hope this letter finds you well and finding the answers you were looking for. As for the other family and friends, they ask about you often. They are all safe and well. Write when you can and please be safe and well.
>
> Sincerely,
> Aunt Lois and Uncle Maxwell

Deb returned the letter to the envelope and walked back toward where she had left Richie waiting. She smiled and said, "It is a letter from the McCall's. They were my neighbors, and Mr. McCall gave me his truck to get away. They haven't heard from me in a while and they are worried. Apparently, the FBI is still watching my mother's house but there haven't been any problems. They also put my mind at ease concerning my friends. I guess I need to write a letter and let them know I am fine."

"Well," Richie said, smiling. "At least it wasn't bad news. I didn't know about the letter or I would have brought it with me last evening."

Deb waved her hand. "No big deal," she replied.

"Did you have a good time?" he asked.

"I did, thank you," Deb said.

"Why did you leave so early?" he asked.

"I felt I should limit my exposure. I needed to get out. It gets so boring here, and I thought if I kept my visit short, it wouldn't hurt. Sorry, if I created any problems for you and your friends," she said.

"There were no problems. However, I don't know what you said to Marshall, but he spent the rest of the night sulking over his beer," Richie said, watching her closely.

Deb shook her head. "I have no idea what that is all about. He asked if he should follow me home and I said I would be fine. We left it at that."

Richie smiled. "Maybe it was something else, but I thought it strange that it started right after you left. I think he likes you. That's saying a lot for Marshall. We've been friends since we were little kids. He doesn't make friends easily," he explained.

Deb smiled and nodded her head. Does Richie know about Donna and Marshall? She thought she should not comment. She looked around and said, "I'd invite you inside, but Joe is sleeping in the front room."

"That's okay," Richie said. "I have to get back anyway. Donna doesn't know I was stopping out here and she is expecting me."

"Oh, I see," Deb said. "Be sure to give her my regards and apologize for my rushing off last night."

"Well, about that," Richie began. "I wasn't going to mention my stopping by to her. She would start asking a bunch of questions and I think the less she knows about what goes on out here the better."

Deb nodded her head in agreement. "You are probably right about that."

A noise from behind her caused her to turn rather quickly. Joe was staggering out onto the front porch. He looked down at them and waved his hand as he staggered down the steps and moved around the back of the cabin.

Deb smiled back at Richie. "Well, he's certainly not much to look at first thing in the morning," she said.

"Are you sure about his being out here?" Richie asked.

Deb nodded her head. "I'll be fine," she said.

"If you say so," Richie replied. "I have to get going. I'll stop by on my way home after the hardware store closes. I think someone should keep tabs on what's going on out here with that character hanging around."

Deb shook her head and laughed. "Okay, but I can assure you I am perfectly capable of taking care of myself," she replied.

Richie waved his hand as he turned and climbed into his truck. Deb watched as he turned around and drove back toward the plank bridge and the main road. She sighed when he was no longer visible and climbed the steps. She would resume her seat on the front porch, listening to the morning sounds coming from the lake.

CHAPTER TWELVE

Deb watched as Joe stumbled up the porch steps, moaning with each step he climbed.

"Feeling poorly, are you?" she asked, smiling.

"You can keep your smart remarks to yourself, thank you," Joe moaned. He made his way into the cabin and fell upon the cot.

Deb rose from her chair and entered the cabin. "You know, the next time you take off on one of your mysterious walks to the lake, you might want to take a dip. It might help to wash some of the stench off," she said, staring down at him.

"Don't hold back," Joe sneered, looking up at her. "Why don't you tell me what you really think. So, are you implying that I stink?"

"I'm not implying anything," Deb replied. "I'm flat out telling you that you smell awful. And you have the cabin smelling awful as well."

Joe moaned as he covered his eyes with his forearm. "Give me a break. I've got a splitting headache," he moaned.

"You have a hangover," Deb said. "You shouldn't be poisoning your body with so much alcohol. It's not right. You've been given a special gift and look what you're doing with it."

Joe looked up at her with one eye opened. "You were the one who said it was a curse. Now you're calling it a gift?"

"Think of the good we could do with our powers, Joe," Deb said, straddling the stool. "There are so many people out there who need help. I don't think our four friends meant for us to hole up here away from the world. I agree we were directed to this place for a reason, but I don't think it is to hide for the rest of our lives."

Joe moaned again. "Look where helping people got you. Need I remind you why you're here? You're lying to everyone about who you are and why you are here because people are looking to lock you up in some facility somewhere and study your brain. I'm trying to make people think I'm a fisherman who likes to drink a lot. We are both trying to convince the world we are someone else. There's a reason for that. You know that better than anyone," Joe said, before rolling over to face the wall. "I'm going to sleep this off."

"So, you can go out and do it all over again tonight," Deb replied.

Joe spoke facing the wall. "That isn't any of your business."

Deb stood staring at his back for some time before marching out onto the deck. She leaned upon the wooden railing looking out over the tall grass for a while before moving toward the lake. The air smelled sweet this morning. The leaves on the trees were opening. Soon they would cover the trees and as far as she could see would be green.

Deb heard the calling of a variety of birds from where she stood looking out over the lake. In the distance she saw a trace of smoke drifting upward from an early morning campfire. She wondered if the three hunters she had met yesterday were still out there or if they had been so frightened by the shooting that they packed up and left the campsite. She thought about walking that way and then thought she shouldn't. She would not want a repeat of yesterday. Even with an orange vest on, she had managed to get herself shot, and she wasn't wearing a vest this morning.

She looked upward at the sky. "Where are you?" she asked aloud. She wondered who the four strangers were and where they were from. Why were they here? So many questions went through her mind. Questions that would likely never be answered.

Deb felt the moisture against her face. She stood with her eyes scanning the sky above until her neck began to ache. She became aware of movement behind her. Expecting anything, she quickly turned around. A muskrat scurried through the tall grass toward the water's edge.

Deb finally decided it was time to return to the cabin. She held her hands outward as she moved along, tilting her head left and right causing the grass to sway along with her movements. When she was within site of the cabin, she turned and made her way toward the bridge, without any inkling as to where she was going.

Before long she found herself standing upon the plank bridge looking down at the water rushing beneath it. The water was running clear this morning and she noticed a fish hovering near the bottom. She smiled as she stared down at the fish. She held her hands outward and raised her palms. The fish began to thrash as it moved upward. Soon it was out of the water and thrashing about in midair in front of her as it struggled to breathe. Deb lowered her palms and the fish was returned to the water.

She closed her eyes and pictured herself drifting upward. She felt the breeze against her face as she closed her eyes tightly. She could barely hear the water rushing under the bridge now. She imagined herself high above the bridge out of hearing distance of the water. In her mind she could picture the ground beneath her. She opened her eyes and looked about her. She was still standing on the plank bridge. She hadn't moved at all.

Disappointment overtook her as she stepped off the bridge. Why wasn't she able to lift herself? Why? She moved toward the gate without any conscious thought of where she was going. She opened the gate and passed through it, securing it behind her. She moved toward the Hickman house. If they invite her inside this morning, she would accept the invitation.

The house was coming into view. The garage door was up, and a car was backing out of the driveway. They were leaving.

The car stopped at the edge of the drive. The driver's window went down, and a man called out to her. "Miss Parks, do you need a ride?" he called out.

Deb waved and shook her head. "No thank you. I'm out for my morning walk," she lied.

"Okay. If you ever need anything, let us know," the man called back.

"Thank you," Deb called out, forcing herself to smile.

The car backed out onto the road and drove past her. Charlotte Hickman waved from the passenger seat as they passed. Deb noticed the two boys in the back seat. She sighed as she continued down the road toward the Patterson's.

"Where are you going?" she asked herself aloud as she continued along. "What are you doing out here?" She turned and began walking back toward the cabin.

The sound of a vehicle coming behind her caused her to move over to the edge of the road. She heard the vehicle slowing down as it neared. She did not look back. She heard the gravel beneath the tires crunching as the vehicle pulled to a stop. She turned to see Mr. Patterson opening the door of his car.

"What brings you out here this morning?" he asked.

Deb smiled. "I was just taking a walk to get some air and a change of scenery," she said.

"What, the scenery out at the lake isn't good enough for you?" he teased.

"It's certainly beautiful out there," she replied. "What are you doing out so early?"

"Mother is sending me into town for a few things. I could use some company if you have a mind to come along," Mr. Patterson suggested.

"I would love to accompany you to town," Deb said, climbing into the car.

Mr. Patterson seemed to have a heavy foot on the accelerator as he maneuvered the car across the country road. From time to time Deb found herself reaching for something to steady herself as they bounced along. In no time they were driving along the main street of town.

"The missus doesn't like the way I drive. She says I drive too fast to suit her. I told her if she doesn't like my driving she can stay at the house," Mr. Patterson said, putting the shifter into park.

"Well," Deb said, forcing herself to smile. "I suppose you are a little more accustomed to the roads in these parts than I am."

"Oh, I've lived here all my life," Mr. Patterson said, smiling. "I've got to stick this paper on the bulletin board here at the trading post. Want to come in and say hello to some locals?"

Deb smiled. "Of course," she replied, smiling politely.

They entered the trading post, and everyone turned to look at them. The room suddenly grew very quiet as Mr. Patterson walked to the bulletin board.

"What've you got there, Dick?" the man from behind the counter called out.

"I cleaned out the attic and I'm selling a few items that were stashed up there over the years," Mr. Patterson called out. He began hanging his poster on the board. He paused to read the many other papers and business cards that had been posted. "Can't take it with me, you know."

"You plan on going somewhere?" a man leaning on the counter jeered.

"Not me. Now Theresa is another story," Mr. Patterson called over his shoulder as he continued looking at the postings. "She's always threatening to leave."

"Where is Theresa going?" the man asked, turning to stare at Mr. Patterson's back.

At that moment, the curtains that hung over a door behind the counter parted and Marshall stepped through them. His face reddened when he noticed Deb.

"Hello, Marshall," Deb said.

"Hello. What brings you into town so early?" Marshall asked.

Deb took a deep breath and let it out slowly before replying. "I was out for a morning walk and Mr. Patterson happened by. He asked me if I wanted to ride into town with him. I had no other plans, so I thought I'd ride along."

A man behind the counter laughed and said, "You must be a mighty brave woman to ride in the car with Dick Patterson. He drives like a maniac."

Deb smiled at the remark and looked toward the floor. It grew quiet again. Then Marshall said to the man behind the counter, "I got a call from a guy who needs some welding done. I must go look at the job and give him an estimate. I'll probably be gone all day."

"Okay," the man said. "You go enjoy your ride. There's nothing going on here today anyway."

Marshall came around the counter and stood next to Deb. "If you aren't doing anything today, you're welcome to ride along. It's about three and a half hours west of here. I'll buy you lunch and maybe dinner," Marshall said, softly.

Deb smiled. "I think I'd like that," she said. She walked over to the bulletin board and told Mr. Patterson she was going with Marshall and would be gone for most of the day. "Should Joe Kearney ask about me, tell him where I went. He may worry because my truck is still at the cabin and I didn't tell him I was leaving," she explained.

"I'll swing by there on my way home and tell him," Mr. Patterson said. "Go have fun. You deserve it."

Deb smiled and turned to find Marshall waiting near the door. He held the door open for her to pass. It had been a very long time since anyone had held a door for Deb. She felt her face growing hot.

"My truck is out back," Marshall said.

Deb opened the door to the truck and smiled. Somehow, she had expected the truck to be a mess inside. It was spotless. She climbed inside and fastened her seat belt. Marshall turned the key and the truck engine roared. She smiled and said, "I hope you don't drive like Mr. Patterson."

Marshall laughed. "I've rode with Mr. Patterson before. I think you'll like my driving a lot better," he said.

They rode in silence until they were outside the town limits. Deb stared at the scenery as they moved along, trying to think of something to talk about.

"It's going to be a nice day," Marshall said. Deb knew he was struggling for conversations as well.

"Yes, I think you are right. I went for a walk this morning. It gets too quiet out there sometimes," she said.

"That Mr. Kearney, he doesn't give you any trouble?" Marshall asked.

"Not really. He could use a good soapy scrubbing though. I'm hoping he takes a bath while I'm gone. I mentioned it to him before I left," she said.

"He sure can't hold his liquor. He only had a couple beers at the bar last night and he was staggering around like he was wasted out of his mind," Marshall said.

"I can only imagine," Deb replied. "Do you go to the bar every night?"

Marshall glanced over at her. "Do you think I'm an alcoholic or something?" he asked.

"Oh, no, not at all," Deb replied. "I didn't mean to imply anything of the sort. I only meant to inquire about your entertainment. I was trying to make conversation."

"It's alright," Marshall laughed. "I know what you meant."

It grew quiet again. Deb was looking out the window again. "Thank you for letting me tag along with you today. It feels good to get away from the cabin," she said, without looking away from the window. Again, it grew quiet.

After some time, Marshall said, "I know about you. What I mean is, Richie told me all about who you really are."

Deb jerked her head to face him quickly. "What did he tell you?" she asked.

"Richie has been my friend forever. Richie, Larry, and I have always been pals. We don't have many secrets between us. He told me all about you and why you are staying out there at the cabin," Marshall said. "Don't worry, your secret is safe with me. I would never betray my friend. And I appreciate what you did for him. We all thought he was going to die before you came along."

Deb sighed. "I don't know what to say," she replied.

"You needn't say anything," Marshall said. Then it grew quiet again.

"Does Richie know about you and Donna?" Deb asked.

Marshall's face turned crimson. "I'm sorry," Deb said. "I have no right to ask such a question. I apologize. It's just that when she arrived, you got so quiet and I thought maybe you still had feelings for her or something."

"It wasn't like that between Donna and me," Marshall began. "At least not for me. She was a mess when she learned there wasn't anything they could do for Richie. She said she couldn't bear watching him die, so she didn't go to see him anymore. She spent much of her time crying on my shoulder. I was Richie's friend. I felt he would want me to be there for her. Then we started spending more and more time together and it seemed so natural. She began to get clingy and I didn't know how to tell her I didn't feel the same way about her. I was about to lose one of my best friends and I felt if she was there, I would still have a part of him. We were intimate once, but only once. It didn't feel right for me. She wanted our relationship to go to the next step and I was dragging my feet. Then you came along, and you know the rest."

"So," Deb began. "Why the long face when they came in the other night?"

"Because I slept with his girl. He knows about it. I don't keep secrets from Richie. He understands, but I still feel guilty," Marshall explained.

"I see," Deb replied. "I'm sorry for prying. You didn't have to tell me."

"No, I need to tell someone. I don't want to talk about it with Richie. It makes me feel worse because he's so damn understanding and forgiving," Marshall said, hitting the steering wheel.

"Tell me about this welding job you're going to look at," Deb said, hoping to change the subject.

Marshall frowned as he stared out at the road ahead of him. "It's a big project. The city park has all these metal lamp posts that need welded at the base. Seems over the years they have become loosened. If I get the job it will pay nicely and open the door for more major projects. I could use the big city exposure."

"Well then, put your Mr. Charming face on and nail the deal!" Deb laughed.

"This face?" Marshall asked. "You've got to be kidding."

Deb laughed again. "Well, it could use a little work, that much is true." They were both laughing now.

Marshall pointed out some points of interest along the way. They stopped at a steel trolley diner for a cup of coffee to break up the long ride. Deb ordered water which caused Marshall to raise his eyebrows.

"You don't drink alcohol, soda, or coffee?" he asked. "What on earth do you eat and drink?"

"I eat fruits and vegetables. I would have thought Richie had mentioned that to you. I prefer them raw, however I will tolerate them steamed or cooked. As for beverages, I prefer water. Not the chlorinated stuff the cities put out. I like the real deal. You know, the hard stuff," she laughed.

"Is there a reason why you eat the healthy foods?" Marshall asked.

Deb smiled and took a deep breath. Something told her she could be honest with Marshall. "I don't know why, but prepared foods and beverages upset my stomach. I can eat them if I must, but they don't stay down long. I don't know exactly why that is, but that's the way it's been ever since my accident. I can tell you it wasn't like that before my accident. I could drink beer all night and I preferred junk food over anything else out there," she laughed.

She watched out the window as a semi-truck pulled into the lot. A hefty truck driver climbed down from the cab and limped his way inside the diner. He climbed onto a bar stool at the counter.

"How are you today, John?" the driver called out to the cook behind the window that separated the kitchen from the dining area.

"I'm good today, Rusty. How about you?" the cook called out.

"I'm fighting this arthritis today. I can hardly walk. Doc says I need to get this knee replaced, but I can't afford the time off," the driver said.

"I know what you mean," the cook called out through the window.

Deb and Marshall went back to talking about the people in the small community they had just left. Soon it was time to leave. They approached the cash register which was to the right of where the truck driver had been sitting.

Deb reached out and placed her hand upon the driver's shoulder. "It's a nice day for a ride," she said, smiling down at him.

He dropped his fork and began to tremble. The waitress frowned as she looked over at him. "Are you alright, Rusty?" she asked.

The driver did not reply. He continued to tremble. Marshall turned to look at Deb and noticed what was happening. His eyes widened.

"Is he having some kind of seizure?" the waitress asked.

Suddenly the trembling stopped and Rusty's head slumped forward until his chin touched his chest. Then slowly, his head began to raise, and he smiled. "Wow! I don't know what that was, but I didn't want it to end. I feel like someone gave me something for my pain and it suddenly kicked in. I don't feel any pain at all. First time that's ever happened to me," Rusty said, smiling widely. He looked over at Deb and asked, "What was that you were saying young lady?"

"I said, a nice day for a drive, isn't it?" Deb repeated.

"It's certainly a nice day," Rusty replied. "The best day I've had in years, although I feel I could use a nap before I hit the road again."

Marshall held the door for Deb as they left the diner. He also held the truck door open for her. After he climbed into the truck he asked, "What was that? Did you do that?"

Deb smiled. "What? What are you talking about?" she asked.

"Richie said you wrapped your arms around him, and he began to shake violently. He said when the shaking stopped, he was healed. Is that what you just did to that man in there?" Marshall asked.

"Something like that. I did not wrap my arms around him though," Deb replied.

"All of that from just touching him?" Marshall asked, as he pulled out onto the highway again.

"Sometimes it's like that. It depends on how severe the affliction is," Deb explained. "At least that is how I think it works. This is all as confusing to me as it is to you."

Marshall stretched his arm out. "Go on, touch me," he urged.

Deb began to laugh. "Not while you're driving, silly."

"I've never seen anything like that in my life," Marshall said.

"Honestly Marshall, neither have I. This is all still very new to me," Deb said.

"So, what other super powers do you have?" Marshall asked.

"That's about it," Deb lied. She didn't feel Marshall was ready for any more information.

"Richie said something about a symbol on the steps out at the cabin. He said you were trying to figure out who put it there because you see this symbol in your head all the time," Marshall stated.

"Not all the time, but sometimes I see it," Deb replied. "I know who put it there now. It was Joe. He told me so."

"Joe. The drunk that's staying there with you?" Marshall asked.

"That's the one," Deb replied.

"How did he know about the symbol?" Marshall asked.

"That's what I'm trying to find out," again, she lied to him. She didn't want to lie to Marshall but wasn't certain how much she should tell about Joe.

"Is that why you're letting him stay there?" Marshall asked.

Deb nodded her head. She laughed. "You sure ask a lot of questions."

"Hell yeah!" Marshall said. "This is some pretty interesting shit!"

"I suppose it is," Deb replied.

"Does it make you uncomfortable, answering my questions?" he asked.

"Somewhat," Deb answered. "It makes me aware of how strange I must seem to normal people."

Marshall pursed his lips. "I'm sorry. I'll give it a rest," he said, as he reached out to squeeze her hand.

Deb felt an electric current shooting up her arm at his touch. Marshall pulled his hand back and shook it. "Holy shit!" he exclaimed. Then they both began to laugh.

CHAPTER THIRTEEN

Deb sat on a park bench watching some very young boys play T ball. It was a warm day. She glanced over to where Marshall stood talking to a couple of older men. He waved his hands about as he talked. She closed her eyes and concentrated on them.

"I will have all the equipment on my truck for the job, but I'll need you to get any necessary permits I might need to do the job. Let's see, you said there were twenty-nine lamp posts in all. I believe I sent you the estimate earlier. Do you need any further approval before we start?" Marshall was asking.

"We got the committee to approve the project. Your estimate was the lowest, so the job is yours if you want it," the heavier man said.

"Well, email me when you have all the necessary permits, and I'll start right away. I'll work from early morning until dinner time. I think I should have it done before summer," Marshall said.

"Sounds good to me," the thin man said. They shook hands and it grew quiet. Deb opened her eyes to find Marshall walking toward her.

"All set," he said, smiling. "As soon as they send me the email saying they have all the necessary permits, we are good to go."

"Good," Deb said smiling. She stood up and looked around. "This is a nice park."

"It is. It's going to be a nice paycheck too," Marshall said. He looked over at the little ones playing T ball. "They are cute at that age," he said.

"They are cute at any age," Deb interjected.

"Oh, I never thought to ask, have you ever had any children?" Marshall asked.

Deb smiled and shook her head. "No, not me. I don't know if I can. Since my accident I have been anything but normal."

"Well," Marshall said with a grin. "That might not be a bad thing. I mean, I know a lot of normal people who should never have had any children."

"Yeah, I suppose," Deb added. "But not all parents are bad. My Mom worked hard to provide for me."

"What about your father?" Marshall asked.

"He hasn't been in the picture for a long time. I have a stepfather. He's really the only father figure I can remember. He was very strict and not very affectionate, but he was good to me," she replied.

"Do you miss them?" Marshall asked.

"I do. I also worry about them," Deb said.

"Come on, I'll buy you dinner. I know a great place on the way home," Marshall said.

"Is it the steel trolley?" Deb asked, as they began walking toward the truck.

Marshall laughed. "No. We are going home another way. It's a little longer, but dinner will be worth it. You aren't in a hurry, are you?"

Deb shook her head. "I've got the whole day," she replied.

"Good," Marshall said, opening the truck door for her.

Deb noticed Marshall shaking his right hand before turning the key. "Does your hand still bother you?" she asked.

"A little. It's just tingling some. It doesn't hurt or anything like that. Just a different feeling," Marshall said.

Deb slid across the seat and opened her arms. "Let's try something," she suggested.

"Am I going to flop around like a fish out of water?" Marshall asked.

Deb laughed. "You might, but I'm the only one who will see it," she replied.

"I don't know if I want you to see that," Marshall said.

"Come on, big boy," Deb said, holding her arms open and smiling.

Marshall leaned toward her and she embraced him. She held him firmly in her arms as he quivered. He made a soft moaning sound and then the quivering stopped. Deb held him a moment before releasing him. She looked up into his clear eyes. He smiled down at her. "Is that it?" he asked.

"That's it," Deb replied.

They sat close staring into each other's eyes. They moved closer and Deb could feel his breath upon her face. She closed her eyes as she suspected he was about to kiss her, but instead he pulled away.

"Are you ready?" he asked.

Deb slid over to sit near the door again. "All set and ready to go," she replied. She wondered if he could hear her heart pounding.

"I hope you are hungry because this place really knows how to put on a spread," Marshall said, putting the truck in reverse and backing out of his parking space.

"Are you sure you're okay to drive, after...?" she asked.

"I'm a little tired, but not really what I would call, drowsy. I think I'll be alright," he replied.

They were driving along a freeway for several miles before he exited. They passed a residential area and soon they were in another city. It wasn't as big as the city with the park, but it was bigger than her home town of East Palestine.

They were sitting at a red light when a police car pulled around them, with lights and sirens blazing. It carefully went through the intersection before speeding on down the highway.

"Hope this wasn't a bad idea," Marshall said, as the light changed, and he began driving on down the street.

Another police car turned off a side street in front of them with lights and sirens. Then sirens came from behind them and Marshall pulled over to let an ambulance pass.

"Where is this restaurant?" Deb asked.

"It's just ahead," Marshall said.

As they continued, the red lights of a police car had the road blocked. The smell of smoke filled the air. Deb looked up and saw a plume of black smoke ahead of them.

"Stop Marshall," Deb said.

"They won't let us through here, Virginia. We'll have to go around," Marshall said, looking in his rear-view mirror.

"Take that side street and find a place to park," Deb instructed.

"Why?" Marshall asked.

"Someone may need my help," Deb replied.

"How are you going to help them?" Marshall asked. Then he looked over at her and said, "Oh, I get it. I doubt they will let you pass the yellow tape."

"I'll find a way," Deb replied. "Just park anywhere you can and hurry."

Marshall turned onto the first street he came to. People where running along the streets trying to get past the police lines to see the action. Marshall found an opening along the street and pulled in. Before he realized what was happening, Deb exited the truck and began running toward the blazing building. He hurried to catch up to her, but she was too fast for him. By the time he reached the police line, he began scanning the area for a sign of her.

"You can't get through here mister," a police woman said, as she was stretching yellow tape to prevent people from passing.

"I'm trying to find my girlfriend. She's around here somewhere," Marshall said.

"Sorry buddy, you can't get through here," the police woman repeated, holding up the tape for him to see.

Marshall looked up at the flames shooting out of the windows on the second floor of the building. The firemen were stretching hoses across the lawn and a ladder truck was swinging a ladder toward the house.

"My children are in there!" a young mother cried out, rushing toward the police line.

A policeman and fireman rushed toward her and led her past the yellow tape toward the firetruck and ambulance.

Marshall scanned the area for Deb but did not see her. He felt his heart pounding as he watched, helplessly. He moved along the yellow tape, stepping past onlookers and those curious to see the activity.

"Here they are," a fireman called out carrying two small children in his arms and walking toward where the woman stood with two other firemen and a policewoman.

"Mommy we were flying," the oldest of the youngsters called out as they drew closer to their mother's open arms.

Marshall stood watching the heartfelt reunion of the mother and her children. "Are you looking for me?" Deb asked, from behind him.

Marshall turned to see her standing there. He sighed. "I thought maybe you went in there," he said. "I was scared out of my skin."

"No, I didn't go inside," she said, smiling and pointing to the yellow tape. "I couldn't get across the tape line. Besides," she shrugged her shoulders. "I didn't have to go in. The children were saved by that brave fireman over there."

"Come on, let's get the hell out of here before something else happens," Marshall said, reaching out for Deb's hand. He pulled her along as he moved back toward the truck.

"I have excellent hearing, by the way," Deb said, waiting for him to unlock the truck and open the door for her.

"What's that supposed to mean?" Marshall asked.

Deb climbed into the truck and waited for him to close the door. Then he was climbing into the driver's seat. He turned the key and looked over at her. "What did you mean when you said you have excellent hearing? Did you hear something?"

Deb smiled. "I did."

"What did you hear?" Marshall asked, as he steered the truck back out onto the street again.

"I heard you tell that policewoman you were searching for your girlfriend," Deb explained.

"What? Oh, that," Marshall's face turned crimson. "I was nervous and upset. I had no way of knowing what the hell I was saying. If I had said I was searching for a woman, it would have sounded strange."

"Oh, I see," Deb said, smiling as she looked out the side window at the buildings they passed.

"Why did you take off like that? What did you think you were going to do?" Marshall asked.

"I didn't know," Deb began. "I only knew I had to do something."

"But you took off before you even knew there were children inside the building," Marshall said.

"I told you I have excellent hearing," Deb replied.

"Are you saying you heard the children inside the building from where we were parked?" Marshall asked.

Deb nodded her head. "That is right. I heard their little voices crying and coughing."

"Wow! That's amazing. I suppose I'll have to remember that," Marshall said, smiling over at her. "It's a good thing that fireman found them, and you didn't have to go inside after them."

"Yes, a good thing," Deb smiled again as she continued to watch out the side window, keeping her face hidden from Marshall. "Do you have any other super powers I should know about?" he asked.

Deb looked over at him. "None, worth mentioning," she replied.

"I'm not exactly sure what that means, but I'll let it ride for now," Marshall said, as he steered the truck into a restaurant parking lot. "We are here. I hope you are hungry."

"I am famished," Deb replied.

They moved toward the entrance where a line had formed. Marshall smiled over at Deb and said, "I hope you don't mind. It's well worth the wait as long as it isn't too long." He peered ahead of the line.

"They are very busy this evening," an older gentleman waiting in line said.

"Did they say how long the wait is?" Marshall asked.

"They told us forty-five minutes," the man replied.

Marshall turned to Deb and said, "Maybe this wasn't such a good idea. I'm sorry. Every idea I've had today has bombed." He looked back at the line and said, "I can wait, but I am hungry."

"Me too," Deb said.

"Well, let's get out of here. There's a little bar down the road. They serve pretty good food," he suggested, guiding her away from the line.

They returned to the truck and soon they were on the road again. It wasn't very long until they were parked at a log cabin style bar. "I've eaten here before," Marshall said. "I hope you don't mind."

"I don't mind at all," Deb replied.

They entered the bar and took a seat in a booth along the wall. Multiple televisions hung upon the wall facing every direction so the seated patrons could watch a variety of sports events. One was a baseball game, however the one closest to them had a news channel on. A video of the fire scene they had left was playing in the background behind a reporter. The words of the reporter were running along the bottom of the screen.

"The two small children were rescued and are safe in the care of their grandparents tonight. The mother has been charged with child endangering, and Neville, I spoke with a fireman earlier who said the children must have suffered from extreme smoke inhalation because they insist that they were floating in air as they descended to the front door where a fireman found them and carried them outside. He explained to me that hallucinations are a sign of extreme smoke inhalation and possibly damage to their young brains." the reporter said.

"I'm happy they are safe," the male behind a desk said into the camera. "Don't you find it odd that they both had the same hallucination? I'm curious, Shannon, were they twins?"

"No, they are not twins, Neville," the female reporter said, on a split screen.

"Well, they are safe, and that is all that really matters. Thank you, Shannon," the male reporter said.

Marshall took a deep breath as he read the streaming news. When the broadcast went to a traffic accident, he looked over at Deb. "Exactly where were the children when you heard their voices?" he asked.

Deb shrugged her shoulders. "I don't know. I can only tell you I heard their voices from somewhere in the house."

"What were they saying?" he asked.

"I don't recall them saying anything. I heard them crying and coughing," Deb replied.

Marshall glanced back at the television screen and then to Deb. "You must have good hearing," he said.

"Oh, I think I do," Deb said, smiling.

The waitress approached their table for their order then. Deb knew Marshall suspected something wasn't right about her account of the earlier events. She wanted to tell him everything but felt she didn't know him well enough. Just how much had Richie told his friend? Perhaps he knew more then he was letting on. She felt it best to keep the full truth to herself for now. Still, there was something about the way Marshall made her feel. She didn't want to frighten him away. At least not right now.

CHAPTER FOURTEEN

Deb laid on her bunk bed staring up at the ceiling. She hardly slept last night, for she could not get her evening with Marshall out of her mind.

Her first impression of Marshall was that he had feelings for Donna. After their conversation on the subject, she now knew that was not the case. Marshall was grief stricken over the fact that he had sexual relations with his friend's girl. Was there any hope for a relationship between Marshall and herself? Deb had to admit that there was something there. She felt disappointment because the anticipated kiss didn't happen, not even when he returned her to the cabin at the conclusion of their evening together.

They sat on the front porch, listening to the sounds coming from the lake and talking for almost an hour before he left. It was just the two of them alone. Still he made no romantic move toward her.

Deb sat up quickly. They had been alone last night. Joe was not here, and she hadn't heard him come in all night.

Deb swung her legs over the side of the bunk and listened. She could hear the birds calling out from the lake. Normally, Joe's snoring would resonate throughout the cabin. It was quiet.

She went to the door and opened it slowly, peering out at the cot along the far wall, near the front door. It was empty. Deb stepped into the front room and looked around for any sign that would indicate Joe had been there sometime during the night and left again. Everything was as it was when she went to bed the previous night.

Deb pulled a shirt on over her night shirt and stepped out onto the front porch. A heavy fog hung about the cabin, making visibility extremely limited. She descended the steps and walked out beyond where her truck was parked, looking for Joe's car. It was not there. Furthermore, there were no fresh tracks to indicate that he had been there anytime during the night.

She instinctively turned to look over the tree line toward the area where Joe had indicated the alien craft had landed the night of his encounter with the four strangers. It was not visible due to the heavy fog.

Deb took a deep breath and climbed the steps again to sit on the white plastic lawn chair near the door. She continued to scan the area for any movement, as her mind went back to the previous evening at the sports bar.

She was certain that Marshall was suspicious concerning her activities connected with the house fire. He did not press the issue, but she could tell he felt something was off. She had been so tempted to tell him everything. She knew she had to be cautious. The more people aware of her abilities, the better her chances of being exposed to the public.

What was the worse that could happen if Marshall was to learn the truth? He might find it appealing. Then again, he might find it threatening. It might frighten him away. She decided to keep the truth to herself.

She heard the low rumble of an engine on the main road. She listened intently as it continued down the road past the entrance gate to the cabin and lake area. Where are you Joe? Are you in trouble?

Deb remained seated on the front porch, staring out into the soupy fog. As the hours passed, the fog began to lift. There was still no sign of Joe. He couldn't be out there somewhere near the lake for his car was gone.

Deb went inside and washed her face. She reached for the scarf she normally would cover her head with. Looking at her own reflection in the milky mirror she ran her fingers through her blonde hair. It had grown out enough to stand between her fingers. She wet her hair and ran her fingers through it again. It stood on end. She tugged a few loose strands around her face and stood staring at herself. It didn't look so bad. She dropped the head covering onto the table and went outside. She would drive into town to search for Joe.

She drove across the plank bridge and on toward the gate near the main road. Headlights came toward her as she drew near the gate. Perhaps it was Joe. She pulled off to the side of the road as far as she could get to allow him to pass. Instead, the vehicle stopped in front of her. It was Richie.

"Where are you going in this fog?" he asked.

"I was going into town to look for Joe. He didn't come in last night and he's usually snoring away by this time. I thought perhaps something may have happened to him," Deb replied.

"That's why I drove out here," Richie said, opening the door for her and stepping back in anticipation of her climbing out.

"What are you talking about?" Deb asked, as she slid out of the truck.

"Joe's car was parked off the side of the road all night. The Sheriff asked me to come out here to see if maybe he walked to the cabin," Richie said.

Deb shook her head. "I haven't seen him. Was he at the bar last night?" she asked.

"I didn't go to the bar last night, so I wouldn't know. We met with the minister last night, and had dinner with Donna's family after," Richie said, rolling his eyes.

"Oh, I see," Deb said, looking about. "I wonder where he could be."

"Sheriff said his car wasn't locked and they found his car keys on the ground right outside the driver's door," Richie said.

"Then something definitely happened to him," Deb said stiffening.

"He could have dropped them," Richie suggested.

"I need to go into town and ask around," Deb said.

"Well, I told the Sheriff I would get back to him right away. Why don't you ride along with me and we will search for him together?" Richie suggested.

"Okay," Deb replied. "I better take the truck back to the cabin and leave a note just in case he makes his way home."

"Home? It's home now is it?" Richie asked.

Deb frowned as she looked over at Richie. "Home is wherever you lay your head at night," she replied.

Richie merely nodded his head. "I'll follow you back to the cabin."

Deb climbed into her truck and turned it around. After leaving a brief note for Joe on the table she climbed into Richie's truck and they proceeded back across the bridge and toward the main road. As they moved along, Deb scanned the area for a sign of Joe. Perhaps he was out there walking somewhere. The fog was lifting, and the tops of the tall grass were visible.

"Perhaps his car broke down and he is out there on foot. He may be trying to get back to the cabin," she said, as she continued looking about.

"This fog has been pretty dense this morning. If you were born here, you would know better than try to find your way on foot when it's this thick. He should have stayed with his car," Richie said.

"I'll get the gate," Deb said, as Richie pulled to a stop. She climbed out of the truck and opened the gate wide so the truck could pass through. Then she closed the gate again and secured it before returning to the truck. Before climbing into the cab, she turned and scanned the area one more time. Soon they were moving quickly along the main road toward town.

"Where was his car found?" Deb asked.

"It's right around the bend up here. It wasn't a good place to pull off. It's a blind curve and with the fog last night, anyone could have plowed right into him," Richie explained.

Red flares had been placed in the center of the road. Richie slowed down as he continued. The Sheriff's car was parked along the right side of the road with his lights flashing. Ahead on the opposite side of the road sat Joe's car. Richie parked the truck and they exited quickly. The Sheriff noticed them and waved them toward where he stood near Joe's car.

"Are you Virginia Parks?" he asked.

Deb nodded her head. "I am. Any news yet?" she asked.

"No, not yet," the Sheriff replied. He turned and pointed down the road. "We discovered boot tracks in the mud leading from the car. They went that way. There are some strange tracks off to the side of the road. We can't make them out. But the boot tracks seem to stop there. We are scanning the area for any sign of tracks. He might have gotten into another vehicle. As of right now, that is what we suspect."

Deb looked toward where he pointed. "Do you mind if I take a look at the tracks?" she asked.

The Sheriff laughed. "I understand you are a writer, not an investigator."

"Sometimes, I'm both," she replied, smiling.

The Sheriff shook his head and rubbed the back of his neck. "Go ahead, but don't touch anything and don't go off the road. We don't want any evidence disturbed," he looked down the road and called, "Mike, come here." A deputy began walking toward them. "This is Deputy Harris. He'll show you around down there."

Deb smiled. "Deputy Harris, I'm Virginia Parks," she said, as they began to move toward the area the Sheriff had indicated the tracks were.

"I know who you are. I saw you at Pappy's once. You are the writer," Deputy Harris said.

"Is the Sheriff always this grumpy?" Deb asked.

"His breakfast was interrupted. That and the fact that he can't figure this one out. He likes a cut and dry kind of case, if you know what I mean," Deputy Harris said.

"Where I come from, we call that an easy case," Deb said, smiling.

"Call it what you want, but this one isn't easy unless this guy pops up in the woods somewhere," Deputy Harris said. "It's right over there," he said, pointing to the bank along the side of the road.

Deb could see the boot tracks. "Those tracks are his," she said.

"How would you know that?" Deputy Harris asked.

"We don't have sidewalks out at the cabin Deputy. Those are the same tracks in the mud all around where he parks his car," she explained.

"Well, they stop right here," Deputy Harris said. "Those are the strange tracks the Sheriff was telling you about," he pointed to some tracks intermingled with Joe's tracks.

Deb knelt low and scanned the area. The tracks were smooth soled. They were everywhere along the bank. Could they have been left by the four strangers?

"Whoever, or whatever left those tracks was all over the bank. Funny thing is, that is the only place we see them. It's like they dropped down out of the sky and swooped your friend up," Deputy Harris said.

Deb rose to stand. She smiled at the deputy. "It certainly looks that way, alright," she replied.

"Actually, we think someone drove by and gave him a ride somewhere," the deputy said, smiling.

"You are probably right," Deb said, looking around. "Do you mind if we move on down the road a bit?" she asked.

The deputy looked back toward where the sheriff was talking with Richie and some of the other officers. He sighed and nodded his head. "I suppose, but we can't move off the road," he replied.

They walked side by side on down the road. A car was approaching, and Deb moved over to the side. Deputy Harris stepped out raising his arms in the air. The car stopped and the driver put his window down. It was Brian Hickman. The deputy told him to drive slowly and instructed him to call the Sheriff if he sees anyone in the area on foot. Brian waved at Deb as he put his window up and proceeded slowly.

Deb moved to the side of the road. She peered into the wooded area, looking for broken branches or trees to indicate a craft may have landed nearby. There was nothing. She recalled the day the four strangers appeared to her in the corn field and told her she had to flee the area. It was as if they just appeared in thin air. Did they take Joe with them?

"This is as far as we go," the deputy said.

Deb smiled and looked around one more time. She nodded her head. "I believe you are right. It looks like someone picked him up." They began walking back toward the area where Joe's car was parked.

Richie walked toward them. "See anything?" he asked.

Deb shook her head. "It looks like someone picked him up," Deb replied, looking back at the deputy.

"Well, I'm going into town. Want to come along or would you rather go back to the cabin and wait for him there?" Richie asked.

"I'll ride along with you if you don't mind," Deb said.

"They are going to tow his car into town," Richie said, as they began walking toward his truck.

They reached the truck and climbed inside. Richie drove slowly as they went past the red flares that glowed in the misty morning. "Where would he likely go if he was in town?" Richie asked.

"I have no idea," Deb replied. "I would guess a bar, but I doubt they are open this early."

"No, nobody serves alcohol this early in the morning that I know of," Richie replied.

Deb continued to scan the wooded areas on both sides of the road as they drove to town. When they reached the municipal limits, she focused on the small businesses that Joe might have cause to visit. Soon Richie was parking at the hardware store.

"I have to tell Donna why I'll be late today," he explained. "You are welcome to come in."

Deb smiled. "Don't mind if I do," she replied.

They entered the hardware store together. Donna was behind the counter, ringing up a purchase. She looked up, smiling, but the smile instantly disappeared when she noticed Deb with Richie. Deb realized that it had been a mistake to come here with Richie.

"Hi," Richie said, going behind the counter.

Donna did not reply as she finished her business with the customer. "Have a good day, Mr. Fletcher," she said to the older man as he left the store. She turned to face Richie and asked, "Where have you been? Daddy is back there moving heavy crates all by himself."

"I'm sorry. Something came up," Richie explained.

Donna looked over at Deb and Deb turned her back and walked behind a counter where she could not be seen. However, her acute hearing picked up their voices.

"What are you doing? You know how important it is that you make this work," Donna urged.

"I know, I said I was sorry," Richie replied.

"Sorry won't help your paycheck. You are not on salary, Richie. We need every penny we can get," Donna said. "Do you expect me to be the bread winner of the family? Is that what I'm to be to you?"

"What? No!" Richie said. He sighed and said, "Look, Donna, I was on my way in to work when the Sheriff stopped me along the road. That drunk that is staying at the cabin with Miss Parks is missing. They found his car, they found his keys, and they saw where he started walking down the road and then he was just gone. The Sheriff asked me to go out to the cabin and see if he was there. So, of course what was I supposed to do?"

"Well, it looks to me like you are not here to work," Donna said.

"I brought her into town to look for the guy," Richie said.

"So, you aren't here to work," Donna remarked.

"I'll be in later, I promise," Richie said.

"I can't depend on you, Richie. Are you going to be on time tonight? Are you going to find some excuse to be late for our rehearsal dinner?" Donna asked.

"I won't miss that, Donna. You know how important this wedding is to me. How important you are to me," Richie declared.

Donna pushed past him and went around the counter to where Deb stood looking at nails. Donna took a deep breath and forced herself to smile. "Miss Parks how nice to see you again. How is the book coming along?" she asked.

Deb smiled back at Donna. "It's coming along well. I've had a few distractions lately, but no more than normal," Deb replied.

"Is there something here I can help you with? Do you need some nails? Is that old cabin falling down around you?" Donna asked, looking back at Richie.

"Oh," Deb suddenly realized she was staring down into a wooden barrel of nails. "No, I'm just amazed at how many nails there are to choose from. I had no idea."

"Well, it all depends on what you need them for. We have a nail for just about any project you can think of," Donna replied.

"I can see that. Amazing," Deb smiled.

"I hear your friend is missing," Donna said, again looking back at Richie.

"Yes, it would appear so. We suspect he started walking and someone picked him up," Deb explained.

"Well," Donna said, taking a deep breath. "That would be understandable. So, are you going to be in town all day?"

"What?" Deb asked. "Oh, no, I'll be going back to the cabin. I just wanted to have a look around town, just in case he needed a ride home."

Donna smiled and looked back at Richie again. She cleared her throat. "Did Richie happen to mention to you that our rehearsal dinner is tonight?"

"No, he did not," Deb said, shaking her head. She looked over at Richie who would not make eye contact. "I am sorry if my being here has caused any problems. I had no idea when I asked Richie to bring me into town. Please, don't blame him for something that was out of his control."

Donna smiled again, as her face began to flush. "Of course. I know my Richie. He is one of the most dependable men I know," she replied. "It is just like him to step up when someone is in need."

"And so, he has," Deb replied, smiling.

"Miss Parks rode into town with me. I better take her back to the cabin and return here so I can help your father in the back," Richie said.

"Oh please, Richie," Deb began. "I can find another way back to the cabin."

"What? That's over eight miles to the turnoff and another three miles back to the cabin," Richie began. "You certainly can't walk that. I can't let you do that. Besides, this fog is going to linger for most of the day. Walking those roads won't be safe."

Donna took a deep breath. "Richie is right," she said. "It wouldn't be safe to walk, and it is entirely too far. You really should let him drive you out there." She looked back at Richie and said, "Then he can turn around and get right back here to work the remainder of his shift."

"I appreciate the offer, but if you don't mind, I think I would like to look around town before I go home. I'm certain I can find someone going that way once I've finished my search," Deb said. "Please, don't trouble yourself any longer, Richie. You stay and help move those crates in the back."

"If you insist," Donna said, before Richie had time to respond.

Richie shuffled his feet and wrung his hands. "If you don't find another ride home, stop in and I will run you back out there. Better yet, once you've looked around, come back here and I'll give my father a call. He can come out after you."

Deb smiled. "We shall see. Thank you for the lift, Richie," she said. "You have a good day and enjoy your rehearsal dinner tonight, Donna."

Donna forced herself to smile. "Thank you. I think I will," she said, stiffening.

Deb left the hardware store. She walked the wooden boardwalk street, peering in the glass windows of the shops that lined the streets. When she reached the end of the business section she turned and began walking down the other side. Soon she was passing the trading post. She took a deep breath and entered. Several men were gathered around the counter. Upon her entry, they all turned to look back at her.

"Good day, Miss Parks," an older man called out to her.

Deb studied the man's face carefully, hoping to recall who he was. "Sir, do I know you?" she asked, smiling.

"Probably not," the man said. "But I certainly know who you are. We all know who you are."

Deb smiled and nodded her head. "I see you have me at the disadvantage," she said.

"I'm Charley. Charley Shoemaker. I own the property that joins Dick Patterson's out at the lake. I believe the hunter who shot you was one of my tenants."

"Oh," Deb said, sighing. "Poor man got the scare of his life, didn't he?"

"He certainly did. They packed up and went home. Left me in a pickle, so they did. I don't have anyone leasing that cabin for another two weeks," Mr. Shoemaker said.

"I'm so sorry," Deb said.

"Why are you sorry?" Mr. Shoemaker asked. "I'm happy you weren't hurt. To hear that man tell it, you took a bullet to the chest. He said, you were bleeding and everything, but when you stood up there wasn't any marks on your body. He said they don't know where the blood came from."

"Some mighty strange happenings go on out there on that lake," a familiar voice said. Deb smiled as she recognized Willy Goldman standing at the counter talking with the older men.

"I believe we have met," Deb said, smiling. "Willy, I believe."

Willy smiled and approached Deb. "Willy Goldman. I'm impressed that you remember me. How are you today, Miss Parks?"

"I am fine, Willy. How are you?" Deb asked.

"I'm fine. I heard a friend of yours is missing," he said.

Deb nodded her head. "That is right, Willy. Joe Kearney is his name. They found his car parked alongside the road and there wasn't any sign of him. I thought I would come into town and search for him," she explained.

"He might have been taken," Willy said.

"Taken?" Deb asked. "Do you mean abducted by someone?"

Willy nodded his head. "Possibly," he replied.

"Oh, no, here we go," an older man at the bar called out. "Don't listen to him young lady. Willy is one of them conspiracy quacks. He thinks aliens land out there near the lake every now and again."

126

Deb looked over at Willy. "Why do you think that, Willy?" she asked.

"They haven't seen and heard the things I've seen and heard," Willy said, lowering his voice.

"What things?" Deb asked.

"Oh, you probably wouldn't understand," he replied, shaking his head.

"Well, why don't you try me?" Deb said.

"I've seen these lights, you see. They are a soft green. I've seen them hovering over that area out near the lake. I've seen them land out there too. Once I thought I saw someone coming out of the craft. Nobody around here believes me. But I know what I saw," he whispered.

Deb leaned close and whispered, "I believe you."

Willy drew back. "You do?" he asked.

At that moment, Marshall appeared next to her. "Is Willy bothering you?" he asked.

"No, not at all," Deb said.

"I wasn't bothering her, Marshall. We were just talking," Willy said.

Marshall looked over at Deb and back at Willy. "Scram Willy!" he said. Willy turned and went back to the counter where the older men began to tease him.

"He wasn't hurting anything," Deb said.

"Are you here about that Joe guy who is missing?" Marshall asked.

"Yes, have you seen him?" Deb asked.

"No," he replied. "The Sheriff was in here earlier. He told us about finding the car abandoned out along the side of the road. He asked us to let him know if we see or hear anything."

"Thanks," Deb said. "I thought I would search a little on my own."

"Are you going back out to the lake right away?" he asked.

"Well, not exactly," Deb replied.

"How about a cup of coffee and a piece of pie at Hannah's?" Marshall asked.

"I didn't know there was a diner in town," Deb said.

"It's not like diners in other towns. It's more of a coffee shop kind of place Hannah has at her house," Marshall explained.

"At her house?" Deb asked.

"Yeah, Hannah inherited her aunts boarding house. There aren't many overnighters in the area, so she has this little dining area in the front room where she serves sweet treats and coffee. It isn't much, but she doesn't have any competition here in town," Marshall explained.

Deb chuckled. "I'm intrigued. I would love a cup of coffee and Hannah's homemade pie."

"Going out for a minute," Marshall called out. He guided Deb by the elbow toward the door. They went to the end of the boardwalk street and turned left. A large Victorian house with a white picket fence sat nestled among some large maple trees with budding leaves on its branches.

"How lovely," Deb said.

They stepped inside. There were six small tables scattered about the front room. Four of the tables were taken. Marshall pulled a chair out for her near the front window. Deb smiled and sat down. Marshall sat across from her.

"Coffee for two, Marshall?" a hefty woman called out to them.

Marshall held up two fingers. "Cream and sugar?"

Deb shook her head. "Just straight up, Hannah," Marshall called out.

As the older woman carried two cups of black coffee to the table Marshall asked, "Got any cherry pie?"

"You know I always save a piece of cherry pie for you, Marshall," Hannah laughed. "Two?"

Deb nodded her head. Hannah made her way into the kitchen and soon returned with two pieces of cherry pie on a plate. "I thought you didn't eat prepared food," Marshall remarked.

"You can take it with you for later," Deb said.

"Thanks," Marshall smiled. "Now, what's the scoop on the missing drunk?"

Deb frowned. "Joe. Joe Kearney is his name. I don't know what happened," she said.

"He'll show up sooner or later. Might have gotten a ride out of town. I wouldn't worry. Sometimes, strangers find this town a little too dull. He seemed like the kind of guy who might like some excitement. Although, he certainly wanted to stay in that cabin as I recall," Marshall said, taking a bite of his pie.

"I suppose you might be right, but it isn't like him to just leave his car like that. They found his keys lying on the ground next to the car. Don't you find that strange?" she asked.

"Maybe, but I got to tell you, I find that guy strange," Marshall replied. "I think you'll find him back at the cabin when you get there. That is just my opinion."

Deb nodded her head. "Maybe. I hope you're right," she said.

"Do you work at the trading post, too?" Deb asked.

Marshall placed a large bite into his mouth, nodding his head. "Yep," he said. "I'm a man of many trades. The trading post is just a part time thing. My welding business is my main income. I'd like to get bigger. This job we went to look at yesterday could be the break I've been waiting for."

"I hope it works for you. If you don't mind, I have a favor to ask of you," Deb said.

"What can I do for you?" Marshall asked.

"Could you get away long enough to run me out to the cabin? I rode in with Richie, and I don't think Donna was very happy about him taking me back to the cabin," Deb explained.

"Sure, I'll take you home," Marshall said, laughing. "I can almost see Donna's face now. She is a little controlling and very possessive when it comes to Richie."

"I think I know what you mean," Deb said. "She said tonight was their rehearsal dinner. Are you a part of that?"

Marshall sighed and nodded his head. He took the last bite of his pie. "Unfortunately, I'm the best man," he replied. "Are you going to eat that?" he nodded toward the pie.

Deb shook her head and pushed the plate across the table toward him.

"Thanks," Marshall said. "You don't know what you're missing."

"I believe you," Deb replied.

Marshall ate the pie and the two of them walked back to the trading post. Marshall told them he would be back in an hour and soon they were driving back toward the cabin. Deb pointed out the area where Joe's car had been found. "They must have towed it away," she said.

She climbed out and opened the gate. It wasn't long before Marshall was pulling up to the cabin. "Do you have time to come in?" Deb asked.

"I have to get back to the trading post," Marshall said. "We have a truck coming in today. I'll keep my eyes and ears peeled for your friend."

"If you haven't anything else going on, you can stop out after the dinner," Deb suggested.

"We shall see," Marshall replied. "Keep your eyes and ears open." Then he was gone.

CHAPTER FIFTEEN

Deb laid on the bed staring up at the ceiling. She couldn't sleep. The hours seem to be dragging as the afternoon and evening wore on. She listened intently at the sounds from outside the cabin, hoping to hear Joe returning from wherever he had been all day.

She had hoped that Marshall would drop by after the rehearsal dinner, but he did not. Perhaps he wasn't interested in Deb after all. She felt something between them, but now she suspected that it was wishful thinking on her part. After all, the kiss she expected never happened.

She could hear sounds of night birds calling out in the darkness. A rustling somewhere under the cabin caught her attention. It was probably an opossum or a raccoon. The numbers in her head began to dance about. Normally, she would try to push them out of her mind, however, she was bored to death and so she paid close attention to them.

2,1,2,3, and then quickly 333. What did it mean? Maybe two raccoons were under the cabin and one left, then two more returned. It could mean anything. The number 3 began to pop up constantly. She concentrated on the numbers, hoping to become drowsy and fall asleep.

Her acute hearing picked up a new sound outside. Someone was walking in the high grass. No, it was more than one person. 3, 3, 3. There were three of them. Could it be the mother bear and her cubs? Deb sat upright. If it was Joe returning, he was most definitely not alone. 3, 3, 3. She swung her legs over the side of the bed and quietly made her way to the door that led to the front room. She was aware of silence underneath the cabin. The animals lurking about there had heard it too.

Deb moved into the front room and placed her hand against the front door, barring anyone from entering the cabin. She had left the door unlocked in the event Joe would return during the night. She heard faint whispering. It was a man's voice. Another man replied. She placed her ear to the door and listened.

"I see a truck," a man's voice said.

"That doesn't mean there is anyone here," a different male voice replied.

"Would you two be quiet?" a third voice said, softly. This voice was female.

Deb continued to bar the door by leaning against it. She heard the wooden steps creaking as the three strangers made their way onto the front porch. She turned and pressed her back against the door as the wooden boards of the porch creaked. Someone was moving toward the window.

The moonlight allowed a shadow to become visible on the far wall as a figure pressed his face against the glass. "I don't see anything or anyone," they whispered to their companions. Then the figure tried to jostle the window open.

The window had not been locked. Deb had thought nothing of leaving the cabin open when she went on her long walks or when she went to town. Anyone could have entered at any time. She hadn't noticed signs of entry in the past. Who were these people and what were they up to?

A leg swung over the window sill and soon a lean body dropped to the floor. The intruder had not noticed Deb right away. As a second leg swung over the window sill, the first intruder noticed Deb leaning against the door.

"Go, go, go!" he called out to the intruder about to drop into the room.

Deb raised her hands and the first intruder began to float upward. The second intruder fell out the window backwards. She could hear the moaning from the front porch and steps and one of them was running away.

"What do you want?" Deb asked the intruder hovering near the ceiling of the cabin.

"Ah! Put me down!" the intruder shouted. "Put me down!"

"What do you want?" Deb asked again. Her voice seemed to vibrate throughout the cabin. She moved closer.

"We didn't mean any harm, honestly," the intruder cried out.

Deb heard the second intruder getting to his feet. He also was fleeing, but from the sounds of his footsteps on the wooden porch, he was limping.

"Don't hurt me, please," the hovering intruder begged.

"Who are you?" Deb asked.

"My name is Josh. Josh Holdem. I'm a free lance reporter," the intruder whined. "Please, lady, don't hurt me. I'm sorry. I didn't expect to find you here."

"Why are you here and what are you looking for?" Deb asked.

"We heard a story about a woman that got shot out here somewhere and we wanted to investigate the story," the reporter said. "Please, could you put me down?"

"What makes you think you can break into someone's home like this?" Deb asked. "What gives you the right?"

"We were just looking for an orange vest with a bullet hole and blood stain, that's all," the reporter said. "Lady, I don't know how you are doing this, but I really would like to be put down now."

"I'll put you down when I get the answers to all my questions," Deb said.

"Oh, please. I promise, I'll leave. I'll go back to the city and I won't come back. I promise," the reporter said.

"Where are you from?" Deb asked.

"We are from New York. We work for a tabloid published out of New York. If we come up with a story good enough, they pay us for the story and even more if we have pictures to verify the story. That was all we wanted. We just wanted to find the orange vest and take a few pictures. Then we were going to leave. We weren't taking anything with us. We weren't going to steal anything, I promise," the reporter who called himself Josh Holdem said.

"Where did you hear about the shooting?" Deb asked, as she moved closer yet.

"Ah, some guy told us. He was a hunter and he claimed he shot this lady out here somewhere. He said he knows he hit her, and there was a bullet hole in the vest. He said she was bleeding and everything. He said she dropped to the ground and he thought she was dead. Then..., please, lady, I don't like hanging up here like this. By the way, how are you doing this?" he asked.

"It's a parlor trick I learned from a magician friend of mine," Deb lied.

"It's a pretty good trick, if you ask me," Josh said, forcing a smile. "But I would feel better if you put me down now."

"I'm not ready to let you go yet," Deb replied.

"Look lady, I promise I won't go anywhere. Just put me down. Please? I'll answer any questions you have for me, just put me down," Josh whined.

Deb sighed. The window was too high off the floor for him to jump through without climbing onto something and she stood between him and the only door. She allowed him to drift to the floor, slowly.

"Thanks, lady," Josh said.

"Where are your friends?" Deb asked.

"Probably at the border by now," Josh said.

"So, tell me about this vest you are looking for," Deb said.

"There was this guy we ran into in a roadside diner," Josh began. "He claimed he was up here hunting with some friends. He said he fired at what he thought to be a moose, and just as he pulled the trigger, he noticed the orange vest. He said he instantly knew he had made a terrible mistake, but it was too late. He said this girl dropped to the ground and made awful gurgling noises. He said she looked right at him with fear in her eyes because she knew she was dying. Then this guy shows up and cradles the girl in his arms. He swears the girl got to her feet and pulled her shirt to the side. He told us there was a bullet hole in the orange vest and the girl's shirt, covered with fresh blood, but there wasn't a mark on her body. It was like a miracle of some kind. Beings we publish stories about odd occurrences we thought it would be a perfect story for the tabloid. But we needed a picture of the orange vest for without the proof, the publisher wouldn't buy it."

"So, what makes you think the vest is here?" Deb asked.

"Well, he said the girl was tall with blue eyes and she wore some kind of scarf around her head like she was a cancer patient or something," Josh said.

Deb took a deep breath. She hadn't worn the scarf all day and she wasn't wearing it now. "Sit down, Josh," she said, pointing to the chair with no back.

"Are you the lady that got shot?" Josh asked.

"Not me," Deb lied.

"You have hair, but not much to speak of," Josh said. "You could very well be the lady he was talking about."

"You got the wrong girl, Josh," Deb said.

"Are you a hunter or fisherman? Fisherwoman?" Josh asked.

"Nope!" Deb replied. "I am a ghost writer. I'm up here for some quiet to write a book."

Josh looked around the room. "It certainly is quiet up here. Say," Josh leaned forward and placed his elbows upon the table. "How did you do that thing where I was hanging in the air back there?"

"I told you, it was a parlor trick taught to me by a dear friend who is a magician," Deb lied.

"Could you show me how to do it?" he asked.

Deb smiled and shook her head. "No, I promised him never to reveal his secret."

"Look, I am sorry about the intrusion. We didn't mean any harm. We are just three friends trying to make a buck, do you know what I mean?" Josh asked.

"I understand completely," Deb replied. "You are three friends who don't want to go out in the world and get your hands dirty, so you sneak into people's private spaces and take pictures to write fictional stories to sell junk magazines in shopping centers. Do you even care if the story is true or not?"

"Hey," Josh protested. "That isn't fair. If we don't do it someone else will."

"I think you better leave now," Deb said, walking to stand near Josh.

"Come on, lady," Josh whined.

"Perhaps I should hang you from the ceiling again until the cops get here," Deb warned.

"Okay, okay," Josh said, putting his hands out in front of him. "I'll go."

"I better not read anything about this in the papers either, or I will come looking for you and your friends. Do I make myself clear?" Deb asked.

Josh smirked. "Are you threatening me, lady?" he asked.

"No, I'm warning you. People around here get shot lurking about in the night. There are things out there in that tall grass that eat people lurking about in the night, too. I would hate to read about three tabloid photographers who got mauled and eaten because they were trying to break into someone's cabin at night," Deb warned.

"I'll keep that in mind," Josh said, walking to the door. "Am I going to be alright getting back to the road?"

Deb shrugged. "I don't know. Honestly, I don't care. Be on your way."

Josh opened the door and peered out into the darkness a moment before stepping outside. "I don't suppose you would consider giving me a lift to the road," he suggested.

"I don't suppose," Deb said, shaking her head. "You found your way here; you can find your way back."

His face paled as he moved out into the darkness. An owl screeched off in the distance and he flinched. Deb sighed. "Oh hell!" she mumbled to herself. "Okay, I'll give you a lift to the road."

Josh was quiet until they reached the plank bridge. "You aren't going to drive across that are you?" he asked, sitting erect to peer out over the hood of the truck.

"You can get out and walk anytime you want," Deb replied.

"I hope you know what you are doing," he asked.

"Why would you three bozos come all the way up here to break into someone's cabin for a picture of a bloody vest?" Deb asked.

"Well, that's not the only story up here," Josh said.

"What other story are you talking about?" Deb asked, glancing over at him.

"Please, lady, watch the road," Josh pointed to the road ahead of them.

"What other story, Josh?" Deb repeated.

"Oh, some guy is missing. We heard that earlier in the day. It might not be anything worth writing about, but then again, you never know," Josh said.

"The guy missing is my friend, Joe. There isn't any story there," Deb said. "He just broke down along the road and hitched a ride somewhere."

"So, there isn't anything unusual about the story?" Josh asked.

"Nope," Deb replied. "Who told you about it?"

"We ran into this guy at the trading post. I think his name was Wally or Willy. He said there is all kinds of strange things to write about up here," Josh said.

Deb had reached the gate and stopped in front of it. "Willy. His name is Willy and he isn't a very good source. He isn't a liar or anything like that, he just has some issues if you know what I mean. If you publish anything based on what Willy tells you, you will come out looking like a fool. Do you understand what I'm saying?"

"I understand. Thanks for the heads up," Josh said.

"The main road is on the other side of that gate. Latch the gate behind you. I'll shine my headlights on it until you are clear of the gate. Out there you are on your own," Deb said.

"Okay, thanks lady," Josh said. "I think our car is somewhere along the road out here. I don't know which way for sure," he stammered. "I don't suppose...."

"You're on your own now," Deb said. "Be careful"

She waited as Josh opened the gate and passed through. After he secured the gate behind him, she turned the truck around and drove back to the cabin.

CHAPTER SIXTEEN

Deb sat on the porch gazing out across the tall grass. She had not been able to go back to bed last night. She had found herself bored as the uneventful days passed out here all alone, and now things were changing. However, they were changing too quickly, and she had a feeling it was not for the good. Perhaps it was time for her to move on.

She looked down at the symbol carved into the step. She had not had a vision of the symbol for several days. Why was she here? She had hoped things would work out between Richie and herself, but they did not. Now she found she had feelings for Marshall, and she was beginning to think they were one sided as well. Maybe she should move on. Was there anyone out there for her? She missed her friends.

Where was Joe? Had the alien strangers taken him? Why didn't they take her too? Is that why she was called to this place? Was this her future fate?

She rubbed her forehead as thoughts raced through her mind. She found her head beginning to itch on the inside. She reached up and began scratching her head with both hands. "What?" she called out into the morning mist. "What do you want of me?"

She heard a vehicle bouncing across the plank bridge. It was not a familiar sound. It was not Richie. She stood up and waited as the Sheriff's jeep pulled up behind her truck.

"Miss Parks, good morning," the Sheriff called to her, as he exited the vehicle. He walked up to stand at the bottom of the steps. He placed his left foot onto the bottom step and leaned upon the wooden railing. "Getting some morning air, are you?" he asked.

"Good morning Sheriff. Do you have any word regarding Joe Kearney?" she asked.

The Sheriff shook his head. "No. No, I'm afraid not. I take it you haven't heard from him either?" he asked.

Deb shook her head. "No, I have not."

"Well, now we have two missing persons and the odd thing is, they both have connections to this cabin and you. You wouldn't know anything about that would you?" the Sheriff asked.

"What are you talking about? Who is the second missing person?" Deb asked.

"Well," the Sheriff removed his hat and scratched his head. "It seems a photographer from New York is missing. His two friends came into the station this morning and said he was last seen out here last night. Would you know anything about that?"

"Yes, I suppose I know a little about the photographer in question, but I assure you he was fine when I dropped him off at the gate last night. You say he is missing?" she asked.

"He is. At least according to his two friends he is," the Sheriff replied.

"Did his two friends happen to mention the circumstances surrounding their being here last night?" Deb asked.

"Somewhat," the Sheriff replied.

"I see," Deb said, as she sat down on the top step, facing the Sheriff. "Well, I caught the three of them trying to break into the cabin by way of my front window over here. One made it inside and his two friends ran for the hills leaving him behind. He told me his name was Josh Holdem and he was a photographer for a tabloid paper in New York. We had a long talk and I drove him out to the gate. He was going to walk to a car they had parked along the road somewhere out there."

"You didn't take him beyond the gate?" the Sheriff asked, writing on a note pad.

"No, I did not. He managed to get to the cabin on foot and break in by way of the window. He was not injured, so I saw no reason why he couldn't make it to his car," Deb replied.

"Well, apparently he didn't make it to the car," the Sheriff said.

"Are you sure the car was there?" Deb asked. "As I recall his friends wasted no time leaving him behind when I caught them breaking in. Maybe they drove off without him and now they can't locate him."

"That's a possibility," the Sheriff agreed. "Forgive me, Miss Parks, but I have to investigate every possible angle."

"Am I a suspect to a crime, Sheriff?" Deb asked.

"Oh, no, not at all," the Sheriff replied. "I was hoping I would drive out here and discover your friend had returned."

"I do wish that were the case, Sheriff, but it is not," Deb said, rubbing her temples.

"How is the book coming?" the Sheriff asked.

"The what?" Deb asked.

"The book you are writing, how is it coming?" the Sheriff repeated.

"Oh," Deb smiled. "It's coming together. I have a few glitches to work out, but I'll get it done. I always do," she continued to smile.

"Well, if ever there is anything I can do to help, let me know," the Sheriff said, removing his foot from the step. "Oh, I don't suppose you would have any objections to me looking around inside the cabin at the area where you say the photographer broke in?"

Deb took a deep breath. "Of course, come on in," she said, standing up and going to stand near the door.

The Sheriff passed through the open door and looked around the room. His eyes fell upon the bunk along the wall in the front room.

"That is where Joe Kearney slept," Deb said. "As you can see it has not been slept in for a couple of days now." She walked to the window. "This is the window the reporter came through. A second man was about to enter when I frightened them and he and a companion ran for the hills, leaving Josh Holdem behind."

The Sheriff went to the window and ran his hands along the sill. "I can see it would take some skills getting inside this little window," he said. "I take it they found it unlocked."

"It was unlocked. So was the front door," Deb said. "I open the window often to air out this smelly old cabin after Joe sweats off his drunken nights. The front door was left unlocked in the event he should find his way home again."

"I wonder why they didn't come in through the door?" the Sheriff asked.

"I have no idea," Deb said. "Possibly they assumed it would be locked."

"How long would you say the young man was inside the cabin?" the Sheriff asked.

"Not long," Deb replied. "I asked him who he was, why he was here, and after threatening to have him arrested, I drove him down to the gate. I was going to make him walk, but there are some dangerous predators out there, so I drove him to the road."

"Interesting," the Sheriff said, writing on his pad. "You weren't worried about predators along the road?"

"They interrupted my sleep. I wanted to go back to bed. Why were they my responsibility? They were breaking and entering," she was beginning to get angry.

"Just asking, Miss Parks. It's all part of the investigation," the Sheriff replied. He looked around the room, frowning.

"Is something wrong, Sheriff?" Deb asked.

"I don't see a typewriter or computer. How do you write?" he asked.

"Well, a computer would be of no use to me out here, would it?" she asked.

"I suppose," the Sheriff said. "Well, I suppose I've seen enough. I will let you know if we hear anything regarding your friend and of course, I will keep you informed about the investigation into our missing reporter."

"Thank you, Sheriff," Deb replied, following him outside. She stood on the porch and watched as he turned the police car around and drove out the muddy drive toward the road. A rumble of thunder caught her attention.

Deb went inside the cabin. As the thunder drew closer, she began to pace the floor. Occasionally, she would catch her reflection in the mirror over the washboard. She would pause, look at herself, and then begin to pace again. As she paced, she found the itching inside her head increased. "What do you want from me?" she shouted, loudly. "What?" She did not hear Richie pulling up outside.

She was mumbling to herself. "Why am I here? Am I here for a reason?" she was asking herself.

Richie knocked upon the wall next to the open door. Deb did not hear him over the roaring thunder outside. She turned to resume her pacing and noticed him there. "How long have you been there?" she asked.

"Not long," Richie said, smiling. "Are you alright?"

"I'm fine. The Sheriff just left," Deb replied.

"I know, I met him at the gate. He said someone tried to break in here last night and now the guy is missing," Richie explained.

"They didn't try to break in. They broke in. He came in through the window," she said, pointing to the small window in the front room. "He was a photographer for one of those junk magazines you see at the check outs in all the stores."

"What was he doing out here?" Richie asked, stepping inside. It was beginning to sprinkle outside.

"He was hoping to get a picture of my orange vest with the bullet hole in it. It seems he heard the story surrounding my being shot and was hoping for a picture to back up his story for the paper," Deb replied, as she resumed her pacing.

"What do you think happened to him?" Richie asked, moving to straddle the stool near the table.

"How do I know?" Deb barked. "I drove him as far as the gate. He said they had a car parked out along the road somewhere. I dropped him off at the gate and came back here, trying to get some sleep, but that didn't work."

"Are you sure you're alright?" Richie asked.

"Yes, I'm fine!" she barked, then, "No, I'm angry. Where is Joe? Did something happen to him? What happened to Josh? Did something happen to him as well?"

"Who is Josh?" Richie asked.

Deb turned to look at Richie. "Oh, Josh Holdem was the photographer who is missing."

"You know his name?" Richie asked.

"Yeah, we had a long talk before I drove him to the gate," Deb explained. "I thought you knew that."

Richie cleared his throat and shook his head. "I'm trying to keep up, but I'm finding it difficult," he said.

"I know what you mean. I was here and I'm having a hard time with it all too," Deb said, scratching her head.

"By the way," Richie began. "I meant to tell you and forgot; I like your hair that way. I brought you something." He placed a small plastic bag on the table.

Deb opened the bag and pulled out a plastic tube of hair gel. She held it up and frowned as she looked at it. "What is this for?" she asked.

"It's for your hair. Donna said, all you need to do is dampen your hair and put a small amount of this in your palm. Work it through your hair, style it and go," Richie said.

"Donna said that?" Deb asked. "You discussed my hair with Donna?"

"It wasn't like that, no," Richie protested. "She just mentioned that you look so different now that your hair is growing in. She said a little gel in your hair, and nobody would ever know you were bald at one time. She said there are girls who keep their hair cut short like that."

"I see," Deb smiled.

"What?" Richie asked.

"Nothing," Deb said. "I just find it very interesting that Donna was discussing my hair with you. The looks she was giving me yesterday at the hardware store, gave me the impression she wasn't very happy with my being there. I really don't think she likes me."

"She was upset with me. That's what you were seeing," Richie said.

"I can't believe you are that naive, Richie. Donna is jealous. I don't know why she is jealous of me, but she is jealous, and possibly a bit controlling. You need to know that before you say your vowels on your wedding day," Deb said. The rain began to fall upon the porch outside.

Richie shook his head. "I know, I know. I don't know what to do. She gets a bit bossy as well. Sometimes I want to call the whole thing off, but I've been in love with Donna for as long as I can remember. I don't want to lose her," he explained.

"Well, it's your life," Deb said. "I've been thinking, maybe it's time for me to move on. There really isn't anything for me here. I haven't been able to help anyone in a long time, and I feel so useless. I don't see having a special gift like the one I've been given and not using it to help others."

"Where do you think you're going to go?" Richie asked.

"I don't know," Deb said. "I haven't thought it through that far."

"Well, stay at least until after the wedding," Richie urged.

Deb nodded. "I suppose I could stay a few more days, but unless something changes, I'm going to move on. I have to tell you; it gets pretty quiet out here and I've had about all the quiet I can take."

"The wedding is Saturday. I'll try to scout around for signs of fliers or something to indicate they are still looking for you. We have to be careful," Richie said.

Deb nodded. "I agree. I just want to see my friends again and my mom. I really miss them," she could not keep her voice from cracking.

"I better go. I'll stop again tomorrow morning. Will you be alright until then?" Richie asked.

"I'll be fine," Deb said, smiling. "Thank you for stopping by."

Richie stared at her for the longest time. "Okay then," he said. "Until tomorrow."

He stepped out onto the porch and looked back at her before leaving. Deb did not get up from the backless chair she occupied on the opposite side of the table. She continued staring at her folded hands on the table in front of her. She was thinking of her mother and her friends. The thought of possibly seeing them again caused the numbers in her head to flash by quickly. And the symbol was back. What was that all about?

CHAPTER SEVENTEEN

Deb lost track of time as she sat staring at her hands. The storm passed overhead without her being aware of it, leaving the rain to pelt away at the cabin. A noise on the front porch caused her to look up as Marshall stepped inside the cabin, soaked to the skin.

"It's really coming down out there," he said, wiping the rain from his face.

"I didn't hear you come in," Deb said, rising from the chair.

"No wonder. I don't know how you hear anything," he said, pointing to the ceiling.

The rain pelted at the metal roof of the cabin, making a loud roaring noise. Deb smiled. "I like that sound. It's almost hypnotic, and it's a welcome break from the constant silence." she said, pointing to the stool. "Have a seat, I'll get you a towel."

She parted the curtains that covered the cupboards and pulled out a dry towel. Handing it to Marshall she asked, "What brings you out here in this storm?"

"I ran into Richie in town earlier. He said something about you leaving. Are you really going to leave?" Marshall asked.

"I'm thinking about it. I think it's time. I get pretty bored out here. I won't leave until after the wedding though," she said, returning to her seat on the backless chair.

"The wedding is Saturday," Marshall said. "How soon after the wedding are you leaving?"

"I don't know," Deb said, shrugging her shoulders. "Maybe a couple of days after the wedding."

"So soon?" Marshall asked.

Deb smiled. "Will you miss me?" she teased.

"Yes, I suppose I will," Marshall said.

Deb stiffened. "What?" Marshall asked. "Not the answer you were expecting?"

Deb shook her head. "No, it isn't," she replied.

"Well, it's the truth," Marshall said. "I thought there was something between the two of us. You know, I thought we were growing rather fond of one another."

Deb was speechless. She sat staring across the table at him.

"Well, I suppose I thought wrong," Marshall said, growing red in the face. "Maybe I better go."

"No!" Deb blurted out.

"No, what?" Marshall asked. "No, you don't want me to go, or no, there isn't anything between us?"

"No, I don't want you to go," Deb said. "I mean, please don't go just yet."

Marshall walked around the table to where Deb sat. He reached down, taking her by the hands, and pulling her to her feet. She couldn't speak. He tenderly kissed her, and she kissed him back. Once again, he was pulling her by the hand, only this time he was leading her to the bunk where Joe normally slept.

Deb and Marshall laid side by side on the narrow bunk bed, wrapped in each other's arms. The rain continued to pelt the roof so loud that nothing else could be heard.

Marshall sat up. "I have to get back to the trading post," he said.

Deb began to dress as Marshall sat on the bunk lacing his boots. "So, are you still going to leave?" he asked.

Deb sighed. "I'll think on it," she replied. "The truth is, I truly miss my mother and my friends. You and Richie are my only friends here and with Richie getting married Saturday, I don't see Donna allowing him to run groceries out here every other morning. And you, you said yourself that this job at the park was going to keep you busy all summer."

Marshall sat down so that he was looking up at her, as she stood tucking her shirt tail inside her jeans. "We can work something out. Maybe you could come with me. I could teach you to weld, or help in some other way," he said.

"I don't think so," she said, laughing.

"I have to get back," he said, standing up. "Why don't you come with me. Later we can stop by Pappy's to meet some friends and I'll bring you back here."

"The people here are nice, Marshall, but they won't replace my friends back home. I miss them," Deb said.

"I understand, but maybe if you got to know some of the locals better, you wouldn't feel so alone out here. Come on, what do you say? Come into town with me," Marshall urged.

Deb sighed. "Okay," she said.

"By the way, I like your hair like that," Marshall said. "I meant to tell you before, but I got side tracked."

"Thank you," she said. "I don't suppose you would know where a girl could get a dress for a wedding."

"No, I wouldn't know, but I know someone who would. You can talk to her at Pappy's tonight," Marshall smiled. "Come on, my lady, your chariot awaits.

Marshall stood in the open door watching the rain as it fell in sheets. Only the edge of the tall grass between the lake and cabin was visible due to the heavy downpour. Deb and Marshall stood staring out across the porch toward the lake.

"It's really coming down out there," Marshall said. "We better wait for it to let up before we run for the truck."

"I can make a cup of tea if you want," Deb suggested.

Marshall smiled. "No, I don't want anything," he said, pulling her close. They stood in the open door holding one another as the rain continued to fall. "It won't be busy in town when it's raining this hard," he said, over the top of her head.

"I don't believe I've ever seen it rain this hard before out here," Deb said.

"The weather up here gets unpredictable at times. I barely made it across the bridge. If the bridge washes out, I might be stuck here," Marshall teased. After a moment he said, "I hope you will change your mind about leaving. Richie told me there were some people searching for you. You are safe here, why do you want to take the chance that someone will discover you?"

"I don't know," Deb said. "I really hate to leave now," she smiled up at him. "But I do miss my mom and friends. I have these crazy friends that were like family. We did everything together. It's been almost a year since I've seen or heard from any of them. They have been on my mind so much lately."

"Maybe we could take a few days and drive down there. Pennsylvania, wasn't it?" Marshall asked.

"Yes, between Gettysburg, and Chambersburg, in a little town called Mont Alto and Quincy. There isn't much there for me, except for my friends," Deb said.

"The wedding is this weekend," Marshall began. "What if we took a couple of days after the wedding and drove down to see how your friends are doing. Then maybe we can stop and see your mom. Where is she at?"

"Mom lives in Ohio. A town called East Palestine, Ohio," Deb said. "That will be the tricky one, for I suspect her house is being watched by the FBI."

"The FBI?" Marshall asked. "You are wanted by the FBI? What the hell did you do?"

"I didn't do anything," Deb said. "It's more like what I can do. They want to place me in a facility where they can study my brain activity. Didn't Richie explain that to you?"

"Hell no! I know you healed his tumor, but I sort of thought that was a coincidence," Marshall said, looking down at her. "He said some people where looking for you, and I thought you might have done something illegal like, I don't know, wrote a bad check or something. He never explained and I really wasn't sure I wanted to know."

"It's complicated. Even Richie doesn't know everything. I'm not dangerous or anything like that," she leaned against the door jam and began to explain. "When I woke up in the hospital things were different. I was different." Deb said.

"You told me that much before," Marshall said.

"Well, my mom noticed it way before anyone else," Deb said.

"You told me the machines wouldn't work when you were awake. You said they had to put you to sleep to get the CT scan," Marshall said. "Are you saying there is more to it?"

Deb nodded her head. "Yeah, but no one else knows. Well, Joe knows, but there is a reason for that."

"Joe Kearney? The guy who normally sleeps in that bunk?" Marshall asked.

Again, Deb nodded her head. "That's the one," she affirmed.

"Why is it he knows and the rest of us don't?" Marshall asked.

"Because," Deb paused.

"Don't you trust me?" Marshall asked.

"I'm not sure I should be talking about Joe. Maybe that part I should keep to myself. He may not like anyone knowing his business," Deb declared.

"Okay, forget about Joe," Marshall said. "What about Deb?"

"Well," she began. "The first time I noticed something different was with this little old man down the hall from me in the hospital. His name was Leonard. He was the sweetest old man and he had been placed in a nursing home and left there to die. He was a WWII veteran and he had been cast aside like a worn shirt. I hugged him, and he began to shiver and shake. At first, I thought I was hurting him. But when I released my hold on him, he stood up on his own, which he couldn't do before."

"So, you really did heal Richie," Marshall said.

Deb nodded her head and replied, "Yes, I did. But that isn't all I can do."

"Maybe I should sit down," Marshall said, pulling her by the hand toward Joe's bunk once more.

"There was a lady in the room next to Leonard's. Her husband was sleeping in a chair, because he didn't want to leave her alone. You see, he beat her terribly. I was told by one of the nurses that it wasn't the first time.

This time he nearly killed her, and the police were trying to get her to file a report against him. He was making certain she didn't talk to anyone. He threatened her. I know this because my hearing is very acute. That is another thing that changed after my accident. I heard them talking all the way down the hall, and they were whispering," Deb explained.

Marshall looked over at her. He had been holding her hand and she became aware that his hands were sweating. "Are you sure you want to hear this?" she asked.

He nodded his head. "I want to hear it all. I am not in this for the short term. I want you to know that. Nothing you could tell me is going to make a difference, so you might as well tell me everything."

"I walked down the hall during the night. It was dark in the room because they were both sleeping. But I could see him sleeping in the green chair with his head off to the side and his mouth hanging open, like the dog that he was. I don't know how I knew to do what I did, but I concentrated on flipping him out of that chair, and that is exactly what happened. He flopped out onto the floor like a fish out of water. He woke up instantly and began cursing at his sleeping wife. Then I concentrated on that large green chair and it lifted in the air and came down on him hard. Again, I lifted the chair and struck him. I pounded him repeatedly with that chair. He was screaming and cursing. I heard some bones breaking, but that did not stop me. I wanted him to feel the pain he had inflicted upon his wife repeatedly," Deb explained.

Marshall shook his head. "Remind me not to piss you off," he said.

"Are you frightened?" she asked.

"Maybe somewhat," Marshall replied. "But I'm not going to let that stop me."

"Well, they wheeled him out of there on a gurney," Deb said. "The police questioned his wife, but of course she didn't see anything, or anyone. They thought it was because she had been drugged with pain meds. The police said he was a shady character and possibly had many enemies out there who finally caught up to him. Once he was out of the room, his wife told them about his frequent beatings. She told them everything and agreed to press charges."

"And that is why they are looking for you?" Marshall asked.

Deb shook her head. "No," she replied. "They finally got me to sleep and ran some tests. They discovered that my brain activity had doubled since my accident. Of course, that made some doctors curious. One came to the house to ask me to check myself into a facility to have my brain activity monitored and examined. I told him no and sent him on his way. While backing out of my drive, he ran over a little girl who lived across the street and killed her. Of course, I couldn't just stand by and do nothing, so I embraced the child. She opened her eyes and stood up like nothing had ever happened. She ran off to play. The doctor witnessed the whole thing. That is how this all started. I was hiding one day when a whole swat team came to the house looking for me. Right after that the four strangers who had chanted over me at the accident appeared and told me to run. With the help of a good neighbor, I ended up here."

"Who are the four strangers?" Marshall asked.

"I don't really know, for sure," Deb said. "I only know that on the night of my accident I was watching this huge craft in the sky. My friend Angela told me that four identical guys showed up at the accident and began chanting over me. That was when I started gasping for breath and they rushed me to the hospital. That was after the coroner pronounced me dead."

"So, you think these four quad triplets are aliens?" Marshall asked."

"What do you think?" Deb asked back. "I don't really know, but they are like no humans I've ever seen before. And when they talk, they all talk together as one. It sounds like a song they are humming, but with words."

"That's some story," Marshall said.

"Don't you believe me?" Deb asked.

"Oh, I believe you, alright. It's just some story," Marshall replied.

"That is about all there is to tell. I can heal people, by embracing them, I can bring people back from death, and I can move objects without touching them. Oh, once I lifted a whole car out of a snowy ditch. That was pretty cool. I also lifted a she bear out there near the lake. She was charging me because I managed to get between her and her cubs. That was pretty cool too," Deb said, smiling.

"Well, what about those children at the house fire? Did you do anything there?" he asked.

Deb nodded. "I heard them crying and coughing from the second floor. I couldn't get by the police and firemen without being noticed so I lifted them and moved them downstairs to the front door where I knew they would be noticed. A fireman happened to see them there and got them out safely," she replied.

"I think I can understand why the FBI might be interested in you," Marshall said. "You may come in handy on the battlefield."

"Well, I don't want to take sides. I don't want the government picking and choosing how I use my abilities. I would like to think I am using them for good," Deb explained. "Besides, I like my freedom."

"It looks like the rain is letting up. Maybe you can tell me more on the way into town," Marshall said.

"There isn't much more to tell, but I'll answer any questions you have," Deb said, standing to her feet.

The two of them rushed outside to the truck. The mud oozed over their shoes and splashed up the back of their legs as they ran. Marshall turned the truck around and drove to the bridge. Water was rushing over it.

They sat staring at the bridge that was about four inches under rushing water. "I don't know about this," Marshall said. "I don't think we should try it."

Deb smiled. "Leave it to me," she said. She concentrated on the hood of the truck. It began to rise. She heard Marshall moaning, "Whoa," as they drifted upward and moved across the stream. Then she slowly lowered the truck to rest safely on the other side.

"That is pretty cool, alright," he said.

"Yeah, but for some reason, I can't levitate myself. I can't figure that one out," Deb said. "How can that be?"

"Levitate? Do you mean like the exorcist girl?" Marshall asked.

"Something like that," Deb replied, with a chuckle.

"Well, I'm new at this super powers stuff, but I'm glad you can't float overhead like that girl in the movies. That would really freak me out," Marshall said, pulling up to the gate.

Deb laughed. "It wouldn't be any different than what we just did," she said.

"Maybe the two of us can figure it out, you know, together," Marshall suggested.

"I like the sound of that," Deb replied, smiling. Maybe it wasn't going to be such a bad day after all. The itching inside her head had stopped and the symbol was no longer visible. That was always a good sign.

Deb hung out at the trading post while Marshall worked in the back. It was a slow day as the rain continued to fall. The hours flew by and Deb was enjoying the fact that she was not sitting at the cabin all alone for another entire day.

Near the end of the day, the Sheriff stopped in the trading post to purchase some tobacco products. He smiled at Deb and asked, "Have you heard from your friend?"

"No, I was hoping you had some news," she replied.

"No, I don't have anything. This is the strangest case I've seen in all my years as Sheriff. I heard about another man who disappeared years ago. I looked up the file and it was pretty much the same as your friend. This guy, Lawrence Woods, was reported missing. They found his car abandoned along the road. Same road too, but further back this way. They never did find the guy," the Sheriff explained.

"Oh, no. I hope Joe turns up soon, somewhere," Deb said, becoming worried. "When was this?"

"Oh, it was a long time ago. 1971, I believe it was," the Sheriff replied.

"Did anyone hear from the reporter?" Deb asked.

"Oh, yes, he turned up. Apparently, his friends drove off and left him behind. He turned up shortly after I left your cabin. He's alright, just shook up. He went back to New York," the Sheriff explained.

Marshall and Deb stayed at the trading post until the lights were turned off and the doors were locked. "Let's see what's going on at Pappy's," Marshall said, leading her by the hand toward his truck. Deb couldn't get Lawrence Woods out of her mind.

Deb's eyes quickly adjusted to the dim light as they entered Pappy's. Two men Deb did not know sat at the bar. "Over here, Marshall," a voice called out as the sound of pool balls bouncing off one another caught Deb's attention. Willy Goldman and Henry Escott were playing pool.

They sat at the long table and Marshall ordered a draft for each of them. He handed Deb a menu. "Aren't you eating?" she asked.

Marshall nodded. "I know that menu backwards and forward. I'm having chicken fingers and French fries," he said.

"I'll have the same," Deb said, slipping the menu in its holder at the center of the table.

The door opened and Jennifer Calvin and Larry Escott entered. As Jennifer noticed Deb sitting at the table, her face flushed.

"There's the girl I was hoping to see," Marshall said, waving at the couple.

"What's up, Marshall?" Larry asked, smiling down at Deb.

"I need to ask a favor of Jennifer," Marshall said, rising to pull a chair out for Jennifer to sit down.

"What can I do for you?" Jennifer asked.

"My friend, Virginia, needs a dress for the wedding Saturday. Can you help her out?" Marshall asked.

Deb noticed little beads of sweat forming above Jennifer's lip. "You're going to the wedding?" she forced herself to smile.

"Of course, she's going to the wedding," Larry bellowed. "She's one of us now."

"I don't know my way around the area, Jennifer. If you could point me in the right direction, I can shop for something on my own. You needn't be inconvenienced," Deb explained.

"Oh, no," Jennifer said, as she continued to smile. "I would be happy to spend a day shopping with you. It will give us a chance to get to know each other better."

"Good," Deb smiled. "I'm looking forward to it."

Jennifer stiffened. "What are you doing tomorrow?"

"I'll make certain I'm free," Deb said. It was all set. Tomorrow Deb and Jennifer were going shopping for a dress she could wear to the wedding.

The night wore on and finally Marshall announced it was time for them to leave. As they climbed into his truck, he asked, "Do you have to go to the cabin?"

"What? Where else would I go?" Deb asked.

"You could stay at my place tonight. You would already be in town and wouldn't have to drive in to meet Jennifer," he hinted.

"What about clean clothes?" Deb asked.

"Oh," Marshall said, putting the truck in reverse and looking in the side mirror. "You are not going to need any clothes."

CHAPTER EIGHTEEN

Deb woke to find Marshall had already left. She laid staring up at the ceiling. It had been a very long time since she slept so well. Marshall's bed felt huge to her even though it was only a double sized bed. She got up and dressed. A note on the night stand told her to come to the trading post after waking. Marshall's apartment was over the trading post so she wouldn't have far to go.

She made the bed and was preparing to step outside when Marshall met her at the door.

"I brought you some breakfast," he said, smiling.

"How did you know I was up?" she asked.

"I could hear you moving around up here," he explained.

Deb's eyes widened. "Are you telling me they can hear us down there?" she asked.

Marshall nodded. Smiling he said, "Don't worry. There wasn't anyone down there when we got in last night." He handed her a box of store-bought donuts and a large black coffee. "I ran down to the mini mart and picked this up for you," he said, placing the purchases on the table.

"Thanks, but you need to understand that I only eat vegetables and fruit and I mainly drink water," she explained. "I could get that down, but it wouldn't stay."

"I'm sorry, I wasn't thinking. I'm trying to finish up down there so I can get out early," he said moving closer to her. He wrapped his arms around her and kissed her tenderly. She allowed herself to melt into his arms.

"I'm going shopping with Jennifer today," she said. "I'm supposed to call her when I am ready."

Marshall smiled. "It's okay. Jenny is downstairs waiting for you," he said.

"What? Why didn't you wake me?" Deb asked.

"She's not in any hurry. Larry is down there," Marshall smiled. "She probably isn't even aware of the time."

Deb kissed Marshall on the chin. "I better get moving," she said, turning toward the door.

"Aren't you eating anything first?" he asked.

"I'm not hungry. I usually eat a few bites of carrot for breakfast and that lasts nearly all day. I don't require much," Deb said, over her shoulder.

Marshall was following her down the stairs. "Well, you'll certainly be a cheap date."

Deb smiled as she reached the bottom. "I'm not a very good cook though. You need to be prepared for that."

"Oh, that could be a problem," Marshall said, following her into the trading post.

A bell over the door rang as they entered, and everyone turned to see who had arrived. Deb smiled. "Good morning everyone," she said.

"Good morning Miss Parks," Willy greeted her with a smile.

"We hope you slept well," one of the older gentlemen teased. Deb felt her face growing red. Everyone here was aware that she had spent the night with Marshall.

"Don't listen to these old goats. They are just jealous," Larry Escott said, stepping closer. Deb looked over his shoulder to find Jennifer growing red also, as her shoulders straightened, and her chin protruded.

Deb smiled. "Jennifer, I am sorry if I kept you waiting," she said.

Jennifer waved her hand, as she said, "No problem." She remained rigid as she glared at Deb.

"Maybe we should go and leave these men to their idle gossip," Deb suggested.

"Sounds like a plan," Jennifer said.

Deb held the door for Jennifer and then began to follow her to an older model Ford station wagon. Jennifer unlocked the driver's door and pressed the power button to unlock the passenger door. Deb climbed in and waited for Jennifer to start the car.

"Where do the locals do all of their shopping around here?" Deb asked.

"At the store," Jennifer replied.

Deb realized that Jennifer was very upset over Larry's being so friendly to her. How was she going to smooth this over between them?

"Are you and Larry an item?" Deb asked.

"Somewhat," Jennifer replied, then it grew silent.

"I really like Marshall a lot," Deb said. This was not going well. She hadn't planned on her statement sounding so blunt. She needed to think this through before saying anymore.

"How long have you and Marshall been seeing each other?" Jennifer asked, without looking away from the road ahead.

"I would say a whole three days," Deb laughed. Jennifer continued staring at the road ahead. She remained stone faced as she drove along. Her face was returning to its normal color, however, her neck remained crimson.

"Is the store far?" Deb asked. Jennifer shook her head but did not reply. Deb looked down at her hands as she tried to think of some way to break through the icy wall Jennifer had put around her.

"What kind of dress are you wearing to the wedding?" Deb asked.

"It's just a dress," Jennifer replied. "If we can't find anything suitable for you, you can borrow one of mine."

Deb looked over at Jennifer. She guessed Jennifer wore about a size eight dress. Deb wasn't sure what size she wore because it had been ages since she wore a dress. There was a time when Deb was about that size, but since her accident she hadn't been eating anything but fruits and vegetables and very little of them. She didn't find food that appealing anymore. She knew one thing for certain, she was about two sizes smaller than Jennifer.

"I can't tell you the last time I wore a dress. It seems like ages that I've been cooped up in that cabin. I don't have many clothes. I suppose I don't need any. Thank you so much for helping me out, Jennifer. I really do appreciate your kindness," she was rambling again. She clamped her teeth together and stared out the side window as the car moved passed the multitude of forest trees. "Where is this store?" she asked.

"About another thirty minutes west," Jennifer replied.

"Oh," Deb replied. It was going to be a long thirty minutes at this rate.

After a long period of silence, Jennifer said, "Your hair looks different without the scarf."

Deb reached up to touch the top of her hair. "It's growing in, but it's so uneven. I was thinking of getting some styling gel and trying to do something with it for the wedding," she said, smiling.

"I suppose you could get into one of those walk-in hair stylist places before the wedding," Jennifer said. "Have you met Hannah Priezz?" she asked.

"Is she the lady who has the little café in the Victorian house?" Deb asked.

"Yes, that's Hannah," Jennifer says. "She cuts most of the guy's hair in town. She might be able to even up your hair if you want her to."

Deb turned to look at the scenery passing by. So, Jennifer was suggesting she see the local barber before the wedding. She could only imagine what kind of dress she would suggest Deb buy for the wedding.

Deb squeezed the fanny pack she held in her lap. She had been receiving money orders regularly from the McCall's. She had about $700 cash in the pouch. It was a lot of money, but it was all she had. She needed to spend it wisely for she never knew when she would have to make a run for it.

"We can start looking at the mall. There is a big one not far from here," Jennifer said.

"I don't need anything fancy. It's not like I'll wear it much. I think a plain dress will do nicely," she suggested. She watched Jennifer's expression. The suggestion of a plain dress seemed to appeal to her. Perhaps there was hope of breaking through the icy wall after all. However, it was not going to be easy. Deb took a deep breath. She was up to the challenge.

They drove a while longer in silence. "How far is this mall?" Deb asked.

"It's not much further. It's the nearest mall to us and it's about forty-seven miles one way," Jennifer replied.

"I didn't realize how far out there we were," Deb said. The houses were closer together now. It was obvious that they were coming into a town or city of some sort.

They were sitting at a red light. Deb was looking into the front window of a book store and coffee shop.

"Are any of your books in there?" Jennifer asked.

Deb hated lying to Jennifer. She was hoping that they would become friends. However, if Jennifer knew the truth, it would likely turn out badly for both of them. "Probably one or two, I suppose," Deb answered.

"Do you ever get recognized for any of the work you do?" Jennifer asked.

Now Deb was in a pickle, for she had no idea how the whole ghost-writing thing worked. She could only hope that Jennifer didn't know anything about it either.

"Behind the scenes, I suppose. Our names are sometimes placed inside the cover in very small print, but not always. However, nearly all publishers have a list of ghost writers they often refer would be novelists to when they need our help writing a book," she lied.

"So, your famous, but only in the publishing world, is that it?" Jennifer asked, accelerating the car to move to the next red light.

"That is exactly right," Deb replied.

"That doesn't bother you?" Jennifer asked. This time she was looking over at Deb.

"Not me, it doesn't. It may bother some, but I don't want to be famous. I like being able to go anywhere I want without crowds and cameras in my face," Deb replied.

Jennifer was parking the car now. "We're here," she said, opening the car door.

Deb walked around the car to begin walking toward the entrance with Jennifer. She smiled and said, "Jennifer, this is very nice of you. Thank you again."

"You already thanked me once," Jennifer replied, without making eye contact with Deb.

They entered the brightly lit mall. They moved along the aisles until they reached the women's clothing section. Jennifer began looking through the dresses as if she knew exactly what she was looking for.

"What about this one?" Jennifer asked, holding up a royal blue sequins dress. "This looks like your color."

"Hmm, I don't think I want anything that fancy. This is Donna's day. I would prefer something plainer," Deb replied.

"Good idea," Jennifer said. "We certainly don't want to out shine the bride."

"Oh, I don't think I could ever outshine Donna," Deb laughed. "She is a beautiful woman."

"I suppose," Jennifer replied. "What size do you wear?"

"I don't know, exactly," Deb replied. "Like I said, it has been a long time since I've worn a dress."

"I wear an eight. Let's start there," Jennifer said.

They chose three dresses, each a different size and Deb tried them on. The size four fit perfectly. It was a plain light blue with a lace collar and light blue rose buttons down the front. It was mid length with a slightly flared skirt.

"I like this one," Deb said.

"Really?' Jennifer asked. "It is rather plain."

"I know. It is something I will be able to wear almost anywhere. This is exactly what I'm looking for," Deb stated.

"Okay," Jennifer said. "That was easy enough. Now for shoes."

Deb tried on several pairs of shoes and none of them were as comfortable as her mud boots. She was beginning to feel disappointed.

"What about a pair of sandals?" Jennifer asked.

"Let's look at what they have," Deb suggested.

"It appears this is going to be easier then I thought," Jennifer said. "I was expecting to spend the entire day shopping. You certainly are easy to please."

"I never was much of a shopper. I suppose I'm used to spending so much of my time alone. It is nice to have someone to talk to, though," Deb said, smiling.

"Maybe when we are done here, we can stop at the food court and have a latte or something delightful to celebrate," Jennifer said, smiling back at Deb for the first time.

"I would like that," Deb smiled back at her.

Deb chose a pair of black roman sandals that laced up the front above the ankle. "These look dressy enough. Let's get checked out and find that food court," Deb said, smiling.

As they were checking out, the lady behind the counter kept watching Deb. "Pardon me, but you look so familiar," she said.

Deb felt her throat constrict. Was her picture still floating around the media world? She shook her head and said, "I'm sorry, I don't think so."

"Maybe your picture was inside a book or something," Jennifer said, from behind Deb. "She's a ghost writer. She writes novels for people," Jennifer said to the cashier.

"Oh, that must be it. I have my nose in a book all the time," the cashier said.

"The food court is this way," Jennifer said, pointing to a brightly lit outlet in the mall.

They ordered their drinks and sat down at a small black and red checkered table to enjoy their drinks.

"This was fun," Jennifer said. "I have to tell you, I was expecting you to be a snob, you being a literary writer and all. I am a plain Jane sort of girl. Larry said that is what he likes best about me. He doesn't have to try to impress me or anything like that."

"I think you are a delightful young lady and I truly enjoy your company," Deb smiled.

Jennifer leaned across the table and whispered, "Frankly, I didn't know what to expect today. You surprised me. I really do like you."

"I like you too Jennifer. I hope we can be good friends," Deb said.

"What do you think of Larry?" Jennifer asked.

"I think he is a pleasant young man. I like both he and his brother Henry," Deb said.

Jennifer surprised Deb by asking, "As much as Marshall?"

Deb swallowed her latte and shook her head. "I think I might like Marshall more, but let's keep that between us. I'm not certain where Marshall and I are going yet. But I hope there's a future for the two of us."

Jennifer smiled ear to ear. She beamed with happiness and Deb knew she had broken through the icy wall.

Shouting broke their moment. "Run, there's a shooter!" someone called out.

"Quick, everyone, hide!" a man was waving his arms. Suddenly a loud shot broke through the air and the man fell on his face.

Deb tugged on Jennifer's arm. "Get down," she yelled. She looked around for somewhere to hide that wasn't out in the open. "Over there! Run over there and hide behind that counter," she yelled, as she pointed to the counter where burgers and drinks were served.

Jennifer crouched low and began moving as quickly as possible. Deb stayed behind her, trying to protect her from the flying bullets. A burley man was running past and knocked Jennifer over. He jumped over her and kept going. Deb was trying to help her up when a bullet whizzed past her head. She threw herself over Jennifer's body. "Stay down," she whispered to Jennifer. "Play dead."

She scanned the area for a sign of where the bullets were coming from as they fired one after the other in all directions. Was there more than one shooter? The sounds of shots caused her ears to ring. Numbers were moving quickly as she looked around. In her panic she ignored them for she did not have time to concentrate on them and try to figure out what they meant.

She noticed a lean young man dressed in black. He had a handgun strapped to each thigh and a high-powered rifle over his shoulder. About the same time as Deb noticed him, he noticed her. He began to move the barrel of the rifle in her direction, spraying bullets everywhere as he changed the direction of his aim.

Deb concentrated on the barrel of the rifle. It began to move upward. The young man had a shocked and frightened look upon his face as his gun barrel kept moving upward until it was pointing directly upward. Bits of the ceiling dome were falling as he was shooting straight upward. He struggled to keep his hands on the gun as it moved toward the ceiling.

The young man's trigger finger was caught in the trigger of the gun and he was wincing in pain as his full body weight was pulling on a single index finger. He was out of ammo now and the shots had stopped. Higher and higher the gun went upward. The dome ceiling of the mall was approximately sixty feet above them. The young man suddenly found himself dangling near the ceiling, looking down at the marble floor below. He was helpless, as he struggled to hang onto the rifle. He was screaming for someone to help him.

A crowd was gathering beneath him. Everyone was focusing their attention on the spectacle high above them. No one took notice of Deb. She was conscious of Jennifer climbing to her feet, however, her attention remained on the young man in black hanging in midair above them.

Deb heard voices around her as shoppers were gathering to see what was happening. No one had made the connection between Deb and the shooter. She dropped her eyes to the floor and the young man came crashing down to the floor. The sound of bones breaking as his body hit the marble floor was the only sound Deb heard. She took Jennifer by the elbow and tried to turn her away. Some men were rushing to where the gunman laid dead. Deb heard sirens. As she urged Jennifer toward the table where their belongings were, Jennifer turned to look over her shoulder at the crowd gathering around the broken body of the shooter.

"Come on," Deb said. "let's get our things and get out of here. If the police interview everyone, we will be here all night."

She helped Jennifer gather their purchases and they quickly moved toward the exit. When they stepped outside into the sunlight, they found the mall surrounded by people who had rushed outside. Some were shouting names, trying to find friends and family that got separated in the moment. Police were parking their cars near the curb and fire trucks and ambulances were blocking their way. They moved along the sidewalk and quickly disappeared in the parking lot. It took some time for Jennifer to find her car, but soon they were moving toward the exit. She was quiet but trembling terribly as she maneuvered the car toward the exit.

The exits were all blocked by police and fire vehicles. No one was coming or going without being stopped by the officers blocking the exits.

Jennifer rolled down her window. "Yes officer, we weren't in the mall when it started. We were on our way to the car when we heard the people rushing outside," Jennifer said to the female officer. Her voice trembled so that it was difficult to understand her.

The officer looked over at Deb and frowned. "Do I know you?" she asked.

Deb shook her head. "I don't think so." She replied.

"She's a writer," Jennifer said. "You may have seen her face on TV when one of her books came out."

"Are you alright young lady?" the officer asked, looking at Jennifer.

"I'm just shook up. I'm not hurt, and the danger is past. I'll be alright," Jennifer replied.

The officer smiled. "Maybe you should pull over and compose yourself before you drive any further,"

"I'll be fine. I think I will do better once I'm away from here, if you know what I mean," Jennifer said.

The officer shined her flashlight into the back seat. "Would you mind popping the trunk, young lady?" she asked.

Jennifer pressed the button, and the trunk popped open. The officer stood behind the car and they could hear her moving things around.

"What is she doing?" Jennifer asked.

"They are probably searching every car before they let them leave," Deb explained.

The officer closed the trunk and called out, "Okay, you may go." She stepped back and pointed her stick in the direction to the exit. "Move along," she called out as they passed.

Jennifer drove to the red light. As they waited for the light to turn, she rested her head upon the steering wheel. She was crying.

"Are you alright?" Deb asked.

"No!" Jennifer snapped. "I'm scared shitless." She wiped her eyes and drove to the next light. "How is it you don't appear to be shook up?" she asked.

"I deal with stress differently," Deb said. "I was scared out of my skin back there."

"You probably saved my life; you know that don't you?" Jennifer asked.

"I'll gladly drive if you want me to," Deb said, not knowing what she should say.

"I think that is a good idea. At least until I stop shaking," Jennifer said, as she pulled into a gas station parking lot. "I could use a drink on the way home, if you don't mind."

"I think we could both use a drink," Deb said, climbing into the driver's seat. Deb drove the entire journey back. Jennifer instructed her to pull into Pappy's parking lot.

"It looks like everybody is here," Jennifer said.

Deb was certain they were here because Larry Escott's car was parked in the parking lot. Fortunately for Deb, Marshall's truck was also there.

They entered the bar, and everyone turned their attention toward the door. Before the door closed behind them, nearly everyone inside the bar was on their feet and surrounding them. Deb moved toward Marshall and the two of them moved toward a booth in a darker area of the bar.

"Are you alright?" Marshall asked, taking both her hands in his.

"I'm fine," Deb replied.

"We were watching cell phone video on television," Marshall said. "We weren't certain you girls were at that particular mall until Jennifer texted Larry."

Deb sighed. She smiled and replied, "I wasn't aware she texted anyone. She was shaking so badly; I don't know how she managed to send a text."

"What happened?" Marshall whispered, leaning close.

"We finished our shopping and went to the food court. We were about to leave when this kid started shooting people," Deb explained.

"The video showed him dangling from the dome. Did you have anything to do with that?" Marshall asked.

"Marshall," Deb began. She closed her eyes and sighed. "I probably shouldn't have told you about the strange things I can do. Please, I just want to live a normal life."

"You said you wanted to help people," Marshall whispered. "You did. That is exactly what you did today. If you did that, and I'm guessing you did."

"But we can't tell anyone. No one must ever learn about what I can do," Deb said, looking toward the crowd gathered around Jennifer as she explained what happened.

Suddenly the crowd turned to look back at Deb. "Oh no," Deb moaned.

The crown began to move toward them. "Jennifer said you saved her life. She said you threw yourself over her to shield her from the bullets," Larry said.

"She also said the guy running toward you was shot," Stoney said.

"How many are they saying died?" Deb asked, looking back at Marshall.

"Three dead, four critical, and one treated and released with a gunshot to the forearm," Henry recited.

Deb covered her face with her hands.

"They authorities are investigating the crime scene," Stoney said. "They think he had some kind of hoist device that he intended to use to lift him, so he had a better view of his intended victims. They think the device malfunctioned, and that is why he fell to his death," Larry said.

"I saw him rising straight up in the air," Jennifer began. "Whatever he used; it was attached to his gun."

"We saw it too," Henry said. "Someone recorded it on their cell phone."

Stoney added, "From the look on the kid's face, you could tell something went wrong right away. He was just as frightened as the people he was shooting at. He lost control of his gun, and emptied his clip shooting wildly. Shards of that dome were falling down all around him."

Marshall squeezed Deb's hand. "See? It's going to be alright," he whispered.

Deb remained silent as everyone inside the bar stated their opinions. Jennifer seemed to be calmer now. Soon, she and Larry moved to a booth and after some conversation, the crowd broke up and Stoney returned to the bar to pass out drinks. Before long, pool balls were clanging together, and the bar fell into normalcy.

"I better get back to the cabin," Deb said, looking up at Marshall as he sat with one arm around her and the other holding his draft.

"You better stay with me tonight," he said.

"Why?" Deb asked. "I'm not in any danger, and I need to check the cabin. Joe may have returned. I need to go home, Marshall. I appreciate your offer, and I have to admit it is inviting, but I need to go home."

"I'll drive you out to the cabin and we can talk about it on the way," Marshall replied. "Let me finish my beer."

Deb sat quietly, listening to the different conversations throughout the bar. They were conversations that Marshall and the others could not hear. All the while, the numbers in her head moved quickly and the symbols were back. Something was going on. What were they trying to tell her? She needed to be alone to figure it out.

"She threw herself across my body, Larry. She saved my life," Jennifer was saying. "We were trying to get to cover behind the burger counter. This guy ran past me and knocked me to the ground. I was about to get up again when another man came running toward us yelling about the shooter and he dropped dead right in front of us. That kid shot him in the back. He dropped right in front of me. I was scared out of my mind. Virginia plowed right over me and covered me with her body. I saw the shooter look right at us. He aimed his gun at us and suddenly he started moving straight up. You could tell something went wrong by the look on his face. I could hear his gun firing until it stopped. Pieces of the dome were falling all around us. How I didn't get cut is beyond me. I thought that Virginia was certainly cut to pieces by the falling glass, but she didn't have a mark on her."

"It's a good thing she was there," Larry said.

"Yeah, I suppose you are right," Jennifer said. "But we were there because of her."

It was quiet for some time and then Larry asked, "What? What's wrong?"

"I was shaking so bad; I could hardly control the car. Virginia was upset, but not that much. I can't explain it, but it was so unnatural," Jennifer said.

"What are you trying to say?" Larry asked.

"I don't know," Jennifer said. "It's just that something doesn't feel right."

"Hey," Henry called out. "There's more video from the shooting. Look, Virginia, there you are covering Jennifer!"

Everyone arose and went to stand around the television behind the bar. As Henry had said, someone had live time video of the shooting. It showed Deb leaning over Jennifer, looking up at the shooter.

"Wow!" Stoney said. "You really were protecting her."

"Look," Jennifer said, pointing to the screen. "See that man laying there? He was the one that got shot in the back right in front of us."

"They've blurred his face," Larry said. "I wonder if his family has been notified."

"You are a hero, Virginia Parks!" Stoney shouted. "Anything you want, it is on the house!"

Deb smiled. "I'd really like to go back home," she said.

"Are you leaving us?" Larry asked.

Deb could see Jennifer's face paling. Deb shook her head. "I mean to the cabin. I could use some quiet time right about now."

"I can drive you out if you want," Larry suggested. Deb noticed Jennifer stiffening as she glared at Larry.

"Thanks, but Marshall is taking me home," Deb said, looking over at Marshall.

Marshall nodded his head. "Right," he said. "I'll see you guys later. Come on, Virginia, let's get you home."

They left the bar and didn't speak until they were on the main road moving toward the lake and cabin.

"I could probably stay the night if you think you might need someone with you," Marshall said.

Deb shook her head. "That won't be necessary. I'm exhausted and I'll probably go straight to bed."

"Okay," Marshall replied. It grew quiet again.

They were passing over the wooden plank bridge before Marshall spoke again. "Looks like the water's gone down," he said.

"Now we have to deal with the mud," Deb said.

Marshall parked behind Deb's truck. "It's awfully dark in the cabin. I'll come in and have a look around before I leave."

Deb chuckled. "Really? After what happened today you still don't think I can take care of myself?"

"If you don't want me to come in, just say so," Marshall said.

"It's alright. It isn't necessary," Deb replied. When Marshall didn't say anything, she began to suspect she had hurt his feelings. "Oh, I would like for you to come in and say goodnight before you leave," she added, with a broad smile.

Marshall smiled back at her. "I think I can handle that."

They climbed the steps and entered the unlocked door. "Don't you ever lock this door?" Marshall asked.

"I could, but I don't think it's necessary," Deb replied.

Marshall shook his head as he waited for her to light the oil lamps. When the cabin was lit, he walked through it to ensure it was empty. He wrapped his arms around her and kissed her tenderly. "I don't like leaving you out here alone," he said.

"I am never alone," Deb said, smiling. "I always have the voices in my head to keep me company."

They both laughed before Marshall kissed her good night. She went out to stand on the porch until he was gone. She waited until she heard his truck bouncing over the plank bridge. "Alone at last," she mumbled to herself as she entered the cabin again.

Deb hung her new dress on a nail in the back room. She placed the bag containing the new sandals on the windowsill. She pulled on a flannel shirt and stepped into her mud boots, before hurrying toward the front door.

A light fog had formed over the tall grass. It was a quiet night. She stood motionless, with her eyes closed, listening, and smelling the small droplets of heavy fog that fell around her. After a few moments, she turned and went down the steps and toward her usual path through the tall grass.

It was a dark night, with very little moonlight to show her the way. She didn't need it. She knew where she was going. She continued to move through the tall, wet, grass toward the lake. Once she reached the waters edge, she stopped, and closed her eyes, again, listening to the water slapping against the shore. The fog was all around her now.

The numbers in her head continued to move. She paid them no mind. It was the symbol that she concentrated on. It was growing brighter as she turned right and began moving toward the area Joe had said the alien craft had landed years ago. She felt no fear. There was nothing out here that could hurt her. That is what she continued to tell herself as she moved through the tall grass. It was coarse and wet. It cut at her arms and hands as she moved through it, yet she continued. She reached up to scratch her head, but it did not suffice the itch, for it was on the inside. It was an intense itch. She knew something extraordinary was about to happen. She hastened her pace. She moved toward the tall pine trees. Something was there. The fog had a green hue glowing through the trees.

CHAPTER NINETEEN

Deb stood amidst a green glow looking upward through the dense fog. The fog concealed what was hanging over her head, yet the green glow shone through the fog, surrounding her.

The illumination was brilliant, so Deb closed her eyes, outstretched her arms and stood waiting for something to happen. The hair on her body stood on end, and the illuminating light put off a warmth that seemed sooth and calm her. She could hear her lungs expanding and contracting with every breath. Her heart beat sounded like it was connected to a loud speaker, as she stood bathing in the green light from above.

Then suddenly, the fog felt cool and refreshing. She opened her eyes to find the green light was gone. She was standing amidst a thick blanket of grayish white fog. It had been silent only a moment ago. Now she heard every creature that inhabited the area around the lake. She could hear the she bear and her cubs breathing as they slept somewhere far off to her right.

The symbol in her head was gone, but the numbers continued to move and change indicating life forms in the area surrounding her.

Deb took a deep breath, allowing the damp air to fill her lungs. She held her breath for a moment before turning to return to the cabin. She had hoped to learn where Joe had gone. Instead, she had learned nothing. However, she felt different. It was something she could not explain. It was like she was energized. She quickened her step. She didn't know why, but something told her she needed to return to the cabin right away.

Deb held her arms out at her sides as she moved through the tall grass. It did not cut at her arms and hands like it did before. It bent low as she passed through it making her way toward the glow of the lantern, she had left on the table.

She reached the cabin. The sound of her boots sinking in the mucky mud was amplified. She climbed the steps, reaching down to touch the symbol carved in the wood as she reached the wooden porch.

She remembered leaving the door unlocked. A breeze must have blown it open for it rested against the wall inside the cabin as if she were being invited to enter.

Deb stepped inside. There was a prickly feeling on her neck. She reached up to rub it when she noticed Joe sitting on his bed in the front room to the left of the door.

"Well, look what the cat drug in," Deb said.

"I'm not staying," Joe said, pushing himself to his feet. "I have to go. I won't be back, but I wanted to thank you for letting me stay here."

"Where are you going?" Deb asked, taking a step closer.

"I am needed elsewhere," Joe said. "So are you, but it's not time for you to go yet. You are needed here for now."

"How do you know this?" Deb asked.

"I just know. I think you know it too," he said, moving toward the door. "I am glad I got to meet you. There are others like us out there. I suppose we will bump into one another on occasion. I wish you well, and thank you, again." He stepped out onto the porch.

"You can't leave now!" Deb called after him. "You won't find your way to the road in this fog. Besides, Joe, do you know anything about a man named Lawrence Woods?"

"I will be fine," Joe said, turning to smile at her. "Listen to the calling in your head. They will keep you safe." Then he descended the steps.

"Joe," Deb called after him from the porch. "You don't have a car!"

He moved into the fog and disappeared. Deb hurried down the steps and ran in the direction he had gone. "Joe!" she called into the night. "Joe, where are you?" Only the sounds of the night could be heard. Deb closed her eyes and listened. She could hear the water rushing under the plank bridge. She could hear animals of the night moving along the murky banks of the creek and lake. She could hear the tall grass swaying in the slightest night breeze. However, there was no hint of anyone walking in the muddy drive, or in the tall grass. No sounds of human breathing. No sounds from Joe. He was gone.

She went inside to stand facing the door. She closed her eyes and tried to will him to return. Nothing. She looked over at her own image in the milky mirror that hung over the wash board. She had a reddish glow about her. It almost looked like a sun burn. She rubbed her cheeks as if she was trying to remove it. She dipped her hands in the water bucket and rubbed her cheeks again. It felt cool and refreshing, however, the glow remained. Was it from the green light in the fog?

Deb went to Joe's bed and flopped down, staring across the room, but seeing nothing in particular. Her mind raced over the events of the day. What a day it had been! Perhaps she should stay close to the cabin for a couple of days. She didn't need anything in the line of supplies. She would tell Richie to pass the word along that she was trying to finish the book.

She allowed herself to fall back on the bunk. She was so tired. She closed her eyes and slept soundly.

The next morning Deb went to the lake early. The heavy fog made it nearly impossible to see anything, however, Deb noticed that if she closed her eyes, everything was clearly visible. She still felt different. She stood on the familiar bank with her eyes closed and her arms outstretched.

In her mind's eye, she could see the bears climbing a rocky hill on the other side of the pines. She saw two young bull moose squaring off with one another in the tall grass. She saw geese nesting in the grass, and she noticed the eggs were beginning to crack open.

She smelled wild flowers, honeysuckle, and pine. High above, she heard the engine of jet planes flying over. She also heard the voices of several fishermen rising to begin their day in the campsites on various areas of the lake. She heard an engine traveling along the main road off in the distance.

She closed her eyes tightly and outstretched her arms. She began to imagine herself floating upward. She felt herself beginning to grow lighter, then she heard Richie's truck bouncing across the plank bridge. She quickly turned and ran toward the cabin.

Deb was amazed at the speed she was able to travel as she made her way back to the cabin. She was sitting on the porch steps when Richie pulled to a stop behind her truck.

"Good morning," he called out as he carried a bag of fresh vegetables in each hand. "It's a nice morning," he said.

"The fog was pretty heavy last night," Deb said. "It's not going anywhere for a few hours."

"Yeah," Richie said, "But that is normal around here. The fog is just part of our day."

"Come inside," Deb said, turning to enter the cabin.

Richie sat the packages on the table and sat down on the backless chair. He looked up at Deb and smiled. Pointing to his own face, he said, "I like the whatever it is you did to your face." He laughed and said, "It reminds me of the first time I saw you. You had used that self-tanning stuff on your face, and you were orange."

Deb laughed. "Yeah, don't believe those ads on television," she said.

"This isn't like that," Richie continued. "This looks healthy. It looks good on you. What did you do different this time?"

"I didn't do anything," Deb replied. "I went for a walk last night and when I returned to the cabin this is what I saw in the mirror."

"Where did you go?" Richie asked.

"Just out beyond the lake," Deb replied.

Richie grew solemn. "You really shouldn't do that. I really wish you wouldn't go out there by yourself in the daylight and certainly not at night. I would think you of all people would know better."

"I'm perfectly capable of taking care of myself, Richie," Deb said, somewhat annoyed. "Besides, I don't want to talk about that. I have other news."

"What?" Richie asked.

"Joe was here when I got back," Deb declared.

Richie looked around the cabin. "Where is he now?" he asked.

"He left again," Deb said. "No, I do not know where he went nor do I know where he was."

"Is he coming back?" Richie asked.

"No," Deb replied. "He said he wasn't coming back."

"Was he with anyone?" Richie asked.

Deb sighed. "No. At least I don't think so," she replied.

"You better tell the Sheriff," Richie began. "He is still looking for him, as far as I know."

"I don't think we should say anything to anyone," Deb said. "he isn't coming back. I can't prove that I saw him and that may cause the Sheriff to become suspicious. I certainly don't want him snooping around."

"Does this have anything to do with what happened at the mall?" Richie asked.

"No," Deb declared. "Have you seen the news? Was I in any of the videos?"

Richie shook his head. "Not that I know of. There are two videos they keep playing over and over. The main one is a closeup of the shooter pointing the gun at someone and then pointing it straight in the air and rising to the dome. They are looking at everything to see what he used to hoist himself. They think he wanted a better vantagepoint to shoot from, but something malfunctioned. There are all sorts of theories out there and the reporters are saying it may take a week before the FBI come to a conclusion."

"As long as my face doesn't appear on the news. There was a phone video on the television last night that showed my face. I certainly hope the FBI don't see it," Deb said, pacing the floor. "I'm going to stay here until the wedding. I won't be going into town. Are you going to be able to bring food out tomorrow?"

"I'll make time. It will be my last trip out. Donna and I are going on our honeymoon straight from the reception," Richie said.

"That's fine. By then all the mall news will have died down," Deb explained. "I may not be here when you get back. I am considering going on a trip of my own."

"You mean, you and Marshall," Richie said. He smiled. "Marshall is my friend. He tells me everything."

"I keep forgetting that," Deb said, smiling.

"As long as Marshall is with you, I think you'll be fine. I also think you will be coming back," Richie said. He stood up and looked out the front door. "It's still foggy out there. I want you to promise me you won't go out after dark," he said, turning to look back at her. "I mean it."

Deb shook her head. "I can't promise you that, Richie. I will be fine. Don't worry. Something has changed. I don't know what it is yet, but something is very different," she stepped closer and hugged him. He trembled, but only slightly. "I want you to forget about me and think only about the wedding Saturday. Everything will be fine. This is a special day for you and Donna. You have enough to think about without worrying about me."

Richie shook his head. "You don't get it," he began. "I need something to take my mind off the wedding. If I don't, I'll go nuts. Maybe you and Marshall have room for one more when you hit the road."

Deb shook her head and laughed. "Not on your life! Now go! You have things to do. If you don't get out of here Donna is going to be arriving at my door giving me that look." Before Richie could speak, she added, "You know what look I'm talking about."

"Okay, okay," Richie said.

He began to leave, and Deb called out to him, "Hey, don't forget. Not a word to anyone about Joe."

"I promise," he called back to her before climbing into his truck. "See you tomorrow."

Deb watched him leave. She went back inside and gazed at her image in the mirror again. Something was very different about her and it wasn't just the red glow. Her eyes looked clearer. Even her teeth were whiter. What had happened out there last night?

She put the vegetables away and carried the wilted vegetables from the day before out to the lake. She tossed them into the high grass where the nesting geese were. Then she returned to the cabin to sit and pass the long hours away.

Richie was late bringing the supplies the next day. Donna was with him. She raved over Deb's glowing complexion and told her how healthy she looked. Deb credited it to her defeat against cancer. They sat at the table and talked for some time and when Richie and Donna left, Deb felt utterly alone.

After a brief nap, Marshall arrived and the two of them took a walk to the lake before returning to the cabin and climbing into the single bed in the front room. When Marshall left, Deb felt energized. So much so that she couldn't find enough to do.

She grabbed a hammer and made some repairs to the cabin. After all, it would be sitting empty until she returned from her trip with Marshall. She needed to ensure that it was secured and that no critters could take up residence while she was gone.

That night she found it difficult to sleep. She wanted to walk out to where the green light had been before, but she knew she would not find it there. So, she tossed and turned until finally she slept.

CHAPTER TWENTY

It was Saturday morning. Deb woke early and took her normal walk to the lake. She lingered a little longer than usual, taking in every sound and site, trying to burn it into her memory. She had discovered her hearing was even more acute than before, since her encounter with the green light in the night. That wasn't all. She seemed to sense things that were about to happen.

Before, the symbol would become very prevalent, acting as a warning that something was about to happen. However, she hadn't seen the symbol in the past two days, and now she was sensing events before they happened. Even the little unimportant things were known to her in advance. She knew it was all connected to the green glowing light she stood under in the forest.

Deb wondered if Joe had gone with the aliens. Was he up there somewhere learning new things, getting new abilities? Would he return? Could he see what she was doing? Was he with Lawrence Woods? He had said there were others like them. Perhaps she should try to find them.

Deb turned and walked back to the cabin. Again, she became aware of the speed at which she was able to travel. She climbed the wooden steps and surveyed the inside of her cabin.

Deb sat down on the single bed in the front room. She jumped back to her feet, for she felt energized. She stood up and began to smooth the blanket that stretched across the top of the bunk. As she lifted the pillow, she noticed a manila envelope. She lifted the envelope in her hand and knew it contained money. She counted the one hundred dollar bills she found inside. There were twenty of them.

She closed her eyes and pictured Joe placing the envelope under the pillow. He looked to his left and right as if he was insuring, he wasn't seen. Had he hidden it and forgotten it when he left, or had he left it for Deb?

She folded the envelope and slid it into her back pocket. Somehow, she knew Joe had left the envelope of money for her. It was a lot of money. She had not been aware that he had so much money on hand. After all, he said he was a schoolteacher, and she knew schoolteachers didn't make this kind of extra cash.

The vision was gone now. Somehow, Joe knew she would be forced to leave this place eventually. He knew she would need this money to get away safely. She sighed as she thought of Joe. He was a grumbler, but he had a kind heart.

Once again, Deb felt the urge to walk to the lake. It was as if she was being pulled along the path, she walked at least twice a day since arriving here. She stood on the bank with her eyes closed. She had lost track of time, for she heard every creature as it moved about.

Deb stretched her arms out at her sides. She closed her eyes and began to picture herself drifting upward. Today she felt as light as a feather. Voices distracted her thoughts and she opened her eyes to see two men in a canoe paddling through the misty fog and coming toward the bank where she stood.

"Good morning," the man in front called out to her. "Are you camping somewhere near here?"

Deb sensed hostility in these men. She shook her head. "I am not a camper," she replied. Her mind told her to keep the men at a distance.

"We are camping up beyond the bend," the man in back called out, pointing behind him. "We are on a fishing trip. We are expecting a few more of our friends to join us. We thought maybe you were one of them. I'm sorry if we bothered you."

"It's okay. You didn't bother me. This is private property though," Deb explained.

"Oh, we didn't realize we had crossed any boundaries," the man in front said. "Are you alone out here?"

Deb knew they were up to something. She knew she shouldn't trust them. She stepped back and said, "You need to move on now. As I said earlier, this is private property."

"Okay, okay, Miss," the man in front said. He nodded to his companion and the two of them turned the canoe around. There was no more conversation between them. Deb turned and hurried back to the cabin.

Deb knew Richie would not be bringing supplies today. It was his wedding day and he had much to do to prepare for this evening. Deb smoothed her dress out on the bed and placed her shoes next to it. She stood looking down at it, trying to picture what she would look like with it on. She picked up the sandals and turned them over in her hands several times. If only it wasn't so muddy outside. She would have to wear her mud boots to the truck. She was meeting Marshall at the church, as he was best man there would be much to do to prepare as well.

She sat on the front porch, staring out across the tall grass toward the lake. She felt uneasy. There was something about the two men in the canoe that disturbed her. She wondered what they were up to. Something told her they were not fishermen at all. Would they recognize her? Should she venture out to where they indicated their camp was and see for herself?

She sat pondering the idea to investigate their story. She closed her eyes and concentrated on their faces. A vision came to her. She saw the man in the front of the canoe burying a green plastic bag under the very cabin she was standing in. Then she saw Joe crawling under the cabin and returning with the green bag in his hand. What was in the green bag? Had Joe discovered it accidentally, or was he aware that it was buried under there? Deb knew that the two men in the canoe were looking for the green bag.

She opened her eyes and looked out across the tall grass toward the lake. She had a strong feeling that the two men would be back. She would have to be careful, for she felt danger in their presence. She looked across the room at the battery powered clock and realized it was time to prepare for the wedding. She bathed, washed her hair in the basin and tossed the water outside over the porch railing. She dressed and stepped into her mud boots, and carrying her sandals in her hand, she held her dress high above her knees as she went to the truck. Soon she was bouncing over the plank bridge and making her way to the highway.

Deb arrived at the church on time. The parking lot was full. She knew several of the guests, and they were all friendly enough. Most of them were still talking about the mall shooting and how Jennifer had told everyone in town that Deb had saved her life.

Marshall stepped out of the back room long enough to say hello. Deb told him how handsome he looked in his gray tuxedo. He leaned close and said, "You look beautiful tonight."

"Thank you," Deb smiled. "Are you nervous?"

Marshall nodded his head. "Not as nervous as Richie. He's been trying to reach his parents for the past forty-five minutes. They haven't arrived yet. We are hoping nothing has happened to them."

Deb frowned. Suddenly, she grew uneasy. Something was wrong at the Patterson's, for she felt it. "Do you want me to go check on them?" she asked.

"No," Marshall said, smiling down at her. "They are probably on their way. They don't have a cell phone, so there is no way of reaching them if they are on the road."

Deb smiled. She did not want to cause unnecessary anxiety, however, she continued to feel anxious. Perhaps it was nothing. Perhaps she was still thinking of the two men she had met earlier in the day. "You look so different in a tux," she declared.

"I'm not very comfortable, that's for sure," Marshall said. He reached out and brushed her arm with his fingertips. "I better get back in there. I'll see you after the ceremony."

Deb nodded her head and watched him hurry back into the little room to the left of the podium. She made her way toward the front and moved into the center of one of the pews. She sat wringing her hands as people moved passed her, smiling as they went. She sat alone for nearly another ten minutes when Marshall slid into the pew next to her. He placed his arm around her shoulders and leaned close to speak into her ear.

"Something is wrong," he began. "The ceremony is all set to start, and the Patterson's haven't arrived yet. None of us can up and leave at this point, and I was wondering if your offer to go check on them still stands?"

"Certainly," Deb said, sliding to the edge of her seat. "I'll go right now."

Marshall reached into his pocket and handed her a cell phone. "Call Richie's phone when you find them," he said.

Deb nodded her head. "I will," she said, rising to her feet. She decided not to take the extra time to explain that the phone would likely not work for her. Marshall walked her to the front door and stood watching as she hurried toward her truck.

Deb crawled behind the wheel of her pickup and turned the key. She felt an anxiousness in her chest. Somehow, she knew the Patterson's were in trouble. They weren't along the road. She knew that but couldn't explain how she knew. They were still at home. She drove as fast as she dared on the narrow and winding road.

As Deb bounced over the rough road, the vision of the two men she had met earlier in the day kept coming to mind. Somehow, they were involved in the Patterson's delay to their son's wedding. She began to slow down as she neared the Patterson's home. Their car had been backed out of the garage and was still sitting in the driveway.

Deb drove past the house slowly. Something told her not to pull in the drive. She drove down the road and pulled off to the side. She slipped her feet into her mud boots and held her skirt high as she climbed the wet bank and made her way through the wooded area toward the back of their house. It was quiet inside.

She crept up to a dining room window and peered inside. She heard angry voices and Theresa Patterson's crying. She hunched low and moved to a second window that viewed the living room.

The Patterson's were seated on the sofa. They were both dressed in their new clothes. Dick Patterson was leaning his head to the side, holding his hand over a wide gash in his temple area which was bleeding heavily.

One of the two men she had spoken to earlier that morning kicked him in the leg and shouted, "You better come up with something old man, or I'll start on the old lady here!" He kicked him a second time.

"I told you," Dick moaned. "I gave you everything we have. We don't keep money here at the house."

The man reached out and grabbed Theresa Patterson by the hair and flung her to the floor. Dick tried to get up, but the second man punched him in the stomach causing him to fall onto the floor on his hands and knees. At this time, the first man began kicking Theresa in the chest and back.

Deb hurried around to the back door. She turned the knob, but it was locked. She closed her eyes and pictured the lock on the inside of the door. It turned and she slowly opened the back door, stepping into the kitchen. Both men stood in the living room with their backs to her.

The first man kicked Theresa again, and she screamed out in agony. Deb stepped closer and her reflection came into view on the wall mirror. The first man looked up and saw her. He spun around just as Deb lifted him off the floor. As he dangled from the ceiling, he reached into his waistband for a hand gun. He pulled the gun out, just as the second man turned and charged at Deb.

Deb raised her other hand and he too, began to rise to the ceiling. "Shoot that bitch!" the second man called out to his friend as he fumbled with the gun. In his anxiousness, he dropped it. The man began screaming and kicking while his friend dangled in shock at what he was witnessing.

"Sam!" the first man called out. "Sam, do something!"

Sam hung helpless, his eyes wide and his jaw hanging open. He was unable to speak.

Deb narrowed her eyes and concentrated on the first man's temples. She could see every heart beat in the veins in his head. She shifted her gaze to the man's chest. His heart beat faster, and his veins were pounding as the blood flowed to his head. Suddenly the man was screaming and grabbing his chest. His heart exploded in his chest and he went limp. Deb allowed him to fall to the floor.

Sam was squirming now as he looked back at Deb. He realized she was responsible for his dangling from the ceiling. He was shaking his head and mumbling, "No, no, no," he said. "It wasn't me. It was Art. I didn't want to hurt them. You have to believe me, lady. I didn't do anything to them."

"I saw you kick them," Deb said. She had been looking up at him, narrowing her eyes with a rage that grew more intense at the sight of him. Suddenly, she realized that she was no longer looking up at him, for she too was dangling from the ceiling. In her rage, she had levitated herself until she was looking him straight in the eye.

She drew a breath and jerked her head to the side. The man's neck twisted, and he fell limp. Deb allowed him to drop to the floor, also. She remained hovering near the ceiling, looking around for signs of any other intruders. Dick Patterson had rolled over onto his back and was staring up at her with his jaw agape. It was then she allowed herself to drift to the floor.

She hurried to the Patterson's who both were watching the events from their living room floor. She cradled Dick Patterson in her arms, and he began to quiver intensely. Soon his eyes rolled back in his head and he began to settle down. Once the quivering stopped, he opened his eyes and smiled up at Deb, the gash in his head was gone. "Thank you," he whimpered. He began to crawl toward his wife.

Deb moved over to cradle Theresa Patterson in her arms. She too, began to quiver. Deb could feel her frail bones shifting as they set themselves. Theresa rolled her eyes back into her head and fainted for a brief time.

"We have to call the police," Dick said. "These guys broke into the house and demanded every penny we had. They kept insisting I had money stashed somewhere."

"What will we tell them? How are we going to explain this?" Theresa asked, rising to her feet.

"They are both dead," Dick said. "I heard the guy's neck snap. We have to have some kind of story for the Sheriff."

Deb took a deep breath. "You need to call Richie. Everyone is waiting for you. What do we tell them?" she asked, handing Dick Patterson Marshall's cell phone.

"We have to call the police," Dick repeated. "You get Richie on the phone and let me talk to him."

"I can't use the cell phone," she said, holding the phone out toward Dick Patterson again. He frowned as he looked up at her. She did not try to explain.

Dick called Richie's phone, and he answered right away.

Deb stood listening to Dick explain about the home invasion to Richie. He told his son that he was calling the police and for them to have the ceremony without them. Deb could hear Richie disagreeing with his father.

The house phone had been torn off the wall. Dick called the Sheriff's office from Marshall's cell phone and explained that there had been a home invasion at his address. He told them that both intruders were dead. They were told not to touch anything until the Sheriff arrived. They moved out onto the front porch to wait.

"What are we going to tell them?" Theresa asked, again.

"We will say the two of them got to arguing and turned on one another. One was going to shoot the other and they started fighting for the gun. This guy," Dick pointed through the open door toward the heart attack victim. "This guy broke his buddy's neck and then he grabbed his chest and died from a heart attack." He looked over at Deb.

She did not like lying. Somehow, that always caused more problems, but this time, it was necessary.

"We have to get our story straight and we have to stick to it," Dick said. "You can tell them you fainted and didn't see any of it, Theresa. I will tell them everything. Deb, you happened by after the fact. You weren't here until everything was over."

Deb pointed to the blood on his shirt. "I'll tell them it came from my nose," he said. He looked over at Theresa. "You know what to say, Theresa. You got scared and fainted. You didn't see or hear a thing."

Theresa nodded her head. "Alright, Dick. If you say so. What about Richie? Are we going to lie to our son too?"

"It's his wedding day. We don't want to ruin it for him. This will be bad enough without him knowing the details," Dick said.

The sirens could be heard approaching. As the police cars pulled into the drive, Richie and Marshall arrived in Marshall's truck. Ambulances were backing into the driveway. Deb stood on the porch as Richie rushed past her toward his parents. Marshall hurried to Deb, embracing her in his arms.

"What happened?" he whispered in her ear.

"Later," Deb replied. She was not sure she should tell him everything. However, she was certain he would not believe the story Mr. Patterson had concocted. Everyone was instructed to wait on the porch. Marshall and Richie were still wearing their tuxedos. Theresa and Dick Patterson were questioned inside the house. After some time had passed, they were told they could join the others on the porch, however, no one was permitted to leave.

Richie had made repeated calls to Donna, who was still waiting at the church. He paced the porch until it became too crowded, at which time he moved to the front yard, pacing back and forth, while talking to Donna on the phone.

After nearly forty-five minutes had passed, Richie arrived on the porch, sweating heavily, and red faced. "Well," he began. "It looks like the wedding is a bust. Donna said nearly everyone is leaving." He sat down on a lawn chair and held his head in his hands. "How am I ever going to make this up to Donna?"

"Dude!" Marshall gasped. "What are you thinking? Do you honestly think your parents planned for those two clowns to break into their house on your wedding day?"

"No, Marshall. I know better than that!" Richie snapped. "But try explaining this to Donna. She is so upset that her wedding day is ruined."

"Then maybe, just maybe," Marshall snapped. "Maybe she isn't the girl for you. Did you ever think of that? She's so damned controlling! What the hell, Richie! She's been a nag ever since you proposed to her. You can't sit there and tell me you've had one happy day since you've proposed. Man! I say the hell with Donna Staples, the hell with her father, and the hell with a job stocking shelves at the hardware store."

"You don't understand, Marshall," Richie said, rising to his feet and pacing again.

"You're right, I don't understand," Marshall said.

Deb looked over at the Patterson's. They sat quietly listening. Neither of them offered to join in the conversation, however, Deb could see they agreed with Marshall. Donna was not the right girl for Richie, and the marriage would be a mistake.

It was at this time; they began bringing the bodies of the two intruders outside to place in the ambulances. The Sheriff stepped outside and looked down at his note book as he said, "Apparently, these guys are not from around here. The guy with the broken neck is, or was, Samuel Veon, and the heart attack victim was Author Taylor. Both are from Connecticut, USA."

"Did you say Author Taylor?" Dick asked.

"That's who his ID says he is. Do you know him?" The Sheriff asked.

"Author Taylor has been calling about renting the cabin. He's rented it several times before. I didn't recognize him," Dick said.

"Well," the Sheriff began. "His ID says he's 160 pounds and that man weighs at least 240. That may be the reason you didn't recognize him. When was the last time he stayed out at the cabin?"

Dick looked over at Deb and said, "2007."

"2007. You're sure it was 2007?" the Sheriff asked.

Dick nodded his head. "How is it you remember that far back and can't remember or recognize the guy?" the Sheriff asked.

"Well, like I said before," Dick said. "He's been calling about the cabin, so I looked it up."

"I see," the Sheriff said, writing on his pad. "That's interesting." He looked over at Deb. "Seems to me there are a lot of people interested in staying out at that cabin you are occupying. Is there anything you want to tell me?"

Deb shook her head. "I have no idea what that is all about. As for me being out there, I'm going away for a few days and when I come back, I hope to finish that book I'm writing."

"Moving on, are you?" The Sheriff asked.

"Possibly," Deb replied. "I haven't made up my mind where I'm going yet."

"Well, I would appreciate it if you kept me informed about where you are settling. You never know, I may have some questions for you later," the Sheriff said.

"Of course," Deb replied.

"Sure, was quiet around here until you showed up," the Sheriff stated.

"Come on Sheriff," Marshall said. "She didn't have anything to do with what happened here today."

"No, but she showed up," the Sheriff said. "Same thing at the mall shooting. She had nothing to do with it, but she was there. It's just strange. I have lived thirty-eight years around here and not been in two places where someone died. Since she's been here, we've had a man disappear, and three men die. Not to mention the strange ramblings of the hunters who claim they shot her out there in the forest."

Deb felt her face growing hot.

"They didn't shoot her," Marshall said. "It was like you said, they were rambling."

"Just keep in touch, Miss Parks," the Sheriff said. "Richie, you can go get married now. We are done here."

Richie jumped to his feet and turned to his parents. "Come on, Mom, Dad, lets get to the church before Donna leaves.

By the time they reached the church they found Donna, her family, and Jennifer, the maid of honor, waiting inside. It was decided to go ahead with the ceremony, even though there were only a few present. A few phone calls were made and by the time they reached the reception hall, it was full of people waiting to congratulate the newly married couple.

CHAPTER TWENTY-ONE

Marshall packed his truck and drove out to the lake to help Deb secure the cabin. It was midmorning before they were on the road. They stopped at a local grocery mart to purchase food for the trip. It was afternoon when they reached the border and crossed over into the United States.

Deb told Marshall about the many adventures she and her friends experienced together, and after some prompting, she talked about the details surrounding her accident and recovery.

"I often think of Leonard. He was such a sweet man and he had no one. I know he didn't want to go back to that nursing home. I do wish I knew which nursing home we went to, for I would love to check in on him," Deb explained.

"You said you told your mother you wanted him to live with you," Marshall said.

"I did say that," Deb agreed. "And, I would have brought him with me. I really liked him."

"Are you thinking of looking him up?" Marshall asked.

"I wouldn't begin to know where to start," Deb replied. "If I did, I would have already done it."

"We can start by calling nursing homes within range of the hospital and asking if he is a patient there," Marshall said.

"Would they tell me if he was?" Deb asked.

"I think so. I know they won't tell you anything about his condition, but I think they can confirm whether or not he is a patient," Marshall declared. "Would you still want to take him with you, even though you have no safe place for him? Think about it, I don't see him doing well in that cabin, and what if you had to make a run for it?"

Deb looked over at Marshall. She did not know what to say, for she was wondering what she would do if she was put in a position where she would have to leave him without saying goodbye. Would she be able to do it? Her heart felt heavy at the very thought of it.

Marshall glanced over at her briefly before looking back at the road. "What?" he asked. "Are you considering it?"

Deb shook her head. "No, that wasn't what I was thinking," she replied. "I suppose he is better off where he is."

"That doesn't mean you can't look him up," Marshall said. "It won't be that far out of our way."

"Let me think about it," Deb said. Her heart felt heavy now. She sat quietly staring out at the passing landscape as they moved further south.

They stopped for a late picnic lunch in New York and soon they were on the road again. It was dark when they pulled into a motel in northern Pennsylvania. Marshall showered and fell asleep on the bed watching an old western on television. Deb stepped outside for a breath of air.

She walked the sidewalk facing the motel. She did not want to go far, for she assumed Marshall would waken and step out to find her. As she moved along, she noticed a man standing outside the office, smoking a cigarette.

"Good evening," he said, with a broad smile. "It's a nice evening. They said it was going to storm tomorrow, so I thought I better get all the fresh air I could while I could," he said, laughing.

"It's a quiet night," Deb said, turning to look behind her.

"It is at that. It usually is quiet here on Sunday nights. It will get livelier tomorrow night," he said. "You and your husband are only staying tonight, so enjoy the quiet while you can."

"Thank you," Deb said, turning to return to her room. Once inside her room she went into the bathroom and closed the door. She stretched her arms out and concentrated on levitating. She felt weightless. She opened her eyes and found herself standing on the floor.

"What?" she asked, barely above a whisper. "How did I manage to do it before?"

She tried again and again. She remained firmly planted on the floor. She went to the bathroom mirror and stared at her own reflection. She closed her eyes and tried again. Nothing. Her face was flushed, and a lump formed in her throat. Maybe she should try a different approach.

She stared at her bare feet. She willed them to lift off the floor. She grabbed hold of the sink for she began to drift upward. She smiled as she outstretched her hands and soon her head was touching the ceiling. She giggled and wobbled, slightly. "Whoa!" she said, aloud.

"Are you alright in there?" Marshall called from the other side of the door.

"I'm fine," she called back. "You may come in."

Marshall opened the door slowly, peering through the cracked opening as he pushed the door open. His eyes widened when he saw Deb dangling from the ceiling. He stepped inside the bathroom and asked, "How did you do that?"

"I just willed it, and it happened," Deb replied. "I did the same thing at the Patterson's yesterday. I didn't tell anyone because I wasn't sure I could do it again."

Marshall's face was pale. "Can you fly?" he asked.

Deb realized that she must appear strange and frightening. She allowed herself to drift to the floor. "Does it make you want to run?" she asked.

"I'm not sure," Marshall said, watching her closely. "I don't know what to think. Can you fly?" he asked, again.

"No, I can't fly," Deb replied. "At least I don't think I can."

"Are you weakened by Kryptonite?" Marshall asked.

Deb burst into laughter. "I'm not superman, Marshall."

"I'm not so sure about that," Marshall replied.

"Well," Deb began. "I can't leap from buildings at a single bound, I can't fly, I don't have X-ray vision, although my hearing is very good. And as we both know; I cannot repel bullets. So, I think it is safe to say I am not Superman."

Marshall shook his head, turned and walked out of the bathroom. This was not the reaction Deb anticipated. She followed him into the sleeping area. "If you want to run, I understand. It is a little much to take in," she said, following him.

"It's not that," Marshall said. "I've always been a manly man. Do you know what I mean?"

"I don't consider you a sissy, Marshall. Is that what you think?" Deb asked.

"I don't know what to think," Marshall replied. "I really don't. I listened to everything you told me about what you've done and what you are capable of, and I guess I didn't really believe it was real. Now I see it is real, all of it, and it scares the hell out of me."

"What do you want to do?" Deb asked, swallowing the lump that was back in her throat.

"I need to sleep on it, I guess," Marshall said, looking down into her eyes.

Deb nodded her head and with a cracking voice, said, "I understand."

"I'm going to step out for a bit. I need a drink," Marshall said.

Deb waited for him to invite her to accompany him, but he did not. She stood at the end of the bed and watched as he gathered his loose change and truck keys, stuff them into his pockets, and leave the motel room. She sat down on the edge of the bed, feeling deserted and alone. Perhaps she was wrong about Marshall. Perhaps he wasn't the man she thought he was and perhaps she had made a mistake revealing her secrets to him.

She watched television for a while before showering and crawling into bed. It was about 11:30 PM when Marshall returned. He carried a brown paper bag with the remainder of a six pack inside. She rolled over and watched him as he removed his shoes and went into the bathroom. She heard the shower running. When he returned, she was sitting up in bed waiting for him.

"We have a long day ahead of us tomorrow," Marshall began. "We might as well get some sleep."

He undressed and climbed into bed, placing his back towards her. Her heart sank. She fought back tears as she scooted down, pulled the covers up close to her face and closed her eyes.

She was not able to sleep. She tossed and turned until she finally climbed out of bed and moved to a burnt orange chair near the window. She parted the curtain slightly and stared outside into the brightly lit parking lot.

The wind was blowing, and the sky showed no signs of luminaries. The storm clouds were beginning to roll in.

Deb scratched her head. The itching inside her head was intense. She lowered her head to hang between her knees and scratched her scalp hard. The symbols raced through her head. Something was up, but what? She stood up and looked out the window.

As she looked across the highway, she became aware of the freeway beyond the parking lot. Cars were moving along nearly constantly. Streetlights had the area brightly lit and she could see occupants of the vehicles inside the moving traffic.

She went to the door and gently turned the knob, stepping outside and closing the door gently behind her. She stood looking around. Something told her to walk toward the office. She followed her instincts until she was standing outside the office door.

Two men stood at the counter, talking to the man behind the desk. He appeared shaken by their presence. Suddenly, it occurred to her that he was being robbed. She closed her eyes and envisioned the man on the right holding a revolver in his right hand. It was aimed at the man behind the counter. The second man was unarmed.

Deb remained where she was. She closed her eyes and was still able to see what was taking place inside the brightly lit office. She concentrated on the gun, twisting it until it was pointing at the robber's chest.

"What are you doing?" his companion asked.

"I'm not doing this!" the man with the gun said.

"You better not pull that trigger, man!" the unarmed robber said.

They both looked at the man behind the desk. "Are you messing with us?" the man holding the gun asked.

"I'm not doing anything!" he said, holding both hands in the air. "It ain't me!"

"Let's get out of here," the unarmed man said.

Deb crouched low behind the shrubbery as the two men ran from the office. They climbed into an older Oldsmobile and burnt rubber making their way to the freeway.

Deb watched as the man behind the counter lifted the receiver of the phone and dialed 9-1-1. While his back was turned, she slipped out of view and went back to her room. She undressed and crawled into bed. The symbols were gone, and the itching had stopped. She closed her eyes and slept.

Deb opened her eyes and rolled over. Marshall was sitting on the side of the bed looking down at her. "Good morning," he said. "Did you sleep well?"

Deb nodded her head as she pushed herself to a sitting position.

"It's been raining outside," Marshall said.

"The man in the office said it was supposed to rain today," Deb said, smiling.

"Well, perhaps we should get an early start," Marshall suggested.

Deb nodded and pushed the covers back. Marshall did not move from where he sat. "I'm sorry about last night," Marshall said. "I've been thinking that nothing's changed. So, what if you can float up there?" he said, pointing to the ceiling. "How is that any different than what you've already showed me you could do? I don't know why I reacted the way I did, but I'm certainly man enough to admit I was wrong. If you'll forgive me, I'll try harder not to do that again."

Deb smiled. "I forgive you, Marshall. It is a little much, I agree," she replied.

"Is there anything else I should know?" he asked.

Deb shrugged her shoulders. "I didn't know I could levitate until Saturday. It's as much a surprise to me as it is to you. I suppose we are both learning as we go," she declared.

"I'll try to be more understanding," Marshall said.

Deb smiled and said, "And, I'll try to be more up front and honest." She crawled over the pillows she had been holding and kissed him on the cheek. "There is something you should know," she said with a sigh.

"What?" Marshall asked.

"I stepped out last night for some air," Deb began. "There was a robbery taking place in the office and I sort of intervened, however, no one saw me, and they don't know what I did. I expect the police will be hanging around asking questions. I think we should get moving before they have time to detain us."

Marshall jumped to his feet. "Your chariot awaits, my lady," he said. "You can explain everything on the road."

They quickly dressed and left the key on the nightstand. Marshall drove out onto the freeway and once again they were moving toward southern, central, Pennsylvania. They should reach Mont Alto after lunch.

Marshall was quiet for the earlier part of the trip. As they got closer to their destination, he began to open up more. He asked many questions, and finally he began to talk about his childhood, and growing up with Richie as a friend.

It was approaching dinner time when they reached Mont Alto, Pennsylvania. Marshall drove past Deb's house slowly. The grass had grown up in the yard and the front window had been broken out.

Deb instructed Marshall to pull into the McCall's drive. They exited the truck and went to the side door. As she knocked on the door, she could see the McCall's sitting inside at the kitchen table, eating their dinner.

Maxwell McCall rose from the table and went to the door. He opened it, and it was apparent that he did not recognize Deb at first glance.

"Mr. McCall," Deb said, smiling.

"Yes, do I know you young lady?" he asked.

Deb cleared her throat and said, "Uncle Max, it's your niece, Candy."

Lois McCall quickly rose from her chair and rushed to the door. "Open the door Max!" she shouted. She held her arms high in the air and as Deb stepped inside, Lois embraced her. "Candy, it's been ages," she said, near tears.

Maxwell stood staring at Marshall who remained near the door. "Who did you bring with you?"

"This is a friend. Marshall Nemmans meet my aunt and uncle, Lois and Maxwell McCall," Deb said, smiling back at Marshall.

Marshall shook hands with the McCall's. He stood quietly, somewhat confused by what he was seeing and hearing.

"It's so good to see you again, Candy," Lois said. "So much has happened since last we saw you."

"What's going on next door, Aunt Lois?" Deb asked. "I've never seen the place look that bad before."

"Oh, that," Maxwell said. "The girl who lived there is missing. Some folks drop by every now and again asking questions about her, but no one seems to know where she went. I was mowing the grass, but then some teenagers broke into the place and were having all kinds of parties. The police were called out there at least twice a week. So, I started letting it grow up around there to keep them out of the yard. They were having bond fires and all sorts of goings on over there. The high grass deters that sort of activity a bit."

"How very sad," Deb said.

"Come sit down," Lois urged. "Both of you. Make yourself at home, Mr. Nemmans."

"Please, Ma'am, call me Marshall," Marshall insisted.

"Marshall, what a fine name for a handsome young man such as yourself," Lois said.

"Thank you, Mrs. McCall," Marshall said, politely, as he took a seat at the table.

Can I get you something to eat?" Mrs. McCall asked.

"Oh, please don't go to any trouble on our account," Marshall protested.

"It's no trouble, young man," Maxwell insisted. "We remember this one here," he nodded toward Deb. "She doesn't eat anything except fresh fruits and vegetables."

"That's correct, you remembered," Deb said, smiling.

"How could we forget?" Maxwell asked.

"I have some vegetables in the bottom drawer of the refrigerator," Lois said. "It will only take me a minute to wash them off."

"I will help you," Deb said, holding the refrigerator door open for Lois as she passed fresh vegetables to Deb.

"You boys help yourselves," Lois called over her shoulder. "We will be right with you."

Before long they were seated at the table. They continued to refer to Deb as Candy McCall. Once dinner was finished, Deb helped Lois load the dishwasher and the four of them stepped outside.

"Not real sure who can hear us out here," Maxwell whispered. "Pretty darn sure the house is bugged."

"I'm so sorry," Deb whispered.

"Come around back," Maxwell said. "Got someone back here you're going to want to meet."

They rounded the corner and Deb stopped suddenly. Inside a large fenced in kennel, Chelsea laid sleeping. "Chelsea!" Maxwell called, loudly. "She's a little hard of hearing these days."

Chelsea raised her head to look at them. She rose to her feet and stretched, while yawning.

"Chelsea," Deb patted her thighs. "How's my girl?" she asked.

Chelsea walked over to Deb and sniffed her hands. She licked Deb's hands and arms and when Deb knelt to her level, she licked Deb's face. "Do you think she remembers me?" Deb asked.

"It's hard to say," Maxwell said. "She doesn't get too excited over anything lately."

Deb wrapped her arms around Chelsea's neck. The dog trembled. She dug at the ground with her front paws as she shook. Her eyes were bulged, and her ears went back. It appeared as though she was trying to break away from Deb's embrace. Suddenly the trembling and shaking stopped and Chelsea dropped to the ground. At first, Deb thought she was dead. Then suddenly, she jumped to her feet and began barking as she spun in circles. Deb laughed out loud and Chelsea lunged at her, licking her face.

CHAPTER TWENTY-TWO

Deb and Marshall spent the night at the McCall's. When Marshall descended the steps early the next morning, Max told him he would find Deb out back with Chelsea. He stepped out into the morning sunshine. Freshly planted corn and soybean fields stretched along the rolling hills for as far as he could see. Houses and farms dotted the scenery here and there and off in the distance, purple mountain ranges loomed through the early morning fog.

He went around the house to find Lois McCall sitting on an overturned bucket and Deb sitting on the ground brushing Chelsea. Deb smiled up at him and said, "I think she remembers me now."

"I see she is pure bred," Marshall said, pointing to his tongue.

Mrs. McCall laughed. "Yes, Chow Chow's all have a blue tongue. I never did hear why that is."

"There are some other breeds that have blue tongues," Deb said, as she continued to brush massive amounts of hair from Chelsea. "She's losing her winter coat."

"That's a lot of hair," Marshall said.

Deb laughed. "I wish I had this much hair."

"Why did you cut your hair, dear?" Lois asked.

Deb lowered her voice as if others could hear them. "I was hiding my identity, Lois."

"They still show your picture on the television every now and again. Not as often as they did in the beginning, but every once in a while, it pops up," Lois said.

"Have you seen or heard from any of my friends?" Deb asked.

Lois shook her head. "No, not since you left. We do hear from your mother now and again, but not often. She believes she is being watched. We know our house has some sort of listening device hidden somewhere. Maybe even the car. The radio used to work fine, but ever since you left it has been acting up. Maxwell wants to get a new car, but our budget won't allow it," she explained.

"I am so sorry," Deb said, reaching out to touch Lois Maxwell's hand. "This is all on account of me."

"Don't worry your head over such things, dear," Lois said. "You did nothing wrong."

"Is there anything I can do for you while I'm here?" Marshall asked, looking down at Lois McCall. "I could take a look at your car."

Lois shook her head. "No, thank you, young man, we better not tamper with that. It may get us some unwanted visitors." She smiled and said, "Max is fixing breakfast, maybe we should go inside."

"Oh, I don't normally eat breakfast," Marshall stated. "I usually wait until lunch time to eat. I usually just have a Mountain Dew when I get up."

"Do you mean the soda pop?" Lois asked.

"That's the one," Marshall said.

"Well, you'll have to take that up with Maxwell," Lois said, moving toward the gate of the dog run.

Marshall and Deb were left alone. Deb began gathering up the dog hair that surrounded her and Chelsea.

"So, what do I call you while we are here. Deb? Virginia? Candy?" Marshall asked.

"I know it's a lot to take in," Deb said. "You can call me Candy as long as we are here." She stuffed the dog hair in the bucket Lois had been sitting on. She hugged Chelsea again and exited the dog run. Chelsea jumped and spun like a puppy, barking at Deb in hopes she wouldn't leave. "It's going to be hard to leave her again," Deb said, looking down at Chelsea.

"Do you want to take her with you?" Marshall asked.

Deb smiled up at him. "I would love to, but she should stay here. I can't offer her a stable home. Besides, she is protection and comfort to the McCall's. I think we should leave her right where she is. It was good to see her again," Deb sighed, looking over her shoulder at Chelsea one more time before going inside.

"I'm going upstairs to wash my hands," Deb said, as she moved through the kitchen.

"Lois tells me you don't eat breakfast," Maxwell said, turning from the stove.

"No sir, I don't. It smells good, but I normally just drink a Mountain Dew and get moving," Marshall explained.

"We don't have any soda pop here," Maxwell said.

"Coffee will do," Marshall said.

Maxwell smiled and poured a cup of black coffee. He sat the cup in front of Marshall and pushed the creamer and sugar up against the saucer. "Help yourself, young man," Maxwell said.

"Thank you," Marshall replied.

Deb returned and they sat down to breakfast.

After breakfast Deb and Marshall said their goodbyes to the McCall's. Deb explained that she was hoping to find some of her friends before driving to Ohio to see her mother.

They drove into the city of Waynesboro, where most of her friends lived. Upon visiting the upstairs apartment where Angela used to live, they discovered that she had moved. The new tenants did not know where she moved to. Deb felt sad at the thought of not seeing Angela while she was here.

It was Tuesday, and she knew her friends all worked during the day with the exception to Angela. She worked second shift, and beings Deb did not know where to find her, it looked like she would have to settle for waiting until evening to connect with her other friends.

As they were driving to a scenic look out in Pen Mar Park, called High Rock, Deb remembered that Angela's mother lived nearby. They drove to the house and Deb knocked on the door. To her surprise, Angela answered the door.

Deb and Angela squealed with joy as they embraced one another. Angela shook violently as Deb held her in her arms. When the shaking stopped, Deb released her friend. "How have you been?" she asked.

"Not so good," Angela said. "I was bitten by a tick and got Lyme Disease. I've had a hell of a time." She turned and motioned for Deb and Marshall to enter. "I lost my job because of it. Lost my apartment too. I had to move back home with Mom. I don't know what you just did to me, but I feel so good right now."

"Good," Deb said. "If you feel good then I feel good."

"I couldn't stand on my feet all night. I was going to try to find another job, but Mom wasn't doing so well, so I moved in here to take care of her," Angela said.

"What's wrong with your Mom?" Deb asked.

"Lung cancer," Angela said. "They took part of her lung out, but the cancer came back. She's not doing so well."

"Can I see her?" Deb asked.

"Sure," Angela replied. "Let's see if she knows you."

They went to the dining room which had been converted to a bedroom for Angela's mother. Angela stroked her mother's head. "Mom, do you know who this is?" she asked.

"Debbi is that you?" the frail woman asked, stretching her hand out to take Deb's hand.

"It's me alright," Deb said, taking her hand, which felt very bony and frail.

"Who is this young man?" Angela's mother asked, looking past Deb at Marshall.

"This is my friend, Marshall Nemmans," Deb replied.

"What a handsome young man your friend is," Angela's mom declared.

"Would it be alright if I hugged you?" Deb asked.

"Of course," Angela's mom replied.

Deb looked over at Angela and said, "She is going to look like she's going into convulsions. It will be alright. Just wait until the shaking stops."

Deb sat on the side of the bed and embraced Angela's mother. "What did she mean by that?" Angela asked, looking over at Marshall. Marshall did not reply. He and Angela stood watching Deb as she embraced Angela's mother.

The frail woman began to shake. It was all Deb could do to hold her as she flopped violently about in Deb's embrace. Her eyes rolled back in her head and her mouth gapped. Her tongue hung from one side of her open mouth.

"Deb?" Angela asked. She looked over at Marshall and asked, "Is Mom okay?"

Marshall still did not reply. He could not take his eyes away from Deb and Angela's mother. He had seen Deb embrace people before. He had seen the trembling, but never anything like what he was witnessing at this moment. He felt his throat going dry, and his chest growing tight. He began to feel uncomfortable, standing by watching them. Should he do something?

After a few moments, Angela's mother went limp in Deb's arms and Deb lowered her head gently to rest upon the pillow.

"Is my Mom dead?" Angela asked, stepping closer.

"No, she will sleep a while, Angie. When she wakes, she should feel much better," Deb replied.

"So," Angela began, without taking her eyes off her sleeping mother. "You can still do that weird shit."

"Oh, it's even more weird than it was when I left," Deb said, standing up. "You can check her pulse if it will make you feel better."

Angels stepped near the bed and placed her fingers on her mother's throat. "She's alive," she said softly.

Deb chuckled. "Yes, and she will be cancer free when she wakes up."

"Well, that would be really something," Angela said.

Deb could tell that Angela wasn't completely convinced, and she decided to let it go for now. "How are the other girls these days?" Deb asked.

"Oh, let's see," Angela said, reaching down to touch her mother's arm. "Penny got married. She is about six months pregnant, and no, she did not have to get married. He's a real nice guy. I think you would like him. They moved to Maryland. We are all so happy for her. Brianna is an instructor at the fitness center. Go figure that one. Since she lost all that weight, she has become a regular fitness guru. I don't see her too often, and when I do, it is on the local television commercials for the fitness center. She looks great. Oh, she is engaged to the guy who owns the chain of gyms."

"Wow!" Deb said. "That is good news."

"Natalie is still working. She's the only ones who hasn't made radical changes to her life. Don't tell her I said that. Like I've gotten rich and famous. It's a touchy subject with her. She thinks her life is boring and she is going nowhere," Angela said. "I told her I would change places with her any day. She gets bouts of depression. Say, why don't I give them all a call and see if we can meet somewhere while you're here?"

"I would like that very much," Deb said. She smiled over at Marshall and asked, "Do you mind, Marshall?"

Marshall was still somewhat in shock. "Of course, I don't mind. That is why we came isn't it?" he asked.

"Thank you," Deb replied, smiling up at him. "We only have a day or two. He has a business he needs to get back to."

"Where are you from?" Angela asked Marshall.

Before Marshall could reply, Deb interrupted. "Oh, you don't need to know that, Angie. It isn't a big secret or anything, but those agents and doctors are still looking for me and if you don't know, you can't tell them."

"I see," Angie said. She looked down at her mother again, touching her forehead. "She seems to have color back in her cheeks."

"She will be fine," Deb said. "Trust me, she is only sleeping. She is completely cured of the cancer. When she wakes up, she is going to feel as good as you did after I embraced you."

"Yeah, about that," Angela said. "What did you do to me?"

"I cured you. You should be able to go back to work full time after today," Deb said, smiling.

"Oh, maybe you didn't do me any favors after all," Angela said, laughing. "I do feel great, though. It's been a very long time since I've felt this good. I think I feel better now than I did when I was a teenager."

"Good," Deb said. "Now, about meeting the girls. Where should we meet them? I can't go anywhere too public. They may still be watching for me in the area."

"Crackers?" Angela asked.

"Crackers is okay," Deb said, looking over at Marshall.

"Don't look at me," Marshall began. "I don't know anything about this area."

"Crackers at 7:00 tonight?" Angela asked. "Natalie works until 5:00."

"That will work," Deb said. "We need to find a place to stay tonight."

"Stay here," Angela said. "I may need you later to help with Mom."

"Your Mom will be up and walking around before we leave," Deb said, smiling.

"I certainly hope you're right," Angela said. "I'm going to call the girls. I'll be right back."

Deb and Marshall stood quietly as Angela left the room. Marshall looked down at Angela's mother and asked, "What did you do to that woman?"

Deb shrugged. "I can't explain how it works. I only know that every time I embrace someone, they get healed of whatever ails them. The worse their condition, the worse their reaction. She must have been pretty far gone. I'm glad we got here when we did," she said.

"I remember feeling awesome after you embraced me. I haven't had a cigarette in weeks," Marshall said.

Deb laughed. "Good. Glad I was able to help. Are you alright with staying here tonight?" she asked.

Marshall nodded his head. "Yes, but we should get on the road as soon as possible. What are you going to do if you can't meet with your friends tonight?"

"Then we will leave tomorrow anyway," Deb said. "if I don't see them all, I at least know they are alright."

Angela came back into the room. "The only one I couldn't reach was Brianna. Her voice mail said she was unavailable until Monday, so I'm assuming she is out of town," she said. "Penny said they may be late, depending on the traffic and I didn't talk to Natalie directly as she is working. I left a message."

"Well, that settles it," Deb said. "I can't wait."

"Are you hungry? I can order a pizza or something," Angela said.

"No thank you," Deb said. "If you don't mind, I'm going to show Marshall around the area. We will be back in plenty of time for our meeting at Crackers."

Angela reached out to take Marshall's hand. "It's been a pleasure to meet you Marshall. I can't wait for the others to meet you too," she said. They shook hands and she and Deb embraced again. When they parted, Angela laughed. "I was expecting, well, I don't know what I was expecting."

They laughed and Deb and Marshall left. Deb guided him around the city and back out to Mont Alto where she showed him where she used to live and where Dr. Martelli backed over Eva's daughter, Rachel.

"It's pretty busy around here," Marshall said. "I think I like our small community town back home."

Deb smiled. "I do miss my home and friends, but I will admit I like the area in Canada. It's just that lately I've been so isolated for what feels like so long, I don't think I could have handled another year on that lake all by myself," she said.

Marshall squeezed her hand. "You don't have to stay out there all by yourself," he said.

"You don't understand Marshall," Deb said. "If the people searching for me ever discovered where I was, your small town would be turned upside down. I wouldn't want that to happen to you and your friends."

"No, I wouldn't want that to happen either," Marshall said.

They continued to drive around until they decided to rest at the city park. The children were getting out of school and the park was becoming busy. After a close call with a basketball, they decided to return to Angela's mothers. When they arrived, they discovered Angie and her mother in the kitchen preparing dinner.

"Look who is up and about!" Angela said, smiling.

Angela's mother embraced Debbi again. Deb was aware how intently Marshall and Angela were watching them as they held each other. "Thank you, Debbi. Angie told me what you did for me. I don't remember much, but I can tell you I woke feeling so terrific. Thank you so much," she said, kissing Deb's cheek.

"You are quite welcome. I only have one request," Deb said.

"Anything," Angela's mother said.

"Please don't tell anyone what I did. As a matter of fact, please don't mention that I was even here," Deb pleaded.

"Well, people are going to ask a lot of questions," the older lady said. "However, I will tell them I just started feeling better after a lot of prayer and the next thing I knew...," she smiled.

"That is fine," Deb said. "You can tell them whatever you feel comfortable telling them. Just don't tell them what I did or that you saw me. I can't tell you how important that is."

"Would you like some dinner?" Angela asked.

"Marshall is probably hungry. Me, I only eat fresh fruits and vegetables," Deb replied.

"Okay….," Angela said, going to the refrigerator. "What about some cantaloupe?"

"That will do," Deb replied, laughing.

"This household eats a lot of pizza and Colonel Sanders," Angela's mother laughed.

"That's fine with me," Marshall declared.

It was a pleasant afternoon and soon it was time to leave for Crackers. They were the first to arrive. There were a handful of locals sitting at the bar. Some of them Deb remembered, however, none of them recognized her. They told the bar maid that they were expecting friends and that they would take their drinks on the patio out back. They had just sat down when Natalie and her sister Diane arrived. Deb and Natalie embraced.

Natalie trembled in Deb's arms.

"What is wrong with Nat?" Diana asked, looking over at Angela.

"She'll be fine," Angela said.

When Deb released Natalie, she quickly collapsed onto a picnic table bench. "Wow!" Natalie said. "That felt great! What did you do to me?"

Deb laughed. She glanced over at Angela and said, "Nothing really. It just feels so good to see you girls again."

"How's your mom?" Natalie asked Angela.

"Oh," Angela hesitated to answer.

"Oh, no," Natalie said. "I am so sorry."

"No, no, no," Angela said. "She is fine. The cancer is all gone."

"Oh, what a relief," Natalie said, holding her head in her hands. I thought…., well, never mind what I thought."

"We will talk about Mom another time," Angela said, laughing.

"Deb," Natalie began. "I almost didn't recognize you without all that blonde hair. What happened?"

"Oh," Deb reached up to touch her spiked hair. "I shaved my head," she said, lowering her voice. "I tried dying it auburn and it turned dark orange. It was awful looking. So instead of trying something else and ending up with green hair, I just shaved my head."

Natalie laughed. "Your hair was always so beautiful. Wasn't her hair beautiful, Diane?" she asked her sister. Diane sat nodding her head.

It was almost 8:30 when Penny and her husband, Chandler arrived. Deb was hesitant to embrace Penny. She wasn't sure if it would hurt the baby. So, she remained seated at the picnic table until Penny and Chandler were seated across from her and Marshall. Deb was aware that Natalie was watching her closely, undoubtably, wondering why Deb did not hug her old friend as she had done with the rest of them.

Deb and Penny drank bottled water as the rest of them sat drinking their drinks on the patio outside of Crackers. Penny leaned close and asked, "Deb, I'm drinking water because of the baby. Is there something you want to tell me?"

Deb burst into laughter. "No, Penny. I just don't like the taste of alcohol anymore. Besides, I am going to drive us back to Angie's."

"What have you been doing with yourself?" Penny asked.

"I've been hanging out in a cabin and I can't tell you where it is. It's best if you don't know where I am. Of course, I would appreciate it very much if you didn't tell anyone about the cabin. You may remember those FBI agents who were hunting for me when I left, well, they are still searching for me. So please don't mention to anyone that you saw me or even mention my name," Deb explained.

"We won't tell a soul," Natalie said, raising her beer in the air.

They laughed and gossiped about everyone in their past. Marshall and Chandler listened and rolled their eyes as the girls talked about some of their past adventures.

The night wore on and finally it was time to part. Penny went to Deb and threw herself into Deb's arms. Everyone was on their feet as Penny began to tremble. Deb instantly released her friend, standing at arm's length watching her.

"Wow! What a jolt," Penny said. "What the hell was that?"

"Are you alright?" Deb asked.

"Yep! I feel great," Penny said turning toward Marshall. "You will have to have Deb tell you about the night at a bar when these construction workers tried to keep us from leaving the bar. Deb was a real Chuck Norris that night, only, she never lifted a leg or spun around once. It was really something."

Marshall smiled as he looked over at Deb. "I think I know what you mean."

They left the bar then, each going their separate ways. Deb and Marshall took Angela back to her mother's and discovered that her mother had prepared a room for them to spend the night.

Once they were alone, Marshall sat on the edge of the bed and said, "I thought you lost your hair due to cancer. I had no idea you shaved your head."

Deb smiled over at him as she slipped her hand in his. "The FBI agents were searching for me, the doctors were searching for me, and I had this long blonde head of hair that most girls my age would die for. I dyed it auburn, as I said earlier. It didn't turn out well. So, as I told the girls earlier, I decided to shave my head. Once the hair began to grow in, it looked terrible, so I just kept shaving it. Someone assumed I had lost my hair due to cancer, and it was easier to go along with that fact than it was to make up another story, so, I went with the cancer story. It worked," Deb said, smiling.

"I see," Marshall said, reaching up to touch Deb's hair. "I'm trying to picture you with long blonde hair."

Deb smiled. "Well, stick around long enough and you may find out for yourself," she said.

"Oh, I don't think I'm going anywhere," Marshall said, before kissing her tenderly.

CHAPTER TWENTY-THREE

Deb and Marshall were once more on the road, only this time they were driving westward toward the Ohio line. The trip was a total of four hours to East Palestine, Ohio from Mont Alto, Pennsylvania.

They were traveling west along the Pennsylvania turnpike when Marshall's radio went silent and his blue tooth announced an incoming call from Dick Patterson.

"Marshall, this is Dick Patterson," the familiar voice announced. "Don't say a word. We don't know who may be listening. There were some United States Government boys asking questions here this morning. They were asking questions about you and Candy McCall. I thought maybe I should let you know. They may be listening in, so you might want to ditch your phone. We don't know any Candy McCall, so we couldn't be of much help."

Marshall looked over at Deb and sighed. "That's my business phone," he said, frowning.

"Well," Dick Patterson began. "Be careful out there." Then the call ended.

"Okay, maybe you should go home. Just let me out at the next exit and go right back to your life," Deb suggested. "I can handle them, and I'll be alright. I don't want you involved in any of this."

Marshall remained silent as he kept his eyes on the road ahead. After some time, he announced, "I told you I wasn't going anywhere. What is the worst they can do to me? I'm not guilty of anything," he said. "I'm here and I'm not going to desert you just because things get a little rough." He nodded his head and reached over to squeeze her hand. "Toss that phone out the window."

"Are you sure?" Deb asked.

"Toss it!" he exclaimed.

Deb put the window down. Marshall pulled over into the right lane and he began to maneuver through a sharp left curve. Deb tossed the phone and it bounced off the guard rail, spinning on the pavement behind them. A tow truck that had been following them ran over it. Marshall watched the event in the rear-view mirror.

"What are you going to do now?" Deb asked.

"I'll stop at a Walmart somewhere and get a burner phone until we get home," Marshall declared.

"Can they track your truck?" she asked.

"Not unless I use my GPS," Marshall said, looking in the rear-view mirror again. "At least I don't think they can."

"I am so sorry," Deb said.

"Don't be sorry," Marshall said. "You haven't done anything wrong."

They rode in silence for nearly an hour, until they reached the toll booth. Deb sat up straight. Everything was beginning to look very familiar. She looked over at Marshall and in a soft voice said, "They will be watching Mom's house."

"I can drop you off somewhere and go to the house alone," he suggested.

"Do you mind?" Deb asked.

"I don't mind," Marshall declared. "I can knock on the door and slip her a note from you. They won't be able to hear any valuable information that way."

Deb reached into her bag and pulled out a brown paper bag. She tore a piece off and began writing. "I will have you drop me off at the Dairy Queen. Here is a note for my mother, and here are the directions to her house from the Dairy Queen," She said, handing the paper to Marshall. He stuffed both papers into his pocket.

Deb felt her heart pounding as they drove down Taggart Street to Market Street. Marshall dropped her off at the Dairy Queen and pulled back onto Market Street, driving back the way they had come. Deb watched his truck until it was no longer visible, before entering the Dairy Queen.

Deb ordered at the counter. She expected to recognize one of the four employees behind the counter, however, they were younger, and she found no familiar faces among them. She ordered her treat and took a seat in a position where she would see the entrance and parking lot. Cars began to fill the parking lot and soon the dining room was filling up. Deb stared at the faces intently, hoping to see someone she recalled from her days growing up in this town.

An older couple came in and sat at a table in the center of the dining room. They looked familiar, but Deb couldn't be sure. It nagged at her, as she studied them for a recollection of who they could be. She finished her treat, and sat quietly, waiting for Marshall's truck to return. Finally, it pulled in and parked. She watched Marshall as he crossed the parking lot and entered. He scanned the dining room until his eyes fell upon her. Was it her imagination, or, had his face lit up at the site of her? She felt her heart pounding as he walked toward her.

"Was anyone home?" Deb asked.

Marshall nodded his head. "Your Mom read the note and said it was nice to meet me. She wrote this for you," he replied, slipping a note to Deb.

The note said that her mother would meet her at the Dairy Queen in ten minutes. Deb smiled as she read the note. "Thank you," she said, softly, as Marshall sat down across from her.

"Should I go somewhere so you two can talk?" he asked.

Deb shook her head. "I have no secrets from you," she replied. "Besides, I want you and Mom to get to know each other."

Marshall went to the counter and ordered a milk shake. Deb sat watching the parking lot for her mother's car. It had been over a year since she was home last. Perhaps her mother had a different car by now.

Deb noticed a woman walking toward the door. She did not see where she came from but knew instantly it was her mother. She sat up straight, smiling as her mother walked through the door. Julie smiled at Deb as she walked toward her.

"What happened to your hair?" Julie asked, as she pulled out a chair and sat down.

"I thought it would help," Deb replied.

Marshall arrived with a milk shake. He handed it to Julie. "No thank you, young man. I'm watching my weight," Julie smiled.

"You look great to me," Deb said, smiling. Marshall pulled out a chair and sat down. "Mom, I want you to meet Marshall," she said. "Marshall Nemmans."

"I believe we have met, although I don't recall getting your name," Julie said, reaching across the table to shake Marshall's hand.

"Where have you been?" Julie asked, smiling back at Deb.

"I don't think I should tell you," Deb declared. "I am somewhere safe."

"Well, that is comforting. I've been thinking about you so much lately," Julie began. "Just when I think they have backed off on watching the house, I notice another dark SUV parked somewhere close, or following me down the street." She smiled, saying, "Don't worry. I wasn't followed. At least I don't think I was."

"Hello Julie," an elderly man said.

"Hello, Bill," Julie said, looking up at the elderly man who had stopped as he was passing the table. He smiled at Deb as if he was waiting for Julie to introduce them. "Oh, excuse me," Julie began. "This is Miss Martin. We are coworkers."

"Nice to meet you Miss Martin," Bill said. "Well, enjoy your sunny summer day. They say rain tonight and tomorrow." Then he moved toward the exit.

"Mom, shame on you. I never knew you to lie before," Deb teased.

"Well, what was I supposed to say?" Julie asked. "Besides, I probably did him a favor. If he tells someone he met my daughter, the SUV's would be following him around."

"How is Dad?" Deb asked.

Julie smiled. "Steve is fine. He retired in March. He putters around in the garage all day doing whatever retired men do," she said. "He went up to visit your Aunt Suzanne today. He should be home after dinner. Will you still be in town?"

"I don't think it is safe to stay. I just wanted to see you. I just needed to hear your voice and know that you are alright," Deb said. Tears filled her eyes. "I really miss you Mom."

"I miss you too, De..., ah..., honey," Julie stammered.

Deb reached across the table to squeeze her mom's hand. "We can't stay," she whispered. "I want to, but it isn't safe for you and Dad."

"I understand," Julie said. "I want you to be safe and happy. I just wish there was a better way of communicating. I get so worried."

"I know. Let me work on that," Deb whispered. She looked around her at the dining room of strangers. "This town has changed so much since I left home."

Julie laughed. "It has, but not as much as you have changed since you left home," she said.

Deb looked up as a man in gray pants and a blue polo shirt entered the front door. He lifted his sunglasses to sit on top of his head. "Oh, no," she whispered.

Julie turned to look behind her. "I don't recognize him," she said, softly. "He might be."

Deb stood up and moved toward the restroom. She reached for the door to discover it was locked. She stood facing the door, not daring to turn around. The man stepped into the dining room and looked around without ordering anything at the counter. Julie held her breath. He looked very suspicious in her opinion.

Suddenly the man smiled and waved at a couple sitting in the corner. He moved back to where they were seated and began conversing with them. Julie let out a sigh of relief. Deb glanced over at them quickly and returned to the table. "That was a close one," she said.

"Was that couple here when I arrived?" Julie asked.

"I think so, but I'm not certain," Deb said.

"They arrived right after me," Marshall said. "I watched them come in while I was ordering my milk shake."

"Do you think it is possible?" Deb asked.

"I don't know," Julie said. "They've had different agents watching the house. I don't recognize those people, but that doesn't mean anything. Do you see any dark SUV's in the parking lot?"

Marshall stood up. "I think I need to step outside for a cigarette," he said.

"I thought you quit smoking," Deb interjected.

"I still have a couple in my pocket, just in case," Marshall said, smiling down at her. "You never know."

Deb watched him as he moved toward the front entrance. He stood at the corner of the building smoking a cigarette. She did not dare to turn around and look at the people sitting in the corner. Marshall turned toward the window and casually pointed toward the lot with two fingers.

"I think there are two SUV's parked out there," Deb said, softly. "Now what do we do?"

"We better get out of here," Julie said.

"Maybe if we split up, we can meet somewhere else," Deb suggested, rising to her feet.

As she rose the man in the corner rose as well. "I think you better get out of town. I will try to delay them if I can," Julie said.

"Mom! How are you going to do that?" Deb asked.

"I'll have an accident in the parking lot," Julie said, smiling. "My car is insured, and I won't be moving fast enough to hurt anyone. I'll just delay them until the police arrive." She squeezed Deb's arm. "Hurry," she said.

Deb moved toward the door. As she neared Marshall she said, "Come on, we have to make a run for it."

They ran toward his truck. Deb was closing the truck door as she saw her mother climb into her car. The couple from inside the Dairy Queen were getting into their SUV as well. The second man from inside was on his phone as he moved toward his SUV. Marshall pulled up to Market Street and waited for two cars to pass before pulling out in front of the third car. At that moment the couple in the SUV was pulling behind them, and Julie slammed into the back of them. The SUV was pushed out into the street and hit by the oncoming car.

To Deb's surprise, they did not stop. They continued to follow Marshall's truck as he moved passed Sparkle Market and toward the red light at Market and Main Streets. The light was red, and Marshall did not stop. He made a quick right turn and then turned left in front of Tom's Tires. The SUV remained on their tail.

As they meandered through the streets of East Palestine, trying to lose the SUV, they heard sirens. The police were also following them. By the time they reached Taggart Street there were two police cruisers behind the SUV and a second SUV behind them.

"What do you want me to do?" Marshall asked.

"Pull over and let me out," Deb said. "They will stop following you if I'm not with you."

"I can't do that. What will they do to you?" Marshall asked.

"I don't know, but I do know I can handle whatever they have planned for me. I don't want anyone hurt and if we don't stop, eventually, bullets are going to start flying," Deb said. "I care about you Marshall. I don't want you or my mother hurt on my account."

At that moment the sound of helicopters overhead filled the air. Marshall leaned forward and looked upward toward the sky. "There are two of them," he said. He continued driving, wrenching his hands on the steering wheel. "I don't want to put you out. I want to protect you," he said.

"I know you do, but you can't this time," Deb said. "Just pull over and let me out."

Marshall took a deep breath and slammed on the breaks. "I'll pull over, but I'm staying with you. Whatever happens, it happens to both of us. Together," he said, looking over at Deb.

"You don't have to do this, Marshall," Deb said.

"Yes, I do," Marshall said. "I wouldn't be able to live with myself if I didn't."

Before Deb could get out of the vehicle, the woman wearing dark pants and a white blouse was flashing an FBI badge against the window of Marshall's truck. The man driving the SUV was talking with the two policemen who had been pursuing them.

"Hands behind your back," the woman was shouting, as Deb exited the truck.

"What crime are you arresting me for?" Deb asked.

"You are wanted for questioning. We have been instructed to take you in for questioning," the woman repeated, reaching for handcuffs.

By this time the man and the two policemen were approaching them. Deb recognized one of the policemen as a young man she graduated with.

He frowned when he recognized Deb. "Questioning about what?" he asked the agent.

"That is a matter for the FBI. You are outranked on this one officer," the FBI agent said.

"I've done nothing wrong," Deb said. They began to handcuff Marshall as well. "He's done nothing wrong either," she barked.

"That's not for you to determine," the woman said, shoving Deb roughly.

Deb narrowed her eyes. She spun sharply and glared at the woman who distinctly reached for her weapon. Deb looked down at the woman's arm and it twisted, causing her to drop to her knees, holding her arm and screaming out in pain.

"What's happening?" one of the police officers asked.

"She broke my arm," the woman shouted.

"She didn't touch you. She is handcuffed for crying out loud!" Marshall shouted.

"Yeah, she is handcuffed," the policeman agreed.

"She broke my friggin arm!" the woman shouted again. "Shoot that bitch!"

"Whoa! Wait just a minute," the policeman shouted. "Nobody is shooting anybody!" He stepped close to Deb and asked, "It's Debbi Farlow, right?"

Deb nodded her head. "I recall your name is Brian, right?"

"That's correct. What is this all about Debbi?" he asked.

"They want to put me in a clinic where they can run tests on my brain," Deb explained. "They have trumped up false charges against me so they can lock me up."

He looked back at the second officer. "I think we should take everyone down to the station and clear this up. I don't want to let them drive off with her without knowing why," he said.

"You have no jurisdiction, officer! We will have your badge for this!" the male agent said.

"Maybe, but she's not the one who fled the scene of an accident, now is she?" the officer said. The second officer nodded his head. "She will ride with us," Brian said, guiding Deb toward his cruiser. "I'll call the paramedics to look at that arm for you," he said over his shoulder to the woman who remained on her knees.

"Thank you," Deb whispered as she climbed into the back of the cruiser. "Can Marshall ride with me?"

"It's not something they approve of," the officer said. "However, I don't see where it will hurt anything."

The two SUV's were following the police cars as they moved toward Main Street where the Police Station and Fire Stations were located. Brian looked in the rear-view mirror at Deb and asked, "Do you want to explain all of this to me now or wait until we reach the station?"

"A couple of years ago, I was in a car accident in Pennsylvania," Deb began. "When I woke from the coma, I began to heal very quickly. The doctors wanted me to go to a clinic where they could monitor my progress and I refused. I am a free citizen of the United States of America, am I not?" she asked.

The officer nodded his head. "As long as you haven't committed any crimes," he replied. "Have you committed a crime?' he asked.

Deb shook her head. "No," she replied. "I've done nothing to anyone. In fact, it is the other way around. After this doctor came to the house, he backed out of the drive and ran over a little girl next door. He killed her. She was dead. Well," Deb glanced over at Marshall who was watching her intently, slightly shaking his head. "I discovered that after my accident, I could heal people by embracing them. I know it sounds crazy, but it's true."

"You heal people?" Brian asked, smiling. "You? Debbi Farlow from East Palestine, Ohio?"

"Yep, that's me, and yep, I heal people," Deb replied.

"So what? You healed the little girl? Like, brought her back from the dead?" he asked.

"Yep, exactly. Well, ever since that day the FBI has been looking for me. They want to lock me in some military base and study my brain. I don't know, maybe even cut it out, who knows," she explained.

"That's some story, Debbi," Brian said, shaking his head and grinning.

"It's true, I swear," Deb said.

"I don't know," Brian laughed. "Are you sure you haven't been smoking something? I mean, I seem to recall you in the old days."

"Well, when we get to the station, you take these cuffs off of me and let me give you a big old bear hug and then see what you think," Deb said.

"I'm not sure I can take the cuffs off. I'm not sure I want to. That agent claims you broke her arm without touching her. I didn't believe her and now you are telling me you brought some little girl back from the dead. Maybe you did break that agent's arm. If you did, I'm not so sure I want you putting your arms around me," the officer said, pulling up to the curb outside the police station.

"I promise you; I will not hurt you," Debbi said.

"Tell you what," Brian said, turning to look back at her. "We have this disabled dispatcher. His name is Ray. He was in a car accident and he was broken up so badly that he walks with a limp now. You heal him and I'll help you in any way I can."

"It's a deal," Deb said with a nod. "Just keep those agents away from me."

"I'll do my best, but for now the cuffs stay on," Brian replied. He exited the cruiser and the second officer joined him as they ushered Deb and Marshall inside the police station. The FBI agents were right behind them.

"I'm going to lock these two up and then we will have a talk," Brian said to the agents.

"We want a man in there with her at all times," the male agent said.

"Suit yourself, but you wait here until we get her locked up," the second officer said.

"I'm afraid I can't do that, officer. As I said, we need someone with her at all times," the agent said, stepping forward.

"Well, I don't have a problem with a female agent back there alone with her. However, you have one female agent and she needs medical attention. After one of our medical team looks at her arm, she will be permitted back there. For now, we will process her and lock her up," the officer said.

Other policemen were gathering around with confused looks upon their faces. "What's the difference in your being back there with her and one of our agents?" the FBI agent asked.

"We have a female officer in the building. She will sit with your prisoner until your agent has been cared for," Brian declared. He led Deb and Marshall through a door and leaned close to a second officer, whispering, "Stall those federal boys for a while. Send Ray back here, I need to see him for a moment."

"Okay," the officer said, frowning. "Are you going to be alright?"

"I'll be fine. Just send Ray back and the rest of you wait out here until I come out," Brian said. Brian and another officer led Deb and Marshall to the cells. He put them in separate cells. "I should be placing you in different rooms, but I'll leave you two together until we process you and then you will be separated," Brian said.

"Thank you," Deb said.

Brian stepped into the cell with Deb and asked, "Now, if I remove these cuffs, are you going to behave yourself?"

"I'll do whatever you say as long as I don't feel threatened. I will give you that much. However, if at any time I feel threatened or I feel Marshall is in danger, I will not make any promises. And, just so you know, the cuffs won't make any difference," Deb explained.

Brian looked down at Deb and shook his head. "What do you mean by that?" he asked.

"Just get your man in here and let's get this over with before those agents get their hands on me," Deb declared.

Brian uncuffed Deb and stepped out of the cell looking over at Marshall. "Are you alright in there?" he asked.

"Why am I cuffed? What did I do wrong?" Marshall asked.

"For now, all we have on you is speeding. I suppose I could remove the cuffs," Brian said. He seemed to pause as he considered it for a moment and then he stepped into the cell and removed the handcuffs from Marshall's wrists. He exited the cell and locked it behind him.

The door opened behind him, causing him to jump. He motioned for Ray to come closer. He nodded at the officer who had helped get Deb and Marshall into their cells, saying, "You can go out front now. Ray and I have this."

The officer paused, looking from Brian to Ray. "Go on," Brian said, sharply. The officer turned and left the holding area.

"Ray, I need you to help me out here," Brian began. "I know this is going to sound crazy, but this girl claims those FBI agents are after her because she has the ability to heal people. I want to see if she is telling the truth. Are you following me so far?" Brian asked.

"Yes, I know where you are going with this," Ray said. He limped close to the door. "What do you want me to do?" he asked. "Do I go in there with her?"

"No!" Brian exclaimed looking back at Deb. "He doesn't have to come in there does he? Can't you hug him through the bars?"

"I think so," Deb stated. Numbers began moving quickly in her line of vision. They were increasing as they moved about. She assumed the agents had called for backup. How were they getting here so fast?

Brian stood next to the door as Ray stepped close to the bars. Deb stretched her arms through the bars and looking over at Brian she said, "Just a heads up, Brian," she sighed and went on, "It is not going to look good. He is going to tremble or shake violently. It varies. I don't want you shooting me or anything like that. When the shaking stops, I'll release him, and he is going to want to sleep for a while. Don't panic, he will be fine."

A female officer stepped through the door. Brian looked up at her and asked, "Would you mind waiting outside a moment?"

She frowned as she turned to go back through the door the way she had entered.

"Okay, let's do this," Brian said, nodding his head at Ray.

Ray closed his eyes and Deb embraced him. She was aware that Marshall was on his feet and standing nearest the door of his cell. Ray began to shake. It wasn't nearly as violently as Angela's mother had shaken, but it was all Deb could do to keep hold of him through the bars of her cell.

She looked up at Brian watching them. His face was white, and his eyes bulged. He was wringing his hands nervously. At that moment, symbols moved into Deb's line of vision. They were the symbols that normally warned her of danger. She swallowed the lump in her throat and continued to hold Ray in her arms.

The shaking stopped and Ray went limp in her arms. Brian stepped forward and grabbed him as he slid to the floor.

"I'll be damned!" Brian said. "What happens now?"

"He will wake up feeling fine," Deb replied.

"Are you sure? He doesn't look fine to me," Brian said.

"Trust me, Brian. His body is healed. He just needs to sleep off the shock of the process. He will wake up feeling great. They all do," She said.

She glanced over at Marshall and said, "We need to get out of here. There are people coming for us." Looking back at Brian who was knelt on the floor holding Ray in his arms, she said, "Can you help us escape?"

Ray was moaning. Brian asked, "How do you feel, Ray?"

"I feel great, but I'm so tired," Ray replied.

"Brian!" Deb shouted. "You have to unlock the cells so we can get out of here."

"I can't do that, Debbi. I'll lose my job, my pension, everything, if I let you go," Brian said. "I wish I could help you, but I can't. I will speak on your behalf, but that is all I can do."

"We are screwed!" Deb shouted over to Marshall. "They are coming for us." She looked back at Brian and said, "Marshall hasn't done anything wrong. You have to let him go."

Brian laid Ray's head on the floor gently. "I'll go talk to them," he said, rising to his feet. "I promise you I will do everything I can to help." Then he helped Ray to his feet. "As soon as I get Ray somewhere safe, I'll speak to the agents." Then he began to guide a half-conscious Ray out of the holding area.

CHAPTER TWENTY-FOUR

Deb leaned her face close to the bars. "I am so sorry, Marshall. I didn't intend to get you involved in anything like this," she said, looking over at him.

"You didn't do anything, Virginia. Don't beat yourself up over something you had nothing to do with," Marshall said. "What makes you think they are coming for us?"

"I see things. It's even harder to explain than the healing thing. I see numbers moving all the time. Like, right now, I see a two. That stands for me and you. Beyond that door are nine people. But it's the numbers that are coming closer that worry me. I see another two and a four. I see a separate four floating overhead. Possibly a helicopter or a plane. I don't know, but there are four more coming from above. I see the nine beyond that door moving about. One is moving toward us. God only knows what that is," she tried to explain. "Then there are the symbols. That is stranger yet."

The door opened and Ray came rushing toward them. He was panting, as he staggered toward Deb. "I don't know how you did it, or what you did," he was saying as he began unlocking the cell. "If they find out I'm doing this, I'm done on the force," he said, opening Deb's door. He rushed over to Marshall's door and began unlocking it. "That door back there

221

leads to a parking lot out back. It's where we transfer prisoners to court and the county jail. You will be on foot, because your truck isn't here. It was taken to Lisbon," he explained, holding Marshall's cell door open.

"Thank you," Deb said, pulling Marshall by the hand.

"You needn't thank me. It's me who should be thanking you. I'm so tired right now I could collapse. Just go and be safe. Find a way back to Canada or wherever you came from. Just remember, they ran your plates on the truck and they know where you live now. Best not go back there," Ray said, leaning against the wall for support. He nodded toward a camera that was hanging near the ceiling in the corner. "I forgot about that. I suppose I'm busted."

"I'll take care of that," Deb said. She concentrated on the camera causing it to come away from the wall. She stood with her arms outstretched as it smashed against the cement floor over and over until it was in small shards of plastic splinters.

"Yep, that'll take care of that," Ray said, staring at the broken shards scattered about the floor.

Deb kissed him on the cheek and she and Marshall rushed through the door. They stepped out into a small parking lot. They ran to a back yard and kept to the shrubbery as they moved eastward.

"Where are we going?" Marshall asked.

"We can't go out into the open. They are up there somewhere coming this way. We will be spotted easily from the air. We have to stay under the trees," Deb said, pulling Marshall by the hand.

They were crossing a back yard when an elderly woman spotted them from her back porch. "Hey, who are you and what are you doing in my yard?" she called out.

Deb and Marshall kept running. The woman stepped down from the porch and began following them.

"We have to shut that woman up somehow," Marshall said. "She will give our location away.

Deb turned and began walking back toward the woman. "I'm sorry, Ma'am," Deb said. "I used to live in this town, and I thought I knew where I was, but I must have been mistaken."

"Well," the woman began. She looked Deb up and down as she said, "Don't I know you from somewhere?"

"I don't think so," Deb said. "I really need to get moving. If you will excuse us..."

"No, no, I'm sure of it," the woman said.

Deb assumed the woman recognized her from the television broadcasts. She was anxious to get as far from here as possible.

"I remember now," the woman said. "It was about two years ago. I remember it clearly. It was a day I will never forget. I was on my way to get donuts at the Pie Factory downtown. I was using a walker. You hugged me and I haven't used the walker since. It was you; I would never forget that face. You had more hair, but it was you, alright."

Deb recalled the incident. "Yes, it was me. I'm glad you are still getting around without your walker."

"Who are you looking for? Lord knows I owe you. Maybe I can help." The woman said.

"Well, we really need to get somewhere safe. You see the police are looking for us. We haven't done anything wrong, but the FBI knows I can heal people and they want to take me to a government facility," Deb explained. She didn't know why she was taking the time to explain so much detail to this elderly woman. Something told her she could trust her.

"You come with me," the elderly lady said. She turned and began climbing the porch steps again.

Deb and Marshall went inside. Deb looked over her shoulder and said to Marshall, "At least they won't find us in here."

"You two sit right down at the table. Can I get you anything?" the elderly lady asked.

Deb and Marshall shook their heads. The elderly lady went to the phone and Marshall jumped to his feet instantly. Deb covered his hand with hers. "It's alright," she said, softly.

"How do you know she isn't calling the police?" Marshall asked.

"I just know," Deb replied.

"This is Tony's grandma," the elderly lady said. "Is Tony there?" There was a pause. "Well, you tell Tony his grandma needs to speak with him right away. Tell him it is urgent."

Deb and Marshall stood watching the woman holding a wall phone. She smiled back at Deb and said, "It will be alright. I suppose you have forgotten that day at the Pie Factory, but I haven't and never will. You changed my life that day, and I owe you. I'm going to do everything I can to help you."

Now she was speaking into the phone again. "Tony, you put a set of plates on one of those new cars and bring it by the house. I have someone here who needs a ride."

"Don't you hem haw around about it. Do you remember me telling you about that young lady hugging me at the Pie Factory two years ago? Well, she is here, and she needs a car to get away from the police," the woman stated.

"Yes, I did say the police. Never mind why. What difference does it make? You yourself said we owe her everything for what she did that day. Now is your chance to pay her back. I'll take the blame if it comes to that. You just do as I say and do it right now!" the woman said, as she slammed the receiver down.

"He will do as I say," she said, pulling out a chair that had been pushed under the table. "My name is Bertha," she said, smiling.

"They call you Bert," Deb said, smiling. "I do remember you."

"That policeman, Ray, witnessed what happened that day. He was more shook up about it than I was," Bert said.

"Ray, of course," Deb said, looking over at Marshall. "I didn't make the connection. It's the same Ray that we met earlier at the police station."

"Oh, he isn't the same, dear. He was in a bad wreck right after that and he has just lately gone back to work. He has to stay at the station and work as a dispatch now because he isn't able to get around that well," Bert said.

"Yes, Ma'am. We met him earlier. Now I understand why he was so willing to step up to the bars without hesitation," Deb said. "He must have remembered me."

"What do you mean?" Bert asked.

Deb smiled over at the elderly lady. "I gave our friend Ray a hug," she said.

"Oh, then he owes you everything as well," Bert said. "He should be the one helping you get away."

"He did," Deb said. "We are here because of him."

"Well, can I get you anything while we wait for Tony to arrive?" she asked, rising to her feet.

"No, thank you, Bert," Marshall said. "We really need to get out of this town."

"Where will you go?" Bert asked.

"You shouldn't know anymore than you already do," Deb stated. "And, the fewer people who know about this, the better off you and they will be. As I explained earlier, it's the FBI and they don't always play by the same rules as the city police do."

"You are probably right," Bert said. "I won't say anything, and I know Tony won't." She stood near the kitchen window, watching. "Oh, this might be Tony now." Bert went toward the front of the house and looked out the front door window. "It's Tony. He is pulling around back," she said, coming back into the kitchen.

A heavy-set young man came waddling toward the back porch. Bert placed her hands on her hips and said, "I thought I told you to bring a new car!"

"I can't just hand out a new car, Grandma," the man said.

"This here is the young lady I was telling you about," Bert said, turning toward Deb.

"How do you do, Tony," Deb said. "I can't tell you how much I appreciate this."

"What am I supposed to say happened to this car?" he asked. "Someone has to sign off on this. I'm likely to lose my job because of this."

"I'm so sorry," Deb said.

"Oh, stop your belly aching, Tony. Let her give you a hug and be on her way. I don't see where you're losing much with that old heap of junk," Bert grumbled.

"Grandma, that car is only three years old," Tony whined.

Deb stretched her arms out. "Come here, Tony," she said.

Tony did not hesitate. He stepped into Deb's outstretched arms and as always, he trembled and shook. When he went limp in her arms, Bert stepped forward. "I don't suppose you would give this old lady one more hug before you go."

Deb stretched out her arms and Bert stepped into them. She trembled, much like Tony, before dropping to her knees. "Thank you," she moaned.

Marshall reached down and picked up the car keys that were lying on the floor next to Tony's sleeping body. "We better get out of this town while we can," he said.

"Thank you, Bert," Deb said, touching Bertha's shoulder before following Marshall out the back door. They climbed into the car. On the back seat were six ball caps with Brittain Motors logos on the front. Deb handed one to Marshall and she pulled one over her head. They backed out into the street and began driving north on Market Street.

"Where are we going?" Marshall asked.

"We can take Route eleven north until we reach Ashtabula. From there we can make our way to Canada." Deb looked over at Marshall. "You can drop me off anywhere in Canada and go home. They may come looking for you, but you won't know where I am so you shouldn't be in any danger."

"Let's just get to Canada first. One goal at a time," Marshall said.

They drove for three hours and soon they were making their way to the Canadian border. It was dark now, and with the rain clouds clustered above them, there was little illuminating their way. "Will they be looking for us at the border?" Marshall asked.

"It's a possibility," Deb said.

"What should we do?" Marshall asked.

"Well, you can put me out and go on by yourself," Deb replied.

"How, we can't even get across the border," Marshall said. "They took my wallet and ID at the police station."

Deb sighed. "Pull over here," she instructed.

Marshall pulled the car over. Deb got out and walked to the side of the highway. She stepped over a guard rail and slid down a steep bank to a stream below. She stood with her hands on her hips surveying their surroundings.

"What are you doing?" Marshall asked, sliding down the bank behind her.

"I'm not sure if it will work, but I have an idea," she said, looking toward the sky.

"Oh, no," Marshall said, under his breath. "I'm not sure I like where this is going."

"Oh," Deb said, smiling over at him. "If this works, we are both going to be surprised. Come on," she said, as she began to climb the bank again.

"Where are we going?" Marshall asked.

"Back to the car," Deb said.

"Virginia, would you mind sharing your plan with me?" Marshall asked.

"You're better off just not knowing the details, Marshall," Deb said. "Just trust me."

They climbed into the car. Deb smiled over at Marshall and said, "Are you sure you don't want to leave me here?"

"I'm not leaving you," Marshall said.

"Okay, hold on to the steering wheel," Deb said, nodding her head toward the steering wheel.

Marshall did as she instructed. Deb looked down at the floorboard of the car and spread her arms toward the roof. The car began to rise off the road.

"Whoa!" Marshall shouted.

"Is anything coming? Can anyone see us?" Deb asked, without taking her eyes off the tree line which was just underneath them.

"All, clear," Marshall said, with a trembling voice.

They were floating in the air, higher and higher. Marshall looked down from his side window and said, "There's a highway down there."

Deb asked, "Is it busy?"

"I don't think they can see us because it's too dark. Should I put the lights on?" Marshall asked.

"No, not yet. Tell me when there is a break in the traffic," Deb said.

"Okay, okay. I don't want to break your concentration. Are we good?" Marshall asked.

"We are fine, Marshall. I've got you," Deb replied, with a smile.

"There's one coming up," Marshall said. "This is scary shit!"

Deb smiled. The car began to slowly descend. Soon they were parked along the side of the road.

"There's traffic coming up behind us," Marshall said.

"You can start the car and turn the lights on now," Deb said.

Marshall turned the key and the engine roared. "Well, we are in Canada now. Where do we go from here?" he asked.

"Are you sure you don't want to go back to your small-town life?" Deb asked.

"Wherever you go, I go," Marshall said. "We are in this together." He smiled and said, "Besides, there isn't anyone out there who gives hugs like you do."

They continued following the traffic as it meandered along a river road. "Do you suppose this is the Niagara?" Marshall asked.

"Have you ever seen the Niagara?" Deb asked.

"No, I have not. I've never been this far west. Like I said before, I like our little community. I have no reason to come this far from home," Marshall said.

"My parents took me to Niagara Falls when I was a girl. We had a good time, I suppose," Deb began to explain. "Of course, I was bored hanging out with my parents back then. If only I knew what I know now. I'd give anything to go anywhere on earth with my parents."

They continued following the line of traffic until a soft light in the horizon lit up the night sky. "That must be city lights over there," Marshall said, pointing in that direction.

"Maybe we should stick to the boondocks," Deb said, looking at the road behind them.

"I'll turn off at the next road we come to," Marshall said.

Deb sighed, and Marshall sensed something was wrong. "Which way should we go?" he asked.

"Any direction, I suppose. I'm not sure it matters," Deb said.

"What's that supposed to mean?" Marshall asked, nervously. "We don't want to attract any attention."

"We need to find a motel or some place to spend the night," Deb said.

"That means either the city or small community near a city," Marshall said.

"Okay, follow the traffic," Deb said.

They continued following the line of traffic as it maneuvered around curves. All the while, the river kept to their right as they went. As the lights became brighter, they discovered a line of cheaper motels. Marshall pulled into the lot. "How am I supposed to pay for this? I don't have my wallet," he asked.

Deb sighed. "We've come so far," she said softly. Then she remembered the envelope she had stuffed in her back pocket. She was still wearing the same jeans. She reached behind her, and her eyes lit up. "I have money," she said.

As she pulled the envelope out of her pocket, Marshall gasped. "Where did you get so much money?" he asked.

"Those two guys that broke into the Patterson's had stolen this money from an armored car last year. They buried the money under my cabin. Joe had leased the cabin and when he was removing some critters from under the cabin, he discovered the money. He took it and hid it in another location. This is what those two guys were after when they broke into the Patterson's. They thought the Patterson's had found the money," Deb explained. "When Joe left, he knew he didn't need any money where he was going, so he left me this envelope. I suspect he left the rest with that girl he planned to marry. He seemed to care a lot for her, and he knew he would never see her again."

"Did he tell you this?" Marshall asked.

"He didn't have to. I saw it," Deb explained.

"How do you know you got it right?" Marshall asked.

"Oh, I know," Deb replied. "In fact, a lot of things are becoming very clear to me now."

"Like what kind of things?" Marshall asked.

"Oh, everything," Deb said. She handed Marshall a one-hundred-dollar bill. "Here, get us a room. I'll wait here."

She watched Marshall as he went inside the motel office. Soon he returned waving a key in the air. He climbed into the truck and drove over to park in front of a door with the number 9 on it. "Honey, we're home," Marshall said, smiling.

The motel was a dingy little place with a lot of drug and prostitution activity. It was not the sort of place they would normally choose to spend the night. However, they needed a place to stop and assess their next move. They watched some television and slept. When the sun came up in the morning, they were more than ready to leave.

As they were preparing to leave, Marshall asked Deb, "What do I call you?"

"What?" Deb asked, looking over at him, strangely.

"I've heard you called by three different names. Back home you were Virginia Parks, the writer. The McCall's called you Candy and your mother and friends called you Deb. Who are you really?" Marshall asked.

"Who would you like me to be?" Deb asked.

"I want you to be you. I like you for who you are, not what you are," Marshall said.

"Does what I am bother you?" Deb asked.

"I'd be lying if I said it didn't unnerve me a little, but I wouldn't say it bothers me all that much. I care a lot about you and I'm more worried for you than anything," Marshall said.

At that moment, the symbol in Deb's head flashed. She reached up and squeezing her head. She closed her eyes tightly and grit her teeth.

"What is it?" Marshall asked. "What is wrong?"

"Something is going to happen," Deb said, between clenched teeth. "Something big."

"What do we do?" Marshall asked, jumping to his feet and rushing to her side.

At that moment, Deb stood up and went to the door. She opened it and the four strangers stood outside, humming a message. "Wait here," Deb said to Marshall, before stepping outside. Marshall went to the window and watched through a parted curtain.

Deb stood facing the four strangers. "You must see the young man safely home. You must try to correct as much damage as possible before you leave," the four said in unison.

"But they took his wallet," Deb began. "They will be there, looking for us."

"It won't matter. You won't be staying. It is time for you to come with us," they said.

"Where? Where are we going?" she asked.

"This world was not meant for lifeforms such as us. We bestowed abilities to a chosen few in hopes it would help your race. However, you people of earth are not ready for us," they explained.

"What about my family and friends? What about my life? It's all I know," Deb pleaded. "Please, isn't there another way?"

"You must return the young man to his home. He will be safe once you are no longer a threat to the authorities of this planet," they said.

"Am I going with you? Am I going to die? When am I leaving? How much time do I have? Why can't you just return me to my normal self before my accident?" Deb asked.

"We cannot return you to your normal self. As for when, you will know," they said. They turned together and in step with one another, they moved off between two parked cars. Suddenly they were gone. They had vanished.

Deb felt tears stinging her eyes. She turned to see Marshall watching through the window. She wiped at her face and opened the door.

"What did they want?" Marshall asked.

"They want me to take you home," she replied.

"But," Marshall paused. "They took my wallet and my truck. They know where I am from. Isn't that the first place they'll look?"

Deb nodded her head. "It probably is," she said. "The aliens said I am to return you to your home and try to repair the damage done. Then," she swallowed the lump in her throat. "Then, they are taking me with them."

"Taking you where?" Marshall shouted. He reached out to take hold of Deb by the arms. "You aren't going anywhere without me," he said, lowering his voice.

"I have to go, Marshall," Deb said. "They are not going to stop searching for me. No one who knows me will ever have a chance at a normal life if I don't go." She placed her arms around his neck and looked into his eyes as she said, "I love you. I love you more than anything. I need you to carry on with your life. Do this for me. Do this for us." She kissed him long and tenderly.

Marshall had tears in his eyes. "How am I ever to live a normal life now?" he asked. "This time we have had together has been amazing. This isn't out there for normal people. Not this."

"Then hold me close in here," she said, pointing to his heart. "We will always be together in our hearts. If ever there is a way I can return to you, I will. However, I doubt they will let me come back."

Marshall sniffled and wiped at his eyes. "My life will never be the same," he said, softly. "Not without you."

"Eventually you will meet someone. You probably won't share the same experiences we have shared, but you will be happy. I know it, and you know

I can see future things others can't see or know. Trust me, you will be fine. It will take some time," she said smiling.

"What do we do now?" he asked.

"First we have to fix some of our mistakes. Some of my mistakes," Deb corrected. "We are going to return this car and get your truck back. That is the first thing we are going to do."

She pulled Marshall toward the door. "Come on, we need to get in the car."

They climbed into the car and Deb instructed him to put the keys into the ignition, but not to start the engine."

"How are we going to go back with everyone searching for us?" Marshall asked.

"Hold my hand, Marshall," Deb said.

Marshall reached out, taking Debbi's hand in his. Everything began to spin, and a greenish foggy mist surrounded them. As the mist cleared, Marshall gasped. They were sitting in the car amidst other new and used cars. "Where are we?" he asked.

"We are in East Palestine, Ohio. This is Brittian Motors. It's where Tony works and where the car belongs," Deb explained.

"Cool!" Marshall exclaimed. "How on earth did you do that?"

Deb smiled over at him. "I've only just begun," she said. "Now, let's get out."

They stepped out of the car. A salesman began walking toward them. Deb reached out for Marshall's hand and once again everything began to spin, and the greenish fog surrounded them. When the fog settled, they were in a fenced in area, standing next to Marshall's truck. "Wait here," Deb said. Just like that she vanished. Before Marshall could look in both directions, she re-appeared holding his truck keys. "Get in," she said, smiling.

Once again, she instructed him not to start the engine. She reached out for his hand and for a third time the green fog swirled around them. When it settled, they were parked outside the trading post in Canada.

"Wow! I didn't know you could do this," Marshall gasped. "All this time we've been running and hiding, and you could have just beamed us somewhere else."

Deb laughed. "I couldn't do this until this morning. It is a gift the four aliens left with me. It is their way of helping me help you."

"Please, Virginia or Deb. Whichever. Please don't go with them," Marshall begged.

"I have no say in the matter, Marshall. If I did, I would choose to stay," she explained.

"I don't want to be without you," he said, with a crackling voice.

"I will miss you. I promise, I will never forget you and I will never stop loving you," Deb said.

People were coming out of the Trading Post to stand on the porch. "Marshall, where have you been?" Willy Goldman called out to them. "There were some people from the states here asking questions about you and somebody named Debbi Farlow."

Marshall smiled as he and Deb got out of the truck. "Hello, Willy. It's nice to see you too," Marshall said, laughing.

"We thought you were off doing some big welding job. We didn't know you and Virginia were together," someone called from inside the Trading Post.

"There's some people from the states looking for you," Willy repeated.

Marshall looked around. A dark SUV was parked at the end of the sidewalk. A second one was moving up the street toward them.

"I better go now," Deb said, softly.

"Please, I need more time," Marshall said.

Deb stepped away from Marshall. At that moment the SUV pulled up to a stop and two men jumped out, pulling side arms aimed at the group standing on and near the porch.

"Hands in the air. Everyone!" one of the men shouted. Two other men came rushing from the hardware store, pulling their weapons as well.

Everyone raised their hands. Deb hesitated but raised hers slowly. "These people don't know anything," she called out to the armed agents.

"We will be the judge of that!" the tallest and heaviest agent spouted, sharply.

Deb narrowed her vision as she concentrated on the lead agent. She felt herself growing weightless as she began to float upward, glaring down at them.

"Don't shoot unless threatened!" the lead agent ordered.

"Damn!" someone below shouted.

Willy began to twitch as he shouted, "I told you. Didn't I tell you? Some heavy shit goes on out there on that lake. Now you see. Don't you see? Is anyone else seeing this?"

Everyone stood looking up at Deb as she rose high above them. A breeze began to swirl, and a greenish fog came from nowhere, swirling around them so violently that it forced them to cover their faces. When the fog settled and the wind stopped swirling, Deb was gone.

"Where is she?" the agent asked.

Marshall jumped into his truck and turned the key. He sprayed loose gravel over the on watchers as he drove toward the road that led to the cabin. He opened the gate and did not bother to close it. He was looking around and upward as he bounced along the rutted drive that led to the cabin. He was not aware of the convoy of vehicles following him as he bounced across the plank bridge. Soon he pulled up to a stop and looked at the vacant cabin before him. He jumped from the truck and stood looking about. Mr. McCall's truck was still parked where Deb had left it. Nothing had been disturbed in their absence.

Deb stood in the area where Joe said the spaceship had landed years ago. She looked around her, listening. She could hear the she bear and her cubs. She heard the young moose grazing in the tall grass far off from where she stood. She heard the Canadian geese on the lake with seven little ones, swimming close to the shore. She also heard the traffic that had followed Marshall to the cabin.

She looked upward to see a ship hovering above her. She closed her eyes and felt the air change around her. She opened her eyes to see Joe standing next to her. They watched out a small round window as the spaceship lifted upward, higher and higher above the lake. Everything became smaller and smaller until she was surrounded by darkness and the earth rotated off in the distance.

She smiled over at Joe and asked, "How bad is it?" she asked.

Joe smiled and said, "It's not that bad, really. It's an adjustment, but I think you're going to like it once you settle in."

She looked out the window again as the earth became smaller and smaller and suddenly disappeared. Just like her old life, it was gone. She felt a heaviness in her heart. "Will I ever see them again?" she asked.

"Maybe. Who knows what the future has planned for us? Whatever it is, it's going to be one hell of a ride!" Joe said, laughing. Deb smiled and suddenly they were both laughing as they looked out into the blackness of space.

Printed in the United States
By Bookmasters

Printed in the United States
By Bookmasters